FUCKUATION

MACKENZIE LAMONT

Printed in the United States of America

First Printing, 2018

eBook ISBN 978-0-578-42053-0
Print ISBN 978-0-578-42052-3

To the one I loved.

The worst feeling in the world is for the person you love to tell you that you deserve better instead of them being the better you deserve.

Prologue

"Who was the bitch in the car with you?!" Callie yelled through the burner phone she just bought. Travis wouldn't answer the phone when her number popped up, so she had to think quick on her feet. Desperate times call for desperate measures.

"What are you talking about? I'm at my boy D house out Ft. Washington," Travis replied.

"Nigga. I just chased you down 295 -- I know you saw me so don't even fucking try it," Callie replied.

"I don't know who you chased down 295, but it wasn't me," Travis replied.

"Really? That's what you're going with? Like I'm just out here not knowing what my man's car looks like or I'm going to be insane enough to chase a car down without checking for your plates?!" Callie was furious and felt disrespected that he'd insult her intelligence.

"Your batshit crazy ass be saying the stupidest shit ever, I swear. How the fuck you check my plates in a high speed chase down 295 in the dark? Fuck I look like copping to some B.S. like that?" Travis was getting irritated.

"It would behoove you to just come out and be a man about your load of crap, but no. You want to sit here and deny it like I'm going to second-guess what I know I saw. Shit looks real sus out here," Callie hissed. "Either that nigga or you trying to test your nine lives."

"Bitch did you just threaten me?!" Travis heaved through the phone.

"No nigga, threats are for kids... I marked your trade ass." With that, Callie threw the burner out the window.

If Travis knew the real Callie, he might have just bit the bullet and owned up to his cheating. Callie was a force to be reckoned with. 5'6" with a slim waist, a cute face, and a phat ass, Callie was undeniably was every man's wet dream and every woman's on sight enemy. She was 23 years old and too wealthy for her own good, but she had a side to her that would scare the devil himself.

DUCHESS

I stood by the stage entrance and smiled. All I could think was *Damn. I'm really about to hit this stage and finesse these thirsty ass niggas right out of their hard earned money.* I heard my signature song -- Bed by Jacquees -- and knew it was going down. I switched my hips and poked my booty out as I walked to the stage and started to dance my ass off. I saw my prey sitting there, drooling on himself like the helpless victim he was. I pointed to him and my bodyguards led him to the stage. Once he sat down in the chair that I conveniently places, I strategically crawled to him. Slowly. Seductively. I spun around and arched my back so deep that my ass was damn near in his lap. He smacked it of course, and right there in front of him, I fucked the floor. I rolled over on my back opened my legs so he could get a glimpse of this fat ass peach. My shit makes any man's mouth water, so I wasn't surprised when he nearly fell on the floor. I helped him by pulling him on top of me. I locked my thick thighs around him and rolled us both over so that I could position myself on top. I rolled his tie up in my hands while I rode him seductively in front of envious onlookers.

Money was flying all over the stage. My team collected it discreetly, without interrupting the show. You see, I learned early that it's not about the dancing, it's about the illusion that you could fuck me. So with that learned, I sold the dream like crack on the first and fifteenth of the month. I allowed my Persian hair to adorn his chest while I rode his dick. Baby let me tell you, King Kong would have covered up if he was beside the anaconda that was hiding in this man's boxers. The dry fuck even got me off. When the song went off, my bodyguards came up and helped me off of him. I didn't need the help but niggas tend to get disgruntled when the dance is over.

He said, “Wait I’ll pay for a private room.”

“No thank you,” I replied

“I only want a dance.”

Normally I wouldn’t care, but lord knows he earned it. He had all of my attention, so I told him to meet me in Room 3.

He stood up. Just to see what them pockets do, I said, “Wait you know the minimum for a private dance is $1500 right?”

He smiled and said, “Be in Room 3 in five minutes.”

“Pay the doorman to enter.” With that, we were both gone.

I walked up to my homegirl on my way to the room. “Hey Tracy, turn on the cameras in Room 3 for me,” I said coolly.

“What? Duchess is doing private dances now?” She playfully asked.

“Girl no, I’m just going to play with his head. Oh! And tell Don to wait outside the door.” I replied as I cavalierly walked away. When I arrived at Room 3, aka Jade’s Room, I saw Don right there as requested. He palmed the keypad to allow me entry. I walked in and asked, “What’s your request?”

He said, “Honestly, I’m buying time.”

“Really?”

He said, “Yes. What you did to me out there was nothing short of amazing, but I need to see if you have the brains to match.”

He piqued my attention. “Why would it matter?”

He looked me straight in the eyes and said, “Nothing turns a real man off more than an uneducated woman.”

“You seemed to be turned on with no words exchanged out there.”

“You are right, but you felt what I wanted you to feel. When you open your mouth, however, that could all disappear.” I understood this to be true so I continued to listen.

“How many dudes can have access to you?”

I replied, “Zero.”

He said, “Okay. Then why work in a place where you seduce men to get what you want?”

“Easy money,” I replied.

“Are you afraid to work hard for something you want?”

“No, I’m not afraid.”

“You don’t talk much.” *Good observation*, I thought to myself. “I talk when there is something to be talked about.”

This time he chuckled and stood up to leave. “It was nice to meet you, Duchess,” he said.

“Likewise.”

He walked out and I followed shortly after.

In his deep, strong voice, Don said, “Easy money.” He even smirked, knowing that this was just another day for me.

“Don, just keep the $1500. I know your daughter’s birthday is approaching. Get her something nice.”

“Thank you,” he proclaimed as I walked off. He paused. “Wait don’t you want the other $8500?”

With a confused look, I asked, “What $8500?”

“He didn’t tell you? That dude dropped $10,000 for that 5-minute dance.”

I chuckled. “Give it to Tracy to lock up.”

“No problem, and thanks again, Duchess.”

Guess his pockets are just as hung as he is, I thought as I walked off.

TRAVIS

FUCK, FUCK, FUCK. What am I doing? I literally flew down 295 weaving in and out of traffic trying to get away from Callie. I knew she saw me, hell, she was right on my ass. Luckily for me I took the exit off Malcolm X Boulevard at the last minute and she couldn't get over in time to catch it. But that's on her. Why would she get over into a far lane when she knew an exit was approaching? Anyway I dropped the lil hoe off at the Popeye's and gave her ass bus fare. She looked at me half crazy as to say where is the rest, but law #1 is to get your money upfront. She failed herself. I sped off into the night. For the past 45 minutes Callie had been blowing up my phone. I didn't answer because my nerves were still shot. When she called from another number I knew it was her, but I was good by then.

"Hey baby, what's up," I asked coolly.

"Who was the bitch in the car with you?" Callie yelled through the burner phone.

"What are you talking about? I'm at my boy D house out Ft. Washington," Travis replied.

"Nigga. I just chased you down 295 -- I know you saw me so don't even fucking try it," Callie replied.

"I don't know. I'm not sure whom you chased down 295, but it wasn't me --"

She cut me off. "Really? That's what you're going with? Like I'm just out here not knowing what my man's car looks like or I'm going to be insane enough to chase a car down without checking your plates?!" Callie asked.

“Your batshit crazy ass be saying the stupidest shit, I swear. How the fuck you check my plates in a high speed chase down 295 in the dark? Fuck I look copping to some B.S. like that?” I asked, getting irritated.

“It would behoove you to just come out and be a man about your load of crap. But no, you want to sit here and deny it like I’m going to second-guess what I know I saw. Shit looks real sus out here.” Callie hissed. “Either that nigga or you trying to test your nine lives.”

“Bitch did you just threaten me?” I asked in an attempt to regain control over the situation.

With a sinister tone, she replied, “No nigga threats are for kids… I marked your trade ass.” With that, Callie hung up.

After that, all I heard was the dial tone. I had to be in a state of shock because I never heard anyone walk up to me. I was standing in front of my mom’s house at the time. I was going to tell Callie I had been there all night, but my mom wasn’t home. All I heard was “Aye my man…”

When I looked up, I felt two bullets rip through my chest. I reached for my chest as three more bullets invaded my torso and after that my last thought was what Callie said. “No nigga... I marked your trade ass.” She wanted me to know it was her. Everything went black.

APPLE

I love dick that is universal. You know, the type I can ride all night and return home to wifey. Most of the times, a nigga won't let his chick touch his ass but he will let me run all up and through it. And trust me -- I run all up and through it.

I meet the oh-I'm-not-gay-because-I'm-on-top niggas, the I-just-like-the-way-niggas-suck-me-off niggas, and the I-ain't-gay-I-love-pussy niggas. Either way, these niggas end up on the tip of my dick, so fuck them all. Literally.

I ran across Travis two years ago at the National Mall. I was down there trying to be normal and he was down there scoping out the scene. He was more obvious than I'm sure he intended to be, but that was his business, not mine. As his target approaches me, still some space away, Travis fine ass walks up to me and kisses me so passionately that my pussy tingles. The gag of it all!

As his target gets closer, Travis pulls a 9mm out of his pants and shoots the man dead in front of his wife and kids. The wife screams her head off while Travis pulls me in the direction of his car. I was scared shitless. I just witnessed this man shoot another man dead in the heart of downtown D.C. but nonetheless, I went anyway. I mean it's not like he gave me a choice. About four blocks up, six police cars box us in. Now Travis is scared shitless. Clearly, he's no professional. He was probably hired because of his phenomenal aim. That's as far as his talents extends. I see the fear in his eyes as we both hear the police say over the intercom, "The suspects are armed and dangerous. Approach with caution."

The officer tells us to step out of the vehicle with our hands up. All the while I'm thinking, *shit Apple think of something quick*. I take my razor out of my mouth and cut the inner part of my thigh in the shape of several X's. I wipe the razor off and slide it back in my mouth. Travis looks at me like I lost my damn mind but he exits the vehicle anyway. I see the gun in the back of his pants. I pull it out and slide it in my bag, ensuring I buried it deep in there. The cop taps the window and tells me to get out as well. I hear Travis say, “All that for illegal tents?” I get out the vehicle slowly. I was not trying to be on the 4 o’clock, 5 o’clock, 9 o’clock, or 10 o'clock news.

We are both outside the vehicle and the police approach us with guns drawn. I’m holding my stomach, but not too dramatically, the entire time. The officer notices the blood and starts to ask if I’m ok, whether I was hit, did I need a doctor, blah blah blah. I looked at him pretending to be confused and followed his eyes down to my blood-soaked pants. I put my head down and say as sadly as possible, “Yes, I’m just bleeding through my pad. It’s hard as hell to find a restroom down here the late in the night.”

The police officer stops searching me and says, “She’s clean.”

I start crying and the officer asks what’s wrong. I explained to him that it was our first date and how embarrassed I was to be on my period and pulled over for no reason. The officer looks at me sympathetically and tells to his counterparts that they have the wrong vehicle.

“Well, shit, at least ticket the motherfucker for illegal tints,” one of the other officers jokes.

“Wrap it up!” Another officer says.

The officer I had been interacting with apologizes and allows us to leave. Them fools didn’t even notice it was coming through lines, not blobs as blood normally does.

He asked when I got a safe distance away, “Hey where is my shit?” I reached in my bag and handed it to him. Smiling, he said, “Oh a nigga kiss you and now you Bonnie ready to take a charge for Clyde.” I looked out the window.

"You don't hear me talking to you?"

I replied, "I live on Benning Road near the shrimp boat."

He responded by turning the music up.

For some reason, at this point, I'm no longer afraid but annoyed. About 20 minutes later we pull up to an apartment off of 210 and says get out. I silently oblige.

Inside the apartment was nice, but I wasn't impressed. I had niggas whose houses for their side pieces and escapades looked more lavishly designed than this. But hey, you do what you can afford I guess.

He walked up to me and tried to kiss me. This time I turned my head away.

"Oh, it's like that?" he inquired.

I replied, "I'm gay."

"And…?"

"You don't understand. If I fuck you, you will be gay as well."

He caught the hint and said, "You think I don't know that already? You're pretty, I'll give you that, but the streets are never quiet."

I thought to myself, *I wonder what they are saying about you then.*

As much as it caught me off guard, I decided to go with it anyway. This time when he leaned in to kiss me, I allowed him.

He laid me on the couch and allowed me to give him oral. I took his dick in my mouth. All nine inches of it. He tried ramming it in my mouth, but this throat runs deeper than the ocean. I two-hand swirled the shaft of his dick, making him moan loudly -- and you know how us girls get turned on when a man moans. I started to massage his balls and finger his ass. I could tell this was his first time so I took it slowly.

I stood up and told him to come get this pussy. He livened up and entered me roughly. Pounding in and out of me. Even I quivered a bit. When my body started shaking I knew I had to get him there. So I grinded and popped my ass to further entice him. Sooner than later he exploded all in me. He didn't even get soft; he just kept pounding so roughly that I started to go in and out of consciousness. After one final pound, he came again. He got up and showered while I laid there. I drifted off to sleep. Moments later, I was awakened by a buzzing phone. When I looked at the screen it said "WIFE". I shook my head as I thought, *another undercover brother.* I turned over and drifted off to sleep.

When I woke up Travis was asleep. I wrote my number on his chest with Ruby Woo lipstick. I even left a note that said 'call me if u have a hard day' before I left out.

Three weeks later I saw Travis all hugged up with my boss Duchess at the Anonymous Anomaly. It's a strip club I work at. Duchess opened it when she was 20. Most don't even know she owns it, but that's my best friend so you know I'm hip.

I walked up to them and said hello. Travis' face was so cool you would have never thought he was caught.

Duchess spoke and said, "Hey Apple."

I said, "Are you dancing tonight?" That was our code for something was up.

She replied, "I was thinking about it." She was still in code.

"They holding and dropping money like it's last call."

She chuckled and said, "Money is constant."

"Well let me get back to the bar. I'll talk to you later."

"Okay, later."

I walked off, but to translate our conversation, I said to her that was the dude was a trade that I had already fucked and he knew what it was.

After the club finally closed at 4am I met Duchess in her office. As soon as I walked in she burst out in laughter.

“He was as cool as a whistle,” she laughed.

“Wasn’t he, though?” I replied, laughing as well.

“Why didn’t you tell me about him?” Duchess asked, pretending to be hurt.

“I did!”

“No... wait... not the ‘I’m on my period’ guy!” She was astonished.

“Yes, him!” I replied.

Girl, I don’t know what I was expecting but that wasn’t it. He splurges on me like crazy and I have yet to give him any. Why even put up a fight with a nigga who clearly only needs me for appearances?”

“Right.” I said.

She confirmed what I already knew. You see, Duchess was a virgin. No matter how wild she got, she never indulged. She was low key saving it for marriage. She always promised her father she would cherish that, and after he died, she stuck to that. The funny thing is that she will never tell a dude that she’s a virgin and she never, ever explains herself.

CALLIE

Apple and I met in 6th grade. My parents had just moved here from upstate New York and enrolled me at Alice Deal Middle School. I was never the type to care about meeting new people so it wasn't a big deal. One day during third period, I left in the middle of class to use the restroom. As I walked in, Apple was exiting the stall. "Is this the boys' room?"

"Nah, why would we be in the boys' room?" he asked.

I looked at him puzzled and said, "true." I walked to the stall and peed. Later that week, I ran into Apple again during a lacrosse game.

"Hey, I'm Callie and you are...?"

"Not a girl, but all woman."

I started laughing uncontrollably. "What does that even mean?"

"My name is Adam, but I like to be called Alameda."

"That is far-gone. Maybe you should come up with something else."

"Why?"

"Because it doesn't sound like a winner," I paused. "How about Apple, because they're so delicious and good for you."

"Ohhhh, I like that. Slutty but well kept. I like it."

He has been Apple ever since. In our freshman year of high school, some real bad shit happened to Apple. I recall him being excited about this guy but he never told me the guy's name. He claimed he didn't want to jinx it. It was the first crush that had shown him some attention. On May 5th, I recall big parties happening all over the city. Apple was pressing me about going to some party over in Yellow Brick. Now I'm no genius, but I'm sure it wasn't the Wizard of Oz. My name damn sure wasn't naïve Dorothy. So I told him no. Everyone knew better than going in someone else's neighborhood, but Apple said it was safe because of the parties.

At 3am I got a call from Apple.

"Yeah Apple, what's up?" I asked dry.

"Girl, they should call this boy thunder!" Both of us were virgins prior to this night so I immediately woke up and paid attention.

"Why?!" I damn near yelled through the phone.

"Let's just say he came like lightning."

"Damn, that bad?" I asked.

"No... I mean it was loud and rough. I loved it!"

"O-M-G, really?!" I was crazy excited. "Did it hurt?" I anxiously waited to hear the details.

"Yeah for a little while, and then I liked it."

"Callie is that you?" I heard my mother call out. I almost fucked up and said no. Instead, I said "Oh shit, I gotta go." I immediately hung up and laid on the bed and pulled the covers over my head. My mom opened the door to make sure that I was asleep. She closed my door and walked back out of the room.

That Monday when I got to school, I sat outside of Apple's homeroom class. I thought it was strange that he never came out. Afraid he may have left before I got there, I stopped his teacher.

"Hey Ms. Gore, was Adam in class today?" I asked.

"Nope, he wasn't," was all she said before turning her attention to another student.

I kept calling him on his cell, but he never answered. Finally, I went to his house searching for him. I knocked on his door with a sense of urgency.

"Who is it?"

"Hi Mrs. Johanna, is Adam home?" I yelled through the door.

She opened the door and looked at me with sympathy. I knew something was wrong instantly.

"What's wrong?" I asked anyway, fearing the worst.

"Adam is in the hospital," she replied. "He was attacked Saturday."

"Attacked!?" I yelled.

"Yes." That was all she said. I was hanging on, waiting for details and this bitch is acting like I'm the Feds. Clearly, I had to request information since she wasn't going to volunteer it.

"Well, what hospital is he at?"

"He's at Washington Hospital Center, room 603. I'll call ahead to tell them you are coming." She closed the door. I ran to my car and rushed to the hospital. When I arrived at his room I heard all of the machines before I even walked in.

"Apple, it's me. Callie." I said as I approached his bed.

He opened his eyes. "Hey Callie, you didn't have to come all the way up here," he said.

"Are you crazy? Why wouldn't I?" I felt my eyes tearing up. "What happened to you?"

Before he could even answer my question, a nurse came in. "Adam these detectives are here to see you. Ma'am, I need you to step out of the room please."

Apple replied, “No. She will stay.” The nurse backed down.

“Hello sir. I’m Detective Owens and this is my partner, Detective Wells. Can you tell us what happened the night of May 5th?” He took out his notepad, prepared to write.

Adam took a deep breath and started to recap what happened that night.

He said he had attended a party where he didn't really know anyone. He said he had gotten restless and decided to call it a night and head home. “I heard some guys behind me. I paid it no mind at first, but then their pace picked up and the hairs on the back of my neck stood up. So I started to walk faster -- not trying to appear too frightened. One of them hit me from behind and I fell to the ground. Next thing I know, I woke up here.”

The detectives asked a few more questions, hoping to get a clearer picture as to what happened, but Adam wasn’t very helpful. They gave him their cards and left. I could have sworn I heard one say ‘this one will be another cold case with this little bit of information,’ but I couldn’t be sure so I didn’t say anything.

“Is that what happened Apple?” I asked once the door closed and they had been a safe distance away.

He shook his head no. We had always been honest with one another so I waited for the truth.

“After you hung up last night... well this morning... I was about to exit the bathroom. It was quiet so I figured everyone had left or found a corner.” He began to explain. “Next thing I know, Ashton pushed me back into his bedroom --”

“ASHTON?” I interrupted

He looked down and continued. “He said that I had the sweetest pussy he had the pleasure of tasting. I blushed because that sounded like something great. By the time he pushed me on the bed, I had noticed Dame and Kevin were there as well. I asked them what was going on. Ashton said that it was nothing to worry about. He flipped me over and rammed his dick in my ass. I tried to run but he overpowered me. He pulled me up on all fours and Dame started sucking my dick. Kevin looked away disgusted. The feeling of it all felt good even though I didn't want it. My body responded," he said embarrassed.

He continued, "I was still trying to run but wasn't going anywhere. Then Ashton yelled 'tonight you're getting your cherry popped.' I thought he was talking to me since it was my first time, but then he yelled to Kevin 'put your pussy in his mouth now,' but Kevin didn't move. So then he said 'do it now before I rip her a new one.' Kevin must have known what he meant because next thing I know he's on all fours in front of me. Ashton grabbed my neck and said 'I'll snap this bitch if you don't start eating. We can fuck a corpse.' I immediately did as I was told. I stick my tongue in Kevin's ass and spit on the hole like I saw in porn. Kevin enjoyed it, but I could tell he definitely did not want to. Dame was still sucking my dick and when I was hard enough he stopped. Ashton then pulled out of my ass. He stood up and told me to fuck him. That's when I noticed the knife in Dame's hand."

My jaw dropped in horror. Apple looked sad, but kept going. "I jumped up and stuck my dick in Kevin's hole. He screamed so loud it scared me, but I didn't stop. When Kevin tried to run, Dame held him down. Eventually, Kevin gave up. Then Dame sucked Kevin's dick same as he did mine. Not too long after Kevin busted a nut in Dame's mouth, I was allowed to stop then but Ashton made me give him oral. For a second, I thought it would be less painful and less embarrassing if I just let them stab me... but I got afraid and became a coward. I bounced on Dame's dick. Ashton was preparing to come in my mouth. The more I cried, the harder they came. They had no mercy for Kevin or me. I thought the three of them were going to rape me. But actually, the two of them raped me and Kevin. Once it was done, I heard Ashton say 'get these bitches out of here'. Dame told us to leave. I damn near ran out the door naked -- all I managed to get was my dress. When I looked back, Dame was fucking Ashton. A part of me wondered if that was his real boyfriend and this was a way to get back at him for cheating. Or maybe they got off on hurting each other, but either way, I got out of there. Kevin did the same. Three blocks later we had both stopped. Too tired to go on, I looked over at Kevin and his eyes were glossed over."

Apple took a deep breath and his eyes got watery. "I yelled at him and said 'Kevin snap out of it. We have to get out of here, let's get on the metro.' He just followed me. I asked where he lived and he didn't respond. Truth be told I was afraid to go home. I had left my keys at the party spot and I was afraid Ashton would come for me, but I had nowhere else to go at such an unpleasant hour. Once we got into the train station I saw a train was coming in one minute. We walked to that one. As it pulled up Kevin ran up and jumped in front of it."

By now, Apple was crying. I covered my mouth in pure shock. "That was Kevin?" Once again, my eyes were filled with tears that threatened to fall at any given second.

"Yes..." Apple replied. "All of us ran away in terror. I passed out not too long after. When I woke up, I was here."

"Why didn't you tell the police?" I asked, finally.

"I didn't want to disrespect Kevin by telling his nightmare. I needed twenty-two stitches. Trust me, they get the point of what happened. If they don't, they are as incompetent as they come."

"Apple, you have to tell the detectives or Ashton and Dame is going to get away with what they did to you."

Apple shook his head. "I'm the judge and the jury now. They didn't rape the justice system they raped me. Why should the justice system get the honor?"

I just replied, "Whatever you have planned, count me in."

Apple agreed to do so. Two weeks later, we attended Kevin's funeral. It was closed casket of course. His mom was sitting in the front row with Dame, Ashton, and a young girl who I assumed was his sister. She looked about 14.

"How could they have the balls to be here after what they did?" I whispered to Apple.

He said, "They are sadists, I expect nothing less from them." We walked up, gave his mother our condolences, and took our seats.

As I was reading the obituary, I was perplexed. "Apple listen to this," I said as I began to read. "Kevin Alexander Sharp is survived by his beloved mother Alexandra Sharp, his elder brothers Ashton Alex Sharp and Damian Alexon Sharp, and his younger sister Alexa Marie Sharp." Our hearts broke. We got up and left after that.

DAME

"Tasha, I will be home shortly," I cooed.

"Okay baby, but hurry because I have a surprise for you," she replied.

"Alright, let me catch Ashton before he leaves ma's house and I'll be right there."

"Okay baby, see you later."

"Later." I hit end. "Ma where is Ashton we need to politic about some shit right quick," I said walking down the hall.

"Damian, watch your mouth in my house." She angrily replied.

Ashton interrupted ma's rant with, "Fuck this house, we bought the shit." Ashton never cared for ma's babble. We both stepped off together, but not before she could try and get the last word. "I don't give a fuck who brought what... what's mine is mine and you better watch your mouth before I teach you some manners!"

"Hey bruh I only got a minute I need to catch Tasha. She's about to tell me she's pregnant!" I said excitedly.

"Yeah. How do you know that?" Ashton asked.

"Man she's been eating like crazy, getting thicker than some down south gravy, and she's glowing. How could I not know is the question." We chuckled but I could tell Ashton's wasn't sincere. I dismissed it though.

"Here's a stack," Ashton said, handing me my money. "Cool down and I will get you out the way Tuesday."

"Alright, later fam." I replied.

I left out and drove a good mile before realizing I had left my phone. I turned around and headed back to ma house. When I got there I saw Ashton's car still in the driveway. This rubbed me the wrong way considering he always gets the hell out of there when business is done. He hates that house with the ambition of the Gods. He would burn it down if it weren't for him needing an alibi often.

However, I shook it off and proceeded to the house. I used my pin to get into the house and walked in to the family room to get my phone -- where I thought I had left it. That's when I heard Ashton say, "Don't try me lil bitch." I got kinda curious, so I headed to the camera room to see what was going on. My eyes almost escaped me when I saw ma push her pussy inside Ashton's mouth. What is going on here, I thought to myself. I saw ma stand up and enter her bathroom as Ashton laid there. She came back with a large dildo. She laid across the bed and started playing with herself. This shit had to be the grossest thing I've ever seen.

She yelled, "Ashton, come fuck me."

"No!" Ashton yelled back.

"I said come fuck me." Ma said, once again

"No." Ashton said, yet again.

"Don't make me get Alexa in here," Ma threatened.

"Fuck her too," Ashton replied.

"I will," ma replied in a sinister tone. "Alexa!"

Ashton looked away unfazed like he was calling her bluff.

Alexa appeared shortly after.

Alexa is our thirteen-year-old sister, a virgin to my knowledge. But with the sick shit I'm witnessing, I could just be out of the loop.

"Alexa, lay down," my mom commanded.

Alexa did as she was told. My mom lifted her waist, proceeded to take her pants and panties off, and then started eating Alexa out. I'm not sure if this was normal or not, but I heard Alexa moan loudly. Ashton just watched. When Alexa was wet enough, my mom turned her finger vibrator on and started massaging Alexa's clit with it. Alexa began to run.

"No Alexa, sit still," ma commanded.

Alexa tried until ma took the dildo and rammed it into Alexa's vagina. The pain was all over Alexa's face. I knew then it was definitely her first time.

"No, that pussy needs the real deal." Ashton finally interjected. He got hard as a rock and pulled Alexa on top of him. Alexa cried in pain.

"Stop," Alexa cried out. "This hurts... please stop! Why are you hurting me like this?" Alexa continuously sobbed. It only fueled Ashton's ego. He began to bounce her on his dick -- the louder she screamed, the harder he thrust into her. I sat there paralyzed watching the shit.

I got up, picked up the 9mm I just brought from Gray on 22nd, and I walked down the hall towards the room that they were in. I pushed the door open and I started shooting and I didn't stop until I was sure not one of them survived. I turned and walked out of the room and straight out the house. I never even closed the door.

On my drive home I thought about Kevin. That day that all that stuff went down has been etched in my memory permanently. I still remember it like it was yesterday. This is what happened:

I was chilling at Tasha's house watching The L Word. She loved that show. Not my thing, but hey it's her world. Plus, it beat me sitting there studying for the history test I originally told her I needed help studying for. My phone rang. I looked down at the screen and realized it was Ashton. I ignored the first three calls, but he was persistent so I decided to answer.

"Yeah Ashton, what's up?" I asked.

"Slide through." Ashton said.

"Right now?" I inquired. The line went dead.

I was agitated because I just got Tasha to let me slide through. We had a fight over some girl saying I was putting the press on her and we were finally back to chilling. Nevertheless, I knew I needed to go or it would be hell later.

"Hey Tasha, I gotta go." I said.

"What's new?" she asked sarcastically.

I just got up, grabbed my books, and left. I heard her mumble, "The lil Becky probably waiting on you. You wouldn't want to hold her up any longer." I shook it off and kept it pushing.

"What's up Ashton?" I asked 20 minutes later when I got to him.

"Fuck you smell like pussy for?" Ashton asked, disgustedly.

"Bruh, what's up?" I asked again.

"Go take a shower."

At that point, I knew what was up. Ashton hated the fact that I was straight. It was like my straightness undermined his peace of mind being gay. Although Ashton was a senior, he always felt inferior when I was around due to me being skipped a grade. I was a freshman at the time. Ashton was gay, but he would never say it out loud. He used to rape me over and over again in junior high school. After a while, it became normal to me and I didn't complain. Whenever he wanted to have sex, he made me take a shower. He had been this way since he walked in on Tasha and I on Valentine's Day. He threw up right there on the floor. Then there was Kevin. Whenever he tried to touch Kevin, Kevin would beat his ass. No mercy applied. Kevin always said be free to be you, but don't try to force me to have sex with you so you can keep your secret longer. On the day that Kevin died, it was because Ashton told Kevin he was going to rape Alexa as brutally as possible if he didn't give himself freely to him. He wanted Kevin to become submissive to him. Weak if you will. Kevin obliged because he knew what Ashton was capable of.

After I got out the shower I heard Ashton say 'Kevin is about to experience a night he will never forget'.

My idea was to handle Kevin and go about my day. The quicker he came the quicker the whole entire ordeal would be over. But something about that night seemed different. That night you could see the lust in Ashton's eyes. He thrived off of Kevin's embarrassment. To me, threats were foreplay. It was what I was used to. Kevin was different. He clearly understood this was wrong and that it was rape. Fast forward to when he killed himself, I just had no remorse. I didn't understand it was wrong or rape. Before Ashton had ever touched me, daddy and uncle daddy loved me this way all the time. Daddy died of lung cancer and uncle daddy's girlfriend Alice killed him after seeing some pictures he hid in his lock box. This was my reality. The older I got and interacted with people, the more I realized that this was wrong. I went to college and moved in with Tasha to avoid this fuckery. I thought Alexa was safe. After all, she was a girl and Ashton wanted boys. But I guess he didn't care, he was a sadist who enjoyed inflicting pain on others.

The world is a safer place without all of them. Alexa died because who could ever mentally survive that truth? Her own family preyed on her. I hoped she would go to heaven. Ma and Ashton could burn in hell.

When I arrived home, Tasha stood at the door with balloons and a box.

I pretended to smile as I walked towards her.

"Hey baby," I said, trying to control my emotions.

TASHA

I've been with Dame since high school. In the beginning, everything was amazing. After his brother's death, he seemed different. Not in a bad way, but more of a distant way.

I stood there ready for my baby to walk in the door. I've been keeping this secret for far too long and today I've decided to tell him. When he walked in, I felt so elated to show him; I handed him the box to open and when he did balloons and sonograms exploded everywhere. He starting crying and I did, too. I'm a ball of emotions these days, however, these tears were tears of joy. I ran in the kitchen to bring back the cupcake that revealed the sex of the baby, which, truth be told, even I was curious to know. I decided that we would share the moment of learning the gender together.

I froze when I heard a loud gunshot go off. When I ran back in the living room, I found Dame on the floor dead. I dropped the cupcake and ran to his side. I had no understanding of what was happening. It was like an out of body experience where I watched myself react, move, and feel -- but in my flesh, I felt nothing. It just burned to breathe. There was blood and brain matter everywhere.

I finally called 911, but he was dead on impact and I knew it. His soul hugged mine on its way out. The only man that I had ever lived and shared my body with killed himself before he got to meet our soon to be daughter.

All night I answered questions from officers, doctors, nurses, and detectives. It was 3am and I was still dressed in the blood stained clothes. I couldn't take them off. They contained the remnants of my love. Our child would never feel this close to him again. How could this be happening to us? We were perfect together; our love was deep and everlasting. We were your goals. Even at a young age, we still fell in love with each other every day. How could this be us? How could this be the end of it all?

Two Weeks Later

After the funeral, I was happy to be finally alone. I thought Dame had killed himself because of the baby news, but I later found out he walked in on his mom and brother having sex with his sister and he had some sort of psychotic break and killed all of them. The baby news must have gave him a flash back -- maybe he felt like he would go to jail and rather die before watching his daughter grow up while behind bars. I wish I knew his last thought. Maybe I would have had some solace, or maybe I wouldn't, but either way, the baby news was bad timing.

I saw my phone light up and I decided to check the messages. The first text I noticed was from Dame. I couldn't retrieve it fast enough. It read:

> I love you, I always have, and I always will. But my heart pumps venom not blood. This baby will be safer away from the sadist monster that they made me. Live and love again. Give my daughter the world, and don't cry over me.

I was at a loss for words. Could he be confessing that he's the same type of monster that his family was? He can't be... I mean I know him. I would know. Maybe he felt guilty by association. Like birds of a feather flock together. Or maybe he was referring to murdering them. I was a complete wreck. I eventually fell asleep but honestly, a nap was well overdue. I was awakened to my phone ringing. When I looked at the screen I noticed the funeral home calling.

“Hello?” I answered.

“Ms. McCall, there has been a tragic incident and we need you to come down as soon as possible.”

Although I couldn’t understand what was so tragic, I mean Dame was already dead, I replied, “I’m on my way.”

When I got there the detectives waited quietly. I looked around, clearly confused. “What is going on. What happened?” I asked For a brief second I was hoping that that they told me Dame was still alive, but I knew better. I had seen it with my own two eyes.

“Ms. McCall, someone set Damian and Ashton's caskets on fire. We were unable to salvage any evidence due to the fire,” one of the detectives said.

My mouth dropped open. This couldn’t be happening.

CALLIE

Yeah, I went to that lil bihh funeral. I never thought I'd see the day. Correction -- his day was coming sooner than expected, but I didn't think I would see it before I got a chance to be the executioner.

Apple turns 25 next month and little did he know, he was going to get his life back as a gift. You see, that night didn't just destroy Apple; it destroyed me as well. Apple refused to tell anyone what had happened to him. Not even his parents know the gruesome details, and after hearing them I can understand why. I wanted to die hearing it, so I could only imagine how he felt experiencing it. I swore to myself that if I had the chance, they would both have to die. Ashton was envied by all of his peers and wanted by all of the girls. That's why I could never understand why he went through such lengths to hurt Apple. What was his vendetta? To be honest I don't care, and Dame? He took me by surprise. He was a good boy. Perfect grades, steady girlfriend, quiet and respectful. Don't get me wrong he was a player and a partier, but good nonetheless.

Anyway, I had to see this family buried beneath HELL. Six feet under wasn't enough. I needed them sixteen feet under. I needed God to come drag them to the pits of hell without the possibility of sympathy. The rage I feel while thinking about these monsters scares me, but I'm so at peace with my decision that I feel comforted at the same time. How dare these monsters get to execute each other? The pleasure was all mine and I assure you I had a fun, eventful day ready to be had for all of us. Well... not necessarily the mom and sister. This was a boy's only trip. Fucking baboons. Good riddance to all them son of a bitches.

APPLE

Look at this woman sitting here crying over this waste of God's talents. Tasha McCall. I will call her a sad, sad case. If only she knew the devil she played between the sheets with. I wish I could have sympathy, but it's not in me. As I walked up to Ashton's casket, I spit in his face with all the phlegm I could gag up. Tasha jumped up but Callie gave her the look of death. I turned to walk away, but decided to pass on a message. "When you lay down with the devil you're destined to get burned. Judging by the bulge under your shirt, I can tell he lit the fire. If I were you I would think about that 'trap him' baby before you get trapped in the grim reapers sights."

She looked at me with pure hatred her eyes. I strutted off alongside a smiling Callie.

Duchess and I went to the gravesite and waited for all the cars to leave. I walked up to the casket and threw the clothes in it from the night they raped me. Even in death, I wanted to remind him how he sealed the deal to his fate. They just did it before we could. Lastly, I threw Kevin's varsity ring in there as well. I hope it burns a hole right threw that cheap ass, two-for-one-special ass casket.

I finally got the closure I needed. I just hate that the monster was able to leave parts of him behind. They should have been extinct after him. As I was walking off, Duchess said, "Just in case they are faking it..."

She poured gasoline all over their caskets lit a match and walked off. I saw the fire for at least 20 blocks. It was my turn to have no remorse. I told Duchess the police are going to think I did that, but I will go to jail just to have that moment over again. Some things are definitely worth the jail time.

Duchess replied, "God hated those miserable fucks. He tricked them into letting them think they were invincible, only for them to die and be fucked in the ass by the devil. The police could give a fuck less about such miscreants."

I shook my head. Sometimes Duchess doesn't realize how severe things really are or how severe they could potentially get, but I was blessed to have a friend like her that had my back always. So for her I would pull up on anyone.

TASHA

I knew Callie and Apple had something to do with Dame and Ashton's casket being set on fire, but I couldn't prove it. The police said it would be hard to prove since Ashton had several known enemies. "Three different women have accused him of rape since 2008. Any one of these women could have done it," Officer Tate informed me.

Fuck what he was talking about. I knew with every bone in my body and every breath I took that it was Apple. That's why people never go to the justice system with their problems. The real ones take it to the streets because street justice is better than anything else. It doesn't work off of technicalities. Hunches suffice, and that's all that's needed.

Two Years Later

Anika's 1st birthday came and went. She was such a precious baby. I rushed home daily just to be with her, but tonight grandma is babysitting and I'm hanging out with my girl Macy.

I met Macy back in college. She was this cool ass White girl from Texas trying to get as far away as possible. Anyway, we had a project together sophomore year and we have been hanging tight ever since. I need to hurry up and finish getting dressed because -- shit never mind she's here. Leave it to the white girl to be cliché and get here on time.

"Hey girl," I greeted her as I opened the door.

"You aren't ready yet?" She asked, pretending to be annoyed.

"Almost. Give me two minutes." I said.

"Hurry up," she replied.

Forty-five minutes and three shots later, we were finally headed out.

"So where are we going? Anthropologie?" I asked.

"Nope," Macy replied. "I was thinking about sliding through Brendan's house. He's having his brother's 29th birthday bash."

"Brendan Daniels?" I asked.

"Yes!" Macy exclaimed.

"Oh hell yes, let's go. How did you get invited?" I asked.

"Camille invited me." Macy answered.

"Who is Camille?"

"She's a nurse at my hospital."

"Oh, and she is Brendan's girlfriend?" I asked, prying.

"No. She's Brendan's cousin." Macy knowingly replied.

I let out a sigh of relief. You see, Brendan was the man every girl needed. Rough, educated, and employed. Most people didn't even know him, but his name rings bells in the streets. I remember one night it was pouring down raining and I was stuck trying to get my screaming baby to the hospital. Brendan stopped at the light and must have heard Anika screaming. He rolled down the window and said, "Hey I don't want to appear crazy, but do you need a ride?"

I looked at him as fine as he was and shook my head no. He drove off parked his car and jogged back over to us. I was standing there holding Anika super close, watching him because obviously this nigga was crazy. He finally got beside me and just stood there. I looked at him and asked, "What are you doing?"

He replied, "I understand why you will not allow me to give you a ride, but I am not going to leave you and this baby out here in the dark while it's raining."

I was shocked but I quickly responded, "We are fine, thank you."

He said, "I get that."

Can you believe he continued to stand there? I was grateful even though I didn't say it right away. The bus finally pulled up and it was packed beyond capacity. There was no way me or this stroller was getting on there. I just stepped back and let it pass. "Shit!" I said out loud.

"Look, here is my name and license plate number." He reached in his pocket for his ID and car insurance.

"What is this for?" I asked.

"Send it to your home girl or deranged father so you can accept this ride."

Not really seeing any other feasible options, I give in and ask him to take us to GW Hospital. He pulled up 30 minutes later. I thanked him and lugged Anika and her stroller inside. As I'm filling out the paperwork, someone sits beside me. I look up and it is him.

He said, "I am waiting to take you back home."

I thought it was sweet, but I was sure he had a motive.

Six hours later, we finally left. He took me home and helped me get Anika inside. I offered him my couch, and to my surprise, he took it.

The next morning when I woke up he was gone. Nothing went with him and I never saw him again. I never even spoke of him again until Macy mentioned this fine young man named Brandon at her job pushing up on her. She was talking and said he had a brother named Brendan who always slid through to see him. At first I got excited, but I calmed down not wanting to appear thirsty. Now, here we are on the way to his party.

We entered the party and headed straight for the pool area. Brandon walked up not too long after to greet Macy. He was all over her, which caused a lot of eye rolling and shady stares. But my girl Macy? She was fine, educated, stacked, and paid. She was the best cardiologist Children's National Hospital had and she knew it. So you can imagine how sick these fans were while they observed from the sidelines. I couldn't tell if they were disgruntled because she was White or because Brandon was all over her. Either way, they needed some business because this was already happening and he didn't seem to have any plans of mingling with anyone else.

"Let me introduce you to Brendan," Brandon said while waving him over. My heart stopped as he walked up.

Macy said, "Okay. By the way, this is my girl Tasha."

"Nice to meet you, Tasha." Brandon replied while extending his hand for a greeting.

I shook his hand and said, "Nice to meet you as well."

Brendan had finally arrived and Brandon introduced us.

"Brendan this is my friend Macy and her girl--"

"Nice to see you again, Tasha." Brendan said as he looked at me.

This time, Macy was shocked. I smiled and said, "Likewise."

He looked over and politely stated, "It's nice to meet you Macy. I've heard nothing but good things about you."

Macy regrouped and said, "Nice to finally meet you." Not too long afterward, she and Brandon crept off and left me alone with Brendan.

I walked over and sat in front of the fire pit with Brendan on my heels.

"How is Anika doing?" Brendan asked

"She is fine," I replied. "By the way, thank you for that night. I greatly appreciate it."

"No problem."

"Why did you leave without saying goodbye?"

"I should have never stayed the night, but I was so exhausted that I could barely keep my eyes opened."

I laughed and said, "Did you miss your curfew?"

"No, but my fiancé Mia did not approve and she ended up calling off the wedding because of it." He confessed.

I stopped laughing. "I am so sorry. I had no idea."

"How could you? We were strangers. What's done is done."

I looked at him apologetically. He smiled and kept the conversation going. "So Tasha what do you do, are you a doctor as well?"

"I am a dentist."

"Why don't you have a car? Last time I checked they made a decent income, if not better than decent."

"My older sister Niylah died in a car accident when she was only 23. A drunk driver hit her. After that I guess I was too afraid to drive. I know that seems childish, but I have a very bad phobia now."

"My mom was struck by a drunk driver four years ago and died" He paused. "But you cannot dodge death. You need to get out there and learn before you allow this fear to cripple you."

"I know how to drive."

“Well, Anika had a fever of 101 and it was rising that night, you could have gotten her to the hospital a lot sooner if you drove.” He was trying to use my daughter to scare me or reason with me. I’m not sure which one, but neither seemed that effective.

“I hear you.” I saw where he was going and I didn’t wish to respond to it.

He dropped it and we ended up talking about everything else under the sun until the wee hours of the morning. He allowed me to sleep in his guest bedroom and drove me home later that day.

“Thank you for the ride again,” I giggled.

“Never a problem.”

I hesitated, but got out of the vehicle. Before I closed the door I turned to him and said, “I make amazing frittatas.”

He chuckled and said, “Sounds good, but I’ll take a rain check.” I can't lie, I was disappointed. However, I agreed and left.

BRENDAN

Being young, successful, educated, and wealthy had woman constantly throwing pussy at me, but I could tell Tasha was different. She wasn't thirsty, but she was feeling me. I turned her down for the frittatas simply because I was not there yet. I'm the lead engineer at my firm and I had a very lucrative project to present to some clients Monday morning and I needed to ensure that it was perfect.

The music stopped playing in my car, so I knew my phone was ringing. I looked at the screen and saw Braylin calling.

Braylin was my other brother -- one of the famous Daniels triplets. Most people didn't know my mom had triplets, but she raised a doctor, a lawyer, and an engineer. Honestly, I always thought Brandon should have been the lawyer and Braylin the doctor. Brandon was much more confrontational while Braylin was gentle and nurturing. But whatever... these dudes like what they like.

"Hey bro, what's up," I asked

"So I guess my room is for fly by now," he replied.

"No... sorry about that. All the other rooms were taken."

"Yours wasn't."

"It was occupied."

"No bruh, you know I don't mind, but you need to give some girl -- any girl -- a chance. She seemed cool, I mean I noticed she held your attention all night."

"Something to kill time," I replied.

"It's more than that, but you got it." Braylin replied.

“Anyway bruh, how is Shelia?”

“Shelia is fine.”

“Are you and Angie good?” I asked, truly concerned.

“Angie and I agreed that Shelia is our priority.” I dropped the subject, knowing it was a sensitive one for him.

“Well my brother, I have to get going. I have a few errands to run and a phone call or two to make if you don’t mind.”

“Aight catch you at dinner.” He hung up.

BRAYLIN

Angie was indeed a very sensitive topic for me. She and I met seven years ago at Ballston Commons Mall. She was there shopping and I just stopped in for lunch. I had business in the area and needed something quick. She was a showstopper -- just drop dead gorgeous. She was very dark skinned, about 5'7", 150 pounds, cute face, slim waist. I sat and admired her for a good five to ten minutes just trying to see if she was worth the chase. She never had a man like me and I was sure of it. As I listened to her, I was amazed at how articulate and graceful she was. I decided to say hello. I walked up to her. "Good afternoon, my name is Braylin," I said as I extended my hand out to touch hers.

She gave me the once over and extended her hand. Once we touched, all I could think about was how soft she was.

"Hello Braylin, my name is Angelique," she replied.

"Well it is very nice to meet you Angelique. Do you mind if I steal a moment of your time?" I asked.

At the moment realized I was still holding her hand. She pulled away and replied, "No, I don't mind; however, it would be rude of me."

I looked over at her friend and said, "I apologize, how rude of me. What is your name?"

Her friend smiled. "Kira."

"Kira it is nice to meet you as well. Well ladies I will let you go. I apologize for intruding on you girl's day. Before I leave Ms. Angelique may I have your number so I can call and take you out one day soon?"

She smiled and blushed. "I would like that."

I took my phone out and handed it to her. After she put her contact information in it she handed it back to me. "Well ladies, enjoy the rest of your day," I said, dismissing myself.

"You too," they replied in unison.

Two days went by and I decided to shoot her a text.

> I don't mean to infringe upon your day but if you are not too busy can we converse for a minute. - Braylin

Fifteen minutes later she texted back "what do you have on your mind sir?"

I responded, "thinking about going out later tonight and I wanted to know if you were interested in accompanying me. FYI it's a company shindig."

"What time is the event and what is the dress code?" she replied.

"I'll pick you up at 8pm and the dress code is evening formal. If it's too short of a notice, I understand."

She text me right back replying, "See you at 8. My address is 5321 K Street NE, Washington DC 20002."

I replied, "See you then."

When I arrived at her home it seemed very cozy. It was a nice, quiet neighborhood on Capitol Hill. I walked up her steps and rang the doorbell.

"One second" I heard her yell.

Two minutes later, she opened the door with a coat and walks out. I walked her to the car and opened the door for her to get in and get comfortable. I closed it and walked over to my side. She leaned over and opened my door for me. That's a very good sign. Her parents taught her something. I got in the car and I thanked her. We made small talk all the way there. At coat check, I finally saw her dress. It was a very nice black gown that had a modest split on the right side, embellished by heels with diamonds around the ankle strap. The dress hung off her shoulder very elegantly. I was impressed and very pleased with my decision to ask her to be my date.

"Hello Mr. Daniels. How are you?" My assistant, Mr. Hong, asked me.

"Hello Mr. Hong, I am well. This is my date Angelique," I replied.

"Hello Angelique, you are definitely a sight for sore eyes," Mr. Hong replied.

"Aww, thank you Mr. Hong." Angelique smiled.

"This is my wife Annie," Mr. Hong replied.

"Looking as beautiful as always." I said to return the compliment. Truthfully she looked like the back of Shaq's ass. "Well let us get going." I quickly ushered Angelique away.

"Would you like a drink?"

"No thank you. I do not drink anything other than water and juice," Angelique replied.

"Ahhh, Mr. Daniels? This is Mr. Brunswick."

"Good evening, Mr. Brunswick and Mr. Johnson. This is my date Angelique." They both spoke. Angelique exchanged pleasantries before finishing herself to head to the ladies room. Mr. Brunswick, Mr. Johnson and I talked briefly before I walked off to find my date. When she came out the bathroom she tapped my shoulder and I turned around happy to see her.

"What do you do?" She inquired.

"I am a lawyer." I replied.

"Oh, really! What type of lawyer?"

“A criminal lawyer. My firm represents high profile cases,” I answered nonchalantly.

“Have you represented anyone I would have heard about?”

“Maybe. Very likely.”

“Interesting,” she stated.

We danced, talked, and ate good food all night. I found out Angelique was an accountant. She was smart and very feminine. I enjoyed talking to her. Time flew by. The next thing I knew, we ended up in a relationship three months later. The day before I proposed, I had just dropped our two-year-old daughter off with my mother.

I was about to go meet Brandon to shoot the breeze, but decided to slide past the house to change. As I was pulling up a girl was running away from our front door. I caught her plates just as she pulled off. I got up to my door and saw a note attached. I opened the unlabeled one:

> Dear Mr. Benton
>
> I'm sorry to be the one that tells you bad news, but I guess you should know. I'm here because your wife is having an affair with my husband. And because of it I hate her guts and will ruin her life like she has ruined mine. Unfortunately you, like me, will be subjected to pain as well, and that is the sad part. I couldn't live happily, so why should you get to?
>
> Sincerely,
>
> A bitch that will get even

Benton was Angelique's last name, so right away I knew the letter writer thought we were married. I read through the whole letter still. The more I read, the more the words fell off the paper. Angelique would never, and who is this husband? I noticed the second envelope and I opened it. All off my doubt and questions were answered. Dozens of pictures of Malcolm and Angelique kissing and holding hands were right there. Then a flash drive that said 'I always come with receipts' fell out. For some reason the pictures were not enough. I had to really torture myself. When I plugged it in dozens of links popped up. I click one and random and there it was a video of Angelique two nights ago riding Malcolm's dick like a pro. Trying to click off the video, I clicked another and another. Over and over I saw Angelique performing a plethora of sexual acts on Malcolm. I just walked out the door and never looked back.

I knew she saw the note and the videos because my phone flooded with text from her. I finally responded with a simple text that said, "With my boss though?"

Malcolm Johnson was my boss. A rather cool individual -- or so I thought. He stayed out of my way and I stayed out of his. We would play a round of gold here and there, but outside of that we were strangers.

After the letters, I didn't talk to Angie for two years. It wasn't until my mom died that we started speaking again. For a while, we just fought all the time. Now, we just exchange pleasantries and keep it moving. Anyway, I'd rather not reflect too much on the past. It might have me at this bitch's door choking her ass out with my 9 -- and I'm not talking about my dick.

I pull up to PG Mall so I could grab some grub at the food court. After I ordered my Sakura, I decided to just sit and eat there. "Do you always drop ten grand on strangers, or was I the chosen one?"

I looked up to see a dancer that captivated me two years ago at the Anonymous Anomaly. I look her up and down and I smile. "I didn't want to waste your time, so I figured I would make it worth your while," I replied. "By the way I'm Braylin."

"Hi, I'm Callie. You left an impression, but worth my while never consists of money," she replied.

"Okay, well what made it worth your while?" I asked.

"The lack of expectation."

"How do you know I didn't expect anything?"

"Simple, you didn't leave a number. I never danced for you and I haven't seen you since," she stated, matter-of-factly.

I chuckled and said, "Okay. I see your point, but why do you still work there?" Mama would not approve of me bringing a dancer home, so I needed to see where her ambition was.

"Who said I worked there?" Now she was laughing.

"You did! You said you haven't seen me since I saw you, which means you, are located in the same spot. If that weren't the case how would you know for certain your theory was correct?"

"But I never said I worked there," she responded.

"Okay so my eyes must deceive me."

"They must and they have."

"Okay, I'll play this little game with you. Where do you work?"

"I own my own business, so that means I don't work. I delegate."

"Oh okay, very interesting." I replied. "Is your business doing well or is it in the infancy stages?"

"It's very lucrative," she answered with a sense of finality. But hell, I wasn't letting her off the hook like that.

I countered with, "Well I would like to support. What area are you capitalizing in?"

"The most lucrative area there is. Sex."

I was laughing so hard at that point. “So what... are you a madam or a porn director?” I joked, but was very serious.

“Neither.”

“Okay, so what is it called? There is a demand for sex and you supply it.”

“I own a margin of business that allows me to sell dreams.”

“Who would pay for a dream in the sex department?” I asked.

She started laughing so hard that I became confused. “What is so funny?”

“You did.”

“I did what?”

“You not only paid for it, you dropped ten grand on it. I own, and have always owned, the Anonymous Anomaly.”

“Really?” I was pissed she just did all that to say that, but I can’t say I wasn’t impressed. “Really?”

“Yes, really.” She sarcastically answered.

“Who would've known?”

“You if you just asked.”

“Touché.”

“I bought it for myself after I graduated from Howard University's School of Business,” she informed me.

This girl was something else -- something that I wasn’t expecting. We talked for hours and even did some shopping. By the time the mall closed we were so engulfed in one another that we decided to go down to the harbor and just chill. The night was perfect.

Months later, I was just so in love that I didn't have one thought that didn't have her in it. I needed her to be my girl, but she was adamant about being single.

CALLIE

Braylon has been a Godsend. Just sweet, sexy, and has presence. He took all the attention when he entered a room. He keeps requesting that we solidify things but after Travis, I'm just not ready. How do I tell him I'm a virgin? Like who sells things that they haven't experienced? Would he even believe me? I know guys love a virgin. That's why I never tell them I am... but Braylin seems like the type of man that is used to a woman that is more experienced and I'm clearly far from that. Why am I worried? He hasn't even asked me for it.

The constant ringing of my phone interrupted my thoughts.

"Hello," I answered.

"What? You answered the phone?" Apple joked.

"I've been so busy Apple, I'm sorry friend."

"Girl you know we are good. You still preserving the cookie?" He asked, only half joking.

I sighed. "What if i'm thinking about giving him the cookie?"

"Girl no. You promised your dad and if this man loves you he will respect that and honor you." Apple was serious.

"He hasn't asked for it, but Apple I'm in love. I can't keep fighting it. What happens when we get into a relationship and he wants it? Remember Travis?" I asked.

"Girl bye. Travis is fucking years ago. Fuck that trade. He's old news. These hoes are not loyal, but a man that loves you shows you. There is no flipping coins on that one, I promise you that. The rush is in your head."

"You are probably right, but no man has gotten this close. I am intimidated by him and comfortable at the same time. He asked me to come meet his family this weekend. That is a big deal, I know it is." I said worried.

"Which means he is comfortable waiting."

I knew Apple was right -- at least I hoped he was right. The thing is, him being right didn't minimize the hypotheticals running through my mind.

That weekend, Braylon and I pulled up to this breathtaking house. I drove just in case I needed an exit. Families are known to get disrespectful. I didn't plan on getting disrespectful, but disrespectful times call for disrespectful measures.

As we walked in, I was greeted by who I assumed to be Braylin's dad.

"Hello, you must be Callie," he greeted while shaking my hand.

I blushed. "Yes sir," I answered.

"Call me Carter Senior. I'm Braylin's dad."

"Well Mr. Carter, you have a lovely home," I replied.

He frowned a bit and smiled at his son. "This is Braylin's house, but it is very nice. Mine is a lot more simplistic. He got his design capabilities from his mother Annika."

"Oh, I apologize I should not have assumed. Please forgive me," I said embarrassed. I had never been to his homes and he's never been to mine. In fact he still drops me off at Apple's place.

He chuckled. "No worries, dear."

Later on that night I met Brandon and Brendan. That's when I found out my man was a triplet. How rare is that? Luckily, they each had a giveaway. Brandon had freckles, Brendan's hair was curly, and Braylin was more caramel complexioned. They were all light skinned, but Braylin had a yank. My man exceeded the standard. As a matter of fact, he was the standard.

I heard Braylin ask Brendan where Tasha was. "I thought we would get to meet her today?"

"Anika had a fever, so she couldn't make it." Brendan replied.

"Aww..." everyone sighed. I nearly choked on my food.

"Are you okay?" Braylin asked full of concern.

"Yeah, I'm fine... I just swallowed my food wrong," I replied

After dinner we all ate dessert and played a few games in the family room. By then, Brandon's girlfriend, a White girl, showed up. They crept off. I didn't care; I was just enjoying the night. Needless to say, we all noticed though. Brendan sat on the phone with Tasha most of the night.

Around ten pm, we escaped for the night.

BRAYLIN

"So you know Tasha?" I asked Callie.

"Why would you ask that?" She replied.

"Just tell me how you know her. We are too old for games."

"I don't really know her, but I know of her."

Fuck I look like to this girl? The Riddler? "Okay... I'm waiting." I said, over it already.

By the time Callie told me the story, I was at a loss for words. Never did I ever expect her to say something so drama filled. I never pictured her as the type to set a casket on fire... but then again, what did the type look like? I was shocked she told me any of this, but I'm glad she is exhibiting signs of trust. Although I understood, it still made me cringe. I felt like I was talking to a stranger -- like all of these months I didn't know her or what she was capable of.

After sitting silently, I finally spoke. "Callie, you shouldn't start wars in other people fights. I get why you did it, but Tasha was an innocent bystander. I assure you she had no idea what he did. Not to mention she has a daughter that is now growing up without a father or his family."

"I know but those monsters ruined my friend's life. He seems normal but he is far from it," she replied.

"But what does that have to do with Tasha?" I asked.

"The only way to hurt him is through the people he loves. Like why should he have a nice service and a clean burial?" She cried. "He was the devil. They probably in hell playing tag as we speak."

I just consoled her. "You have to take Apple's struggles and give them to him to deal with. You can't carry his weight and yours. You should sit down and talk to Tasha. She found out long after you did. She was forced to be pregnant on her own after watching the only man she ever love die in her arms after committing suicide. In real life there is nothing poetic about that. Then to find out the sick things he and his family did AND seeing his casket burned down? Can you imagine how hurt she is? How many questions she has that may never get answered? What if you idolized your dad and at his funeral you find out he raped ten little girls? That's an enormous load to deal with. You don't know which emotion to have. You can hate him because he was a piece of shit, but she had no idea. He killed himself moments after she told him she was pregnant -- she thought he killed himself because she was pregnant. People always want retaliation but never see themselves as the other party."

CALLIE

I'm sitting here crying like a baby, but through the tears, I had to admit that Braylin was right. Hurt people hurt people. That's the sad truth in rare form. I told him I would talk to Tasha as I exited the vehicle and went in the house. When I got inside, I called Apple to tell him about it. The phone rang twice before he answered.

"Bitchhhhh it's 1 am, like... but why?" Apple asked sarcastically.

"You mean to tell me my best friend is not up waiting and anticipating my call because he is marginalized by some stupid hands on a clock? I am shocked," I replied, matching his sarcasm.

"I guess I'll have to call your replacement and tell her about me losing my virginity." I hung up. The line didn't even go dead before it was ringing. I answered on the last ring.

"Hello," I said groggily.

"Oh hoe, you tried it. And I know damn well your hot ass didn't have your ass up in nobody's air so what really happened?" Apple asked.

"My ass WAS in the air!" I said, defending my hoe card.

"Oh bitch please, you got five minutes... ten if it's juicy. We can spend it bullshitting or you can drag me into the play."

"Fine, fuck it. I just had a long talk with Braylin after nearly choking on my steak when his brother -- who is a triplet by the way -- mentioned he was dating Tasha. After my near death experience, Braylin made me spill the beans. I told him everything. Well, long story short, he thinks we attacked Tasha and she is a victim as well. After hearing his perspective I'm really considering hitting her up to apologize. What we did was savage and I never looked at it from her perspective. "

"Bitch I been felt that way, but she won't get any apologies from me. I said my prayers, forgave myself, and left it in God's hands. She should have forgiven me for her own good -- not because I cried her a river. But I respect your wanting to say it to her," Apple said.

I'm not sure if apologizing to God and a person forgiving you is synonymous with them hearing you apologize. "Well Apple, get some rest. I'll kick it with you early on," I replied.

"Goodnight. Bitch next time you call me this late, it better be following a dick induced orgasm," Apple said before hanging up.

The dial tone blew me, but I said fuck it and hung up too.

The next morning, I got up got dressed, stopped at CVS, and headed to Tasha's house. *Better now than never*, I thought to myself. I drove for 30 minutes, in the car just grooving to Sade's Smooth Operator. Her voice was calming and allowed me to groove and think. I was nervous for some strange reason, and to make matters worse, I keep catching every green light. There was not a red light in sight. I pulled up in front of Tasha's house. Of course I searched her on Been Verified, so this was her last known address. It was also the address I remember from when I was stalking Dame sorry ass. I wanted to know his routine like I knew my monthly cycle. I took a deep breath, got out the car, and headed up her walkway. I knocked on the door.

"Hold on, I'm coming," Tasha yelled. When she finally got to the door she looked like shit, but I decided that in attempt to fix the shit I participated in, I would keep that to myself. "What do you want?"

"I came here today to right my wrong the best way I know possible. I wanted to apologize to you face to face for my behavior. Can we sit down and talk for a minute so I can explain myself. Not justify, but explain how we got here?" I almost wanted her to say no so I could take the coward's way out and say I tried.

"Talk about what? My dead sperm donor or my devil child?" Tasha asked, clearly still angry and hurt.

"Look, I don't want to fight. I'm just trying to right a wrong as I previously stated." She allowed me to come in and I gave her the bag of medicine for the baby, along with some oral gel, and some calming bath soap.

She looked at me suspiciously. I said, "It's a peace offering."

She took it and said thank you. We started talking and I told her the truth about the night Apple was raped. By the expression on her face, I knew she didn't know and for that I understood Braylin. She, like most of us, was in love with a stranger.

She showed me the last text she received from him. I thought it was morbid, but still jaw dropping. She had no idea how to decipher that text until this very day.

She was in tears that stained her shirt and flooded her hands. She said, "All these years that we spent together and I didn't know him at all. I loved this man unconditionally. It scares me to think of how I would have responded had he told me. Kevin was a victim of it all. When he died I thought Dame was hurt, but he was really full of sorrow and remorse. Do you think he would have done that to our daughter?"

"No. That's probably why he killed himself -- so he would never even consider it," I replied. I was honestly thinking, *of course he would, he's a fucking predator.*

"What am I supposed to tell my daughter?" She asked, still broken.

I said, "I don't know the answer to that. Tell her about the times you shared or about the love you had before it was over. Google will explain everything else to her, I'm sure."

"I could never allow her to learn those truths that way," Tasha responded.

"Maybe she will never look him up. Just tell her he was sick and he died. Nothing about that would make her go to Google to investigate."

She looked at me and said, "Some days I wish I would have aborted her. Not because she is a burden, but because I am a coward. A coward who is too afraid to face her and tell her that her daddy was the devil and her mother reaped what she had sowed."

I looked at her confused, waiting for her to expound a bit further.

"Before I met the devil, my mom and I would fight all the time. She would beat me so bad and tell me so often how much she hated me. One day when I was sixteen, I was so sick that I took NyQuil. I was sleep so hard that I never heard him come in my room. He lifted my nightgown and started performing oral sex on me. It felt so good that I woke up. I was moaning so loud and dancing all over the bed. He gripped my waist and dug his nails into my skin. That only seemed to magnify the pleasure. I came all over his face but he didn't stop. He waited until I begged him to fuck me to stop. He entered me slowly and stroked in and out of me. At first I was in so much pain but then it felt so good. He picked up his pace a bit and came all inside of me. We stopped after that. He got up and left. I was so disgusted with myself. I had lost my prize possession to my father -- my mother's man. Right after that, I met the devil and my dad and I never did it again. He never tried or brought it up and neither did I. But when he left out of my room my mother appeared in my doorway. She said, 'if you grown enough to fuck my man in my house, you are grown enough to get out of my house.' She walked off and never spoke to me or did anything for me after that."

I sat there stunned listening to her story. I empathized with her, but I also had a burning desire to tell her that sick people attract sick people. I knew her dad had raped her, so that alone kept me from saying something horrible. She continued, "My daughter will never know how her father feels inside of her and for that I am grateful."

We both sat quietly and then Anika started crying. I could tell Tasha was in no condition to help so I told her I would get her. She looked at me strange, but had no energy to fight.

I went and picked Anika up. She was so warm. I ran a cool bath for her and washed her up. I measured the allotted amount, which was 5 milliliters of Tylenol like the directions told me, and I rocked her to sleep while she cranked a warm bottle. When I went back in the living room, Tasha was knocked out. I silently said a prayer over her and hoped God heard me. I felt like shit after today's chat. I was out trying to cause his family pain, and he already did that himself. I guess I never considered her a victim. I always saw the two of them as one. I drifted off to sleep shortly after.

The sun beaming through the window woke me up. I walked in and she was already playing with her toes and making spit bubbles. She said, "bah bah". About fifteen minutes later, Tasha walked in and scared the shit out of me. She simply said, "Thank you." I gave Anika to her and headed out the door. She was the smartest one year old that I've ever seen. Just clever.

What a hell of a night it was.

BRENDAN

Braylin told me everything that Callie told him about Tasha's old dude. It sickened me, but it was nothing that I didn't know. My old girl Tiffany went to Friendship years ago and told me that she suspected Ashton and Dame were not really related because she had sworn she saw Dame giving Ashton head behind the building one day, but I brushed it off because I knew that they were related. I just figured she was hating and let that be that. In fact, I dumped her shortly after because I figured she was jealous and my girl should never be concerned with anyone else to be jealous.

I decided to call Tasha to tell her I was on my way with breakfast. The phone rang about four times before she finally answered.

"Hello," she said.

"Good morning, baby. I'm about to slide through. I have Starbucks and IHOP," I replied.

"Oh my God that would be heaven right now!"

Must have been a rough night, I thought. "Okay, I'll be there in about thirty minutes."

We hung up, and as promised, I was there in thirty minutes. The door was open, so I just walked on in.

"Hey baby," she said, holding a smiling Anika.

"Hey, was that Braylin's girl Callie I just saw pull out of your driveway?" I asked.

"I thought she had been left, but yeah that was her. She came by to check on Anika and I."

"Oh, I didn't know you guys were acquainted."

"Oh, we went to high school together." She replied nonchalantly -- and very dismissively. I knew from Braylin that they were not cordial, but given the circumstances, I could understand her not wanting to go into detail. Time would answer all of my questions. I decided to just drop the topic for that day. We sat on the floor and ate breakfast while Anika crawled between us. We could discuss anything, and we did. This morning's topic was marriage.

"How do you feel about getting married?" I asked her.

"I always dreamed of getting married -- as all little girls do. But after Dame died, I gave up. I realized you never really know someone. They have secrets hidden so deep inside of them that you couldn't unlock it if you tried. Trust doesn't extend to possible co-defendants, who, in these days, could be anybody."

"What about him specifically made you feel so hesitant? What secrets could he had possible had that made you feel so hesitant?"

"Some things are just hard or impossible to recover from," she replied with pain and sadness in her voice.

"Yes, but everything you go through is there to make you stronger and wiser. It's not there to deter you from going forward," I countered.

"When bad things happen in the dark, you feel blindsided but you suck it up because you had no way to stop it -- no warning signs that it was going to happen. However, when you see it, once it's exposed, the world judges you. They shame you and blame you," she confessed.

"So his actions have become yours?"

"His actions were considered our actions from day one until now. I'm the heart of the devil." She looked into my eyes deeply. Her voice shook. “Who could ever love me knowing that?”

“I love you. You are special. You bring quality to the table... that’s something women just don’t have these days. I want to give you the world because he and I are not synonymous. His action and scars are not yours and they don’t define me. You have to let me love you. Let me in. Trust me to be the difference, not the replica.” I replied.

She looked up at me with tears in her eyes. “Love is not easy and it’s best you prevent yourself from feeling it until shit starts looking like crystal on the White House table. Love knocks you off of your balance. Makes you irrational and has you feeling ambivalent about every little thing. And when the smallest difference occurs in their routine, you will see the worst in yourself -- as well as them. Love will break down barriers only to prove that you should keep them up. Love is the first high. Once you feel it, you can't unfeel it and you probably won’t ever feel that magnitude of a high ever again.”

“You speak things into existence. Watch what you put out there,” I replied.

“Well the universe must be whispering loud because a much greater force than me has set that in stone. It’s an immutable fact -- nothing nor no one can change it. We all go through it,” she said.

“Key phrase: go through it. It means we get through it and we live again and one day that love will be right.”

“When God is ready, He will allow me to love and love with no limitations. Right now, I’m restoring the person I am and becoming the person I want to be.”

“Sounds good… but it sounds like one of those barriers if you ask me.” I was joking, but also very serious.

MACY

"Hello... HELLO... STOP PLAYING ON MY DAMN PHONE," I yelled, clearly frustrated.

"Girl, whose man are you sleeping with?" Kelsi jokingly asked.

"Bitch don't try me," I laughed back.

"I'm just saying, the only time I get phone calls with no talk is when one of my arrangements' wives start trying to figure out why large amounts of money is being disseminated," Kelsi replied.

"I know your butt isn't messing with any married men!" I wanted to ask, but somehow I already knew the answer. Kelsi smiled and walked off. "Where are you going?" I asked with a fake attitude.

"To the bathroom. Why? Do you want to come?"

"Girl no... I'm just making sure your sticky fingered ass is in a contained space."

I wasn't expecting anyone, so the sudden interruption and knock at my door had me stuck.

"You going to get the door or does it answer itself?" Kelsi asked sarcastically. I rolled my eyes and answered the door; to my surprise, I was greeted by a bouquet of red balloons and a note that read:

Picasso himself couldn't create a piece of art as a beautiful and timeless as our story. Tonight we will dance under the stars. Wear this and wait for me.

Brandon

"Who is at the door?" I hear Kelsi yell.

"My baby had a gift delivered!" Kelsi snatches the note out of my hand and reads it. "Awwww!!!" she yells out in excitement. "Wait, where is the outfit?" she asked.

"I don't know," I said honestly. "Maybe it will come later."

"Girl, I hope so. I'm about to get out of here. I have to go and check one of my slides." She hugged me goodbye.

As soon as she walked out the door, she trips over a box. "What the hell?!" she yells out. "Bitch you must be blind."

"What?" I asked, annoyed that she keeps calling me a bitch. Fuck she think this is? Payback for the n-word?

"I found your outfit!" she announces. My eyes grew big; I snatched the box right out of her hand. Inside of the black box with the big red bow was a very elegant red dress with the sexiest gold sandal heels that I've ever seen. It was breathtaking. This man's talents were everything in the romance department.

"This man is into you." Kelsi says and walks off.

"Of course he is," I said out loud.

"Girl you better be careful before one of these traps steal your man," Kelsi said.

"That's not a concern of mine. If they can take him they can have him and I can do better." I replied. Her thotty ass act like she can't wait to put her infected pussy all over his dick. I walked around and cleaned up once she was gone, reminding myself to check the house for anything that could be missing. I never trust broke bitches in my house. Everything looked to be in order, no obvious situations. Every time I try to make friends I meet these fragile females with low or no standards for themselves. It's only a matter of time before this bitch exposes which lane she falls in, but from our conversation earlier, my vote is no standards at all.

Anyway, I hit my girl Angela MUA Lewis up on Facebook to book a last minute appointment to do my makeup. For $100 extra, ole girl was there in forty-five minutes. Good thing too, cuz I just hopped my fine ass out the shower when the doorbell rang. I got downstairs in record time.

"Hey sweetie," she greeted me before I could greet her.

"Hey girl, I'm so glad you could fit me in today. The thought of me doing my thang in this dress on my own skills had me in distress." We both laughed.

"You are not that bad," she replied. "I'm on my way to another client's house right after you."

"Tonight is a busy night for you," I said, catching the hint.

"Yes, it's busy but very manageable. That dress is beautiful by the way."

"My boo picked it out for me. His taste is impressive," I said, still admiring his work.

"It is. My man got his own line dropping and my son is doing his thang with his clothing line as well."

"Really?" I said. "A family of entrepreneurs."

"Girl, teach them young," she replied.

"That's nothing but the truth." She was cool, but I was anxious to get into this dress.

"Yaasss, honey. So what look are we going for tonight?"

“I’m thinking wild and subtle,” I replied

“I know just the look.” I really hoped she understood because I wanted to impress Brandon with the same level of expertise as he had. Thirty minutes later and she was done. That’s record breaking for her. I must say so myself... she did the damn thang with my makeup. Even I was mesmerized. I paid her and started getting dressed right after she left.

KELSI

I was happy for my girl Macy. She was into all that lovey dovey stuff, but I had other things on my mind.

Two years ago I met Carter. He swept me off my feet with his charm. He was everything a good girl would want, but I was bad. Rotten down to the core. I hated his ability to charm me. I told him over and over to find another mistake to correct. That's what is wrong with doctors, they think they can fix anything wrong with a human, but the type of doctor I needed has yet to find his calling. Being the wild, uncontrollable female that that I was, I couldn't be what he needed. When the phone calls slowed down, it infuriated me. Who was he to blow me off? I would go to his job to follow him, but he would almost always shake me. It's like he knew I was hot on his ass. Frustrated and tired, I would just go home. I'll never forget the last time we had a normal conversation. He text me and said, "Red or white wine soothes the mind."

I replied, "Wine is for the weak. Pull out some Patron and he will be up all night long. All pun included."

"You can't just ever go with it, can you?" He asked.

"Go with what?" I asked.

"This isn't working."

"What?"

"US! What the fuck you think I'm talking about?"

"As long as your dick still works you don't need to focus on us," I replied. "And when it doesn't work, then you definitely don't need to worry about us because I assure you there won't be an us at that point."

“Excuse me?”

“You read it right.” I challenged.

And then nothing. I waited days for a reply but nothing. I was so sad that I found it hard to focus. I text him seven months later, sending him a selfie of me sticking a huge dildo in me hoping to entice him. Can you believe he never responded? I even faked accidentally calling his phone and dropping it beside my desk so he could eavesdrop on me being busy at work not concerned about him. Even still no call back. When I went to his job because my pride was torn to shreds, I saw his car speeding off and I'm sure he was with a White girl. Ughhh these bitches and our men.

I came back the next day and followed him and the girl to a restaurant called Mixer. I went in and stayed in the corner, making sure not to be seen. When she got up and walked to the restroom, I took it upon myself to follow. She laid her purse down on the sink and went into the stall. Too easy, I used the camera on my phone and took pictures of her driver's license, two credit cards, a work I.D., and lastly, I noticed a keychain on the ring and made a mental note. When I heard the stall flush, I put the purse back and pretended to wipe my face and fix my make up.

She said excuse me and grabbed her bag. “Oh I’m sorry, I hadn’t noticed the bag.”

“No worries,” she replied. She was still checking her bag for any missing items before she washed her hands.

I walked out before her. I had what I needed, so I left the restaurant.

Three weeks later, I joined Cropped gym. It was small, but you can tell it was for more reserved professionals. I had watched her every move for two weeks so I knew her routine, she would definitely be here shortly. I worked up a sweat and waited patiently. She had a routine, so when I saw her enter I casually moved to the machine she always goes to and accidentally bumped into her.

“Oh, excuse me,” I said. “I need to pay better attention.”

She replied no problem and asked if I were about to use that machine. I said, “I was, but if you would like to use it you --” I pretended to freeze. “Hey, aren’t you the girl from the movie 10 Things I Hate About You?!”

“No,” she giggled.

“Oh you look so familiar. I don’t know why. You just remind me of her. But go ahead and use the machine, I need to get out of here anyway. Big meeting in a few.”

She smiled and thanked me. I left with no more words.

Over the course of six weeks, I befriended her. I couldn’t explain why, I just had to be close to her. Maybe because she was close to him. I’m still not sure why but I did it, and I couldn’t stop myself from doing it.

Two days into our friendship, she got into a minor car accident that I may or may not have orchestrated. That’s neither here nor there. The point is, of course, I was there to help. After information was exchanged, we grabbed a salad from Chop’t and talked the day away.

After investigating Carter and Snow White for so long, I felt confident in knowing their schedules. So imagine my surprise when I was prepared to follow Carter to his brother’s house for their weekly game and ended up in front of Jared’s in Tyson corner.

I got so excited I couldn't contain it. Carter must be over punishing me and has decided to propose. I got up all ready to head in, but thought he would get mad all over again. So I peeled off and waited for his phone call. I stopped by his White bitch house just to see if he broke the news to her yet and judging by her perky demeanor, I see he hadn't.

APPLE

“So Callie, how did it go with Tasha?” I asked.

“Girl it went fine. I think we were both over it,” Callie reported.

“Good. We are so much better than trivial bickering.” I said. It was kind of a lie though because anyone who knew me knew I loved me some good ole messy behavior, and I didn’t care how it came.

“Are we?” Callie grinned.

“What am I missing?” I asked hesitantly.

“I’m joking,” Callie stated. ”What’s been up with you?”

“Oh nothing, just running my best friend’s club because she’s been completely smitten by this prince of a man,” I answered honestly. At that point, I didn’t really care how she took it.

“Oh Apple, I’m sorry. I don’t know what has gotten into me. I just feel like somebody else,” Callie admitted.

“Cupid done stuck his arrow in you girl.” I joked.

“Whatever,” she replied, blushing.

“What’s going on with you and Mr. Perfect?” I asked.

“Nothing,” she blushed.

“Callie!” I yelled. I just looked at her. My girl was definitely struck by cupid. It was written all over her.

“He's perfect. Not in the aspect of a perfect human, but in the aspect of what I need and want. The harder I fight this, the more convoluted the situation gets. I feel ambivalent about this. I just want to know what I am getting. So far everything is so light, I just don't know how either of us will deal with something heavy."

I understood her way of thinking. She's very observant and not as naïve as most young girls. Her father did her good by teaching her to pay attention. But he taught her so much that she fears the inevitable.

"Callie, do what your heart requests until you feel like your heart is being disrespected."

She took it all in and said, "Only once."

"Once is all you need." I replied. "You'll either find your happiness or it will teach you what happiness isn't."

I shook my head. I had been in love many times. Once wasn't enough for my adrenaline. I just felt like she wasn't being practical... but then again, who was I to judge? My broken heart was now empty.

"I have a date to start preparing for, so I need to head out," she said.

"Really?" I asked rhetorically, as if I didn't know.

"Yes, really." She smiled and left. "I'll be back in a few hours after I get my nails, toes, and hair done."

Now I had to start working on some things. I felt like in the near future, there would be a wedge drawn between Callie and I. What I wasn't sure about was whether it would be short term or long term. But right now, I couldn't focus on that. I had to get everything right. I prayed I was wrong, but I knew my gut. It was most definitely trying to tell me something. Preparation was a job of the wise.

Once I was done all that, I ran me a nice bath. I mean scorching hot bath with candles everywhere. I poured me a glass of wine and climbed in the bath to read Eldridge Cleaver's Souls on Ice. It was so deep. Some of the book had me just angry. How could this intelligent man -- a so-called great leader -- be a rapist. Because no one cared about the Black woman, he practiced raping Black women so that he could cross over the tracks and rape White woman to get retribution for the Black women being raped by the White man. To me, that sounds just like a man to excuse his own lies with even sorrier lies. If the Black woman wanted retribution, I'm sure that's not how she saw herself being used in the plan. How many women did he rape that had to watch his growth and development In the Black Panther Party? I kept reading until finally the sandman caught up with me. I woke up in the middle of the night to cold water and a floating book. "Awww shit!" I yelled. I've done this so many times that I've lost count. It's the reason I buy two of each book. I already know I'm either going to fuck one up or lose it. Often, I find myself at the bookstore purchasing the same book for the third time.

CALLIE

After I did my girly spa routine, I headed home. To my surprise there was a bouquet of balloons, a big red box with a black bow adorned with an elegant envelope that concealed a note. A tad bit confused and flattered, I decided to open the note to see whom it was from. It said:

> Time does not stand still for anyone, but every time I'm with you time stops to encapsulate the moment. The Gods shone on our union and spare no expense. You are worth more than any man-made riches and I would shun them all just to lie in your shadows. See you at 8.
>
> Braylin

How the hell does he know where I live? I said out loud obviously not talking to anyone. The only place that I have taken him was to Apple's place. I decided to call Apple to see where his head was at with this situation.

"Hello?" He answered.

"Did you tell Braylin where I live?" I asked calmly.

"No, why would I? Was he at your house or something?"

"Damn you nosey," I said half jokingly. "But no. I'll explain later I have to go."

"Bitch... get here early enough to spill the tea," he replied.

"I think I'll be getting ready and waiting here."

"Your ass always getting me wet with no happy ending. Don't call my phone next time until you have time, baldhead."

“It is not that serious,” I replied, laughing as hard as ever.

“Oh, it’s that fucking serious. It’s just not you anticipating on the other end of the damn receiver. Don’t play me like that,” Apple said, laughing at his own dramatic self. “Anyway, if you not coming over I can call me over a playmate.”

“Your ass always in the air. Put some ice on them knees and relax. Damn.”

“Bitch, you know damn well I’m not on my knees. Fuck kind of orthopedic, geriatrics, archaic, B.S. is that? A bitch swings from the ceiling or upside down doing a headstand.”

“I spit the soda out of my mouth. Now you know your ass is on America's most extra,” I replied. “You're one action away from your own reality show.”

“I bet it would be the most watched show on television.”

“Everyone tunes in when it’s time to be ratchet. Ratchet TV sells. Why not pay a bunch of broke motherfuckers to come on TV and make asses out of themselves for the viewer’s entertainment?”

“Now, does it look like I care? They are paying Apple to be Apple, and if it in turn strikes the interest of couch spectators who would rather watch me live than to go live themselves, then so be it. A coin is a coin no matter how you flip it.”

“Some are tarnished,” I said feeling defeated.

“But does it spend the same?” Apple asked

“You always have some smart shit to say, smart-ass,” I replied, now laughing.

“In my opinion, being a smart ass is better than being a stupid ass, a silly ass, or a broke ass. Which brings me back to my point -- get that coin by any means necessary.”

“Any huuuuhhhh? I guess you don’t mind selling ass then?”

"Girl I sell ass faster than a drug dealer sells crack every first and fifteenth."

"The fuck Apple. That shit is illegal, your hoe ass going to jail."

"No, these broke hoes going out here and coming back with wet legs and empty pockets are going to jail. They the ones committing crimes out here. You might not be giving up no ass, but your ass ain't that naïve. These niggas really think pussy is free. If nothing else in the world is valuable, why would I give up my most valuable asset for free? Now that in itself would be a grave injustice for us all." As crazy as Apple sounded these were instructions to live by. I don't care how many women claim he was out of his mind, deep down we all knew. Therefore, I had to respect it.

"Well hun, let me go get ready," I said.

"Bitch you thought you could dismiss me without those magic words? Try again angel dust."

"Ewww, you are so petty!" I replied.

"I've been called worse."

"Your scary ass is right. And although you a trick bitch with no 401K, I got to respect your mental."

"Oh baby, I know that took a lot out of you. But thank you. You are so gracious."

"Oh bye, hoe." I laughed as I hung up. Apple is a trip. But I love his crazy ass.

TASHA

My baby is getting so big. It is just a pure joy being her mother. I watch her in awe, all the time. I tell you what; she's a phenomenal problem solver. The doorbell rang, scaring me out of my thoughts.

Before I could get there, it rang again. "Coming," I yelled.

I wondered who it could be. Brendan and I were going out for a much-needed mommy break mixed with some adult time, so I knew he wasn't here this early. "I'm coming in one second," I yelled. I was frantically searching for some pajamas, a robe, or something. I finally spotted my robe in the bedroom corner sprawled on the floor. "Ah!" I yelled, running to retrieve it and throwing it around me while moving swiftly down the stairs. I barely had it on and tied before I swung the door open. By the time my slow butt got to the door, no one was there. It was a huge set of red balloons and a big box with a silver bow. Under the ribbon there was a note that read:

> When I saw this dress I saw you in it. Be ready by 8. This is the night you wouldn't want to be late.
>
> Brendan

I screamed in excitement. A few of the neighbors looked over trying to figure out what was going on, but they quickly diverted their attention back their prior activities leaving me to my madness.

I pulled the box into the house and slammed the door shut with my right foot. I opened the box almost ripping it to pieces. The box housed a nice pair of gold sandal heels with a beautiful red dress. My mouth was left agape, clinging for some emotions. I was shocked and surprised. My man had taste. I looked into the box to ensure I had gotten everything, secretly hoping there was some jewelry in the box because I had none worthy enough to embellish the elegance of tonight's ensemble. There was a small red dress for Anika with tiny gold gladiator sandals. It was adorable. I was slightly saddened because I thought we would have adult time, but with so much effort placed into tonight, I decided not to whine and just get her ready instead. I put pretty curly pigtails in her hair with a big red bow on each side. Anika was so adorable that I instantly got over my disappointment.

At 7:50 Jody arrived. I answered the door and she said, "Hi. Brendan sent me to entertain Anika."

Oh now I was the fuck confused. If it were adult time, why did he send her an outfit as well? Before I could say it out loud, a Bentley pulled up. I had to be dreaming. I just handed Anika to Jody and said, "Everything you need is on the kitchen counter," and walked out to Brendan. He hugged me and opened my door. Once I got in he closed my door and walked over to the other side to slide in himself.

KELSI

When I left Macy's house, I headed straight home to get ready. I just knew Carter was going to be here soon and I wanted to look flawless. I mean Queen B flawless with Rihanna's attitude.

My phone started ringing. I damn near flew to it, hoping it was Carter. It turned out to be my cousin Grier.

"Hello?" I answered in a callous tone.

"Hey Kelsi, did I catch you at a bad time?" He asked.

"No, what's up?" I said exasperated.

"Well, I'm not sure how to say this, so I'll just say it --"

"I wish you would," I replied, cutting him off.

He paused and said, "Your sister woke up from her coma three months ago and the hospital is ready to discharge her. They said they reached out to you through email and phone but your number was changed and there was no response to the email."

"Okay...?"

"Well... could she stay with you, Kelsi?"

"No." I replied sternly

"No?" He was taken aback. "That's your twin sister."

"And that's your niece. Now that we all know our relationship, how the fuck can I help you?" I asked, agitated.

"Are you hearing yourself?"

"I hear me just fine. Do you hear yourself?"

I heard him sigh.

"You're over there with an attitude, but why can't she stay with you?" I snapped back. "Why are you sitting on my phone trying to convince me to take in someone who's so close and dear to you?"

The phone was quiet. I just hung up. Tonight was not for family problems. That bitch has been in a coma for three years and now she wants to wake up. FUCK HER.

Three years ago I cut the breaks on my parent's car when I found out they were attending the church benefit that night. It was a bonus that the hoe needed a ride to violin practice. Somehow they ended up crashing into a tractor-trailer on 495. The damn benefit was off of 295. I'm trying to figure out how the fuck they got on 495, but you know, whatever. Dead is dead. My parents died instantly, however, Khaleena was rushed to Georgetown University Hospital. The doctors worked on her for hours. Of course, I rolled in late enough not to be able to donate anything -- not even a drop of blood. I turned on the water works when I got there. I was frantic, hysterical, over the top. I could have gotten a Grammy. I would be damned if they suspected me. When they finally finished operating I was happy. I for sure thought that they would never give up. She was in ICU for six months before they were able to stabilize her and move her to own suite with less supervision. My parents by this time had been long buried. Thanks to their other family members, definitely not because of me though. I used to sit by the phone anticipating and praying that when it rang, the doctors would be calling me telling me that this vixen was dead. They say when your twin dies, you feel lost and incomplete; but I felt like when she died, I would finally meet me and I would be relieved. Finally, I could rid myself of the dead weight. But like you guessed, that call never came. I gave up. The trick was invincible, I swear. If I could not kill her, I was going to torture her. That's when I found Browdy.

I use to pay Browdy to brutally rape her. At first he was not down, but I convinced him that she and I were into S&M. I told him we pleased each other on the regular with our spontaneous sex life. He agreed but charged me extra to watch or participate. I would eat her out and position her so he could hit her from behind. I was in charge of putting his dick in her after I was done sucking it. One day I licked her ass real good, put his dick to the hole and told him to go hard or go home. When I say he rammed it in her ass so aggressively it made my kitty tingle... He was like she is always so tight and wet. I laughed because I knew she was bleeding. Of course, Browdy was clueless. He was high off coke. I could image he thought he was higher than God. Come to think of it, that's how I got him to start raping her. Ahh, yes. Now I remember. It's all coming back to me.

He wouldn't fuck her, but he lusted after me. I placed my pussy with it and let him give me head. When I saw him starting to let the drug take over, I placed some in a bag with holes in it and rammed it up his ass with my fingers followed with some Chinese balls. Those balls will surprise a nigga quick, but that g-spot being hit will keep that ass in the air. He was so high and hard that he let me ride that big, monstrous dick all night long. Clearly, it was my obligation to make sure my sister got A1 dick being it was her first time and all. I used to love sucking on her perky nipples. Watching it always made Browdy cum fast. I would open her mouth and ride her face whenever I was about to squirt or he came. She would swallow the evidence every time.

That night was special though, I found another guy to fuck her with Browdy and I. He laid under her while Browdy was on top and I squatted over Mr. Unknown as he ate my pussy like he was in the Olympics going for the gold. I had to get off of the bed and prop my ass up so they would come and devour me. They held me up in the air while one entered my ass and the other entered my pussy. They bounced me up and down with so much power and speed that I came back to back in minutes. I leaned over to share the pleasure with my sister. I sucked her clit and tasted all of her coke. I fingered her while sucking her juices out and licking her off my fingers. Browdy came out of me and put his entire fist in her ass. You could see the excitement on his face. It was like a virgin cumming for the first time. After they had their way with her, I cleaned her up. The nurses were not allowed to bathe her, I told them I didn't trust them. But realistically, they could and probably did fuck her from here to kingdom come, and I would not care one bit.

By the time they found out she was not a virgin and that something must have happened on their watch, they offered me a huge settlement check to keep it hush hush and sent me on my way. That was back then. Today, I'm about to head out the door. I do not want to be late and miss the fireworks.

CALLIE

Braylin picked me up in his Corvette. After he blindfolded me and told me to promise I would not peek, he lead me inside. When he finally took the blindfold off, I was outside with Tasha and Brendan, as well as Macy and Brandon. I had no idea what was going on. It looked like we were at a vineyard of some sort with lights everywhere. I also couldn't help but to notice Tasha, Macy, and I all looked like the three stooges in red dress and gold heels. Different styles but the same color scheme. Judging by the looks on their faces they had no idea what was going on either. I heard Eric Benet singing Spend My Life With You. We all turned around and there he was. I was so moved. When he was done, we all clapped and turned around in search of our men. They were all down on one knee proposing. I nearly passed out. This man looked into my eyes and said:

"Never have I ever run across something so beautiful. I cherish every moment I have with you and if I died today I would die a happy man. Callie would you do me the honor of being my wife?"

He held up the biggest diamond ring that I have ever seen. My eyes were filled with tears. I looked up for one second to thank God and my father, and when my eyes came back down there was Apple, Don, and Tracy cheering for me to say yes. So I said yes and he slid the whole continent of Africa onto my finger. He got up and pulled me to him as he locked me in the most passionate kiss. Indeed, time had stood still.

Apple and Tracy rushed over to me to see the ring. I proudly displayed it. Only God and I understood this moment. I never thought I would be here doing this with these people. I am truly blessed.

TASHA

Here I am watching Braylin propose... shocked that I see my man down on one knee about to confess his love for me. He looks up to me and says, "Tasha you and Anika mean the world to me. If you and Anika will have me, I would love for you to be my wife and Anika to be my daughter."

Before I could respond Anika ran up and hugged Brendan. He put a baby diamond ring on her finger and a large matching one on the tip of mine waiting for me to reply. He said, "I know you don't believe in marriage but let me be the man that shows you the meaning and the action of marriage. I'll show you the dedicated and loyal side of marriage. I will never be the root of your pain, but the faucet of healing within."

I jumped in his arms and screamed yes. I could never deny this man. He had opened my heart after I was sure God himself would fail at that mission.

MACY

I know motherfucking well this nigga -- yeah I said nigga -- is not about to do what I think he is about to do, I thought in my head.

"Macy you mean the world to me. If I could make a woman from scratch, she would never measure up to even a strand of you. You are a man's dream come true. You are this man's dream come true. Will you be my wife?" Brandon asked, still down on one knee.

"Slides do not get to ask for my hand in marriage, are you fucking crazy?" I asked.

His face turned red with confusion. "What do you mean a slide?" He asked.

"You don't know what your position is. You're a slide. Only good for sliding in and out. Do you honestly think my family will accept you as one of us? I mean you are handsome eye candy and a good fuck, but that it. Your wealth let you taste the cookies, but it doesn't solidify your seat at the table." I responded.

"Macy!" Tasha yelled

"I'm sorry Tasha, you are one smart, intelligent, Black girl, but honey come on. I treat you like a Grade A charity case," I replied.

"A charity case? One thing for sure I have, and always will, take care of myself. I think you need to calm down. Maybe this is too much for you but --"

"Calm down? I'm calm, I'm just here to mix the truth with the reality. Truth is y'all are cool. Reality is that's not enough. I was fucking him and he got caught up. That's on him. Sex and relationships are not synonymous," I replied. "And you girl, you were just my little sidekick. We all have one Black friend."

I heard Brendan say, "I'll call you a cab Macy, enjoy your night."

"Why would I ever need your help? Call this monkey a cab," I replied laughing.

I looked at him disgusted. "You played yourself," I said. "When did I ever give you the idea that I would ever marry you?"

He just looked at me with a cruel, acrimonious stare. Unfortunately for him, a bitch didn't care. I stepped off like I never knew him.

KELSI

Seems like I arrived just in time. To my surprise, the ring was for his lil bihh and not me. I saw the whole proposal. I burned with envy inside, but I was collected at the same time because I knew she would never make it to that alter. As I continued to watch, I grew intrigued. This woman didn't have the look of love and wow on her face. It was wearing something much more intense -- it was wearing a look of disgust, humor, and disdain all mixed into one. When she turned his weak hallmark sale proposal down, I almost died laughing. At the same time, my heart ached for his broken ego. She was going to have to pay for playing with my man. She should have accepted and died like a real bitch. But later for that. That was going to take so calculations.

I couldn't even walk up to him and tell him I would accept it because he was down. I'm going to use this moment to fix what this bitch interrupted, with her ungrateful ass. This bitch feels entitled but the only thing that hoe is entitled to is her demise.

A week went by before I slid through to see Macy's bitch ass. I knocked on her door.

"Oh hey girl," she said when she answered the door.

"Hey," I said. "You look happy, like you are floating on air." All the while, I was ready to kill her on sight.

"Girl..." she blushed. "Have a seat in the living room. I'll be right back I need to turn the stove down and check the food in the oven."

"Oh, girl take your time." I said. Macy returned ten minutes later with two cups of Henny. "Oh we turning up early," I said taking a sip. "How was your date that day?" I asked even though I already knew.

She replied, "HORRIBLE."

I acted shocked as she started to recap the night. I took a big gulp of my Henny pretending to be processing the information. Little did this hoe know, she was speaking out of pocket for the wrong one. And of course you know she left all that racist talk out as well… but I know you didn't expect anything less.

Two glasses of Henny later, and I started to feel woozy. "Girl my speech slurred, I think I'm turning into a lightweight."

I was out cold after that.

MACY

All of you opinionated bitches might think I'm a fucked up individual, but I am not. I'm just honest. I knew this sneaky bitch was up to something when I saw her in my purse taking pictures -- which, by the way, I left out for her to snoop through. If a bitch was looking for me then I was to be found. You'll never catch me hiding from no sneaky, scary hoe. I dared her to come look for me. Next thing I know, she's at my gym trying to befriend me. My memory is good, no fuck that, phenomenal. She thought the first time she saw me was when she followed us in Brandon's car. Nope.

I'm the nurse that got in trouble for her sister's rape. Y'all, when I say I filed complaint after complaint about her sister being raped and it would never go anywhere I mean it. One day I put cameras in her room and it was horrifying. Her sister must have really enraged her. I got released from that job and, to tell you the truth, I was damned disturbed. I moved on and the severance check was very good to me. However, I decided to play this hoe's game. She may have written the rules, but I'm the reason rules are necessary. This bitch heart dropped when Brandon proposed to me, but I could say yes to being his wife. I had plans for him. In fact he was the plan -- he was plan b.

Six Hours Later

"Where am I?" I heard her say as I tasted her warm pussy. I ignored her and kept licking her. She moaned out loud -- involuntarily, I'm sure. I stood up and placed my pussy in her face. She turned away. I placed nipple clamps on her nipples as she cried out loud.

“What’s the matter? I thought you liked S&M.” I said, laughing at her own tormented soul. “They are adjustable if that would be more fitting for you. Would you like me to tighten them?” I ask, almost seriously.

She still didn’t comply, so I tightened them. She yells out. “Aww, what’s wrong baby?” I said in a patronizing tone. I leaned down to her ear and said, “Here’s a secret for you. I’ve grown to like S&M as well. Browdy indirectly taught me well. You see,” I said as I put my pink pussy back in her face -- this time putting a gun to her temple. This time she complies when I say please me... I continue my story as she devours me. Baby had skills; I came on her face at least three times in the process of telling the story. Browdy was my man... correction, the head isn’t that good. “Browdy was my man. After you got him addicted to crack, he only wanted to fuck you and your sister. But thankfully after all the sick videos I made of y'all interactions I noticed how turned on I became. When he left me, I begged him to come back. I reenacted all the things y'all would do, but he still was not biting. I would even sneak in your sister’s room with him and help him rape her, as I’ve seen you do many of nights. I became as sick and demented as you,” I said slightly disgusted with myself. She ate me so good I stopped when I lost my place and I start to ride her face. When I came in her mouth that last time, I took out the toys and put the double-headed dick in us. One side in her and the other in me. She was tight and I liked it. She cried a little, but why would I sympathize with the devil. She made me. I placed the vibrator on our clit as I leaned in to cum with her. She came hard. I said, “I had to hurt you the way you hurt me. Brandon was just a casualty of war.” I saw the rage in her eyes. I said, “Oh look at me, I almost forgot. I jumped up like it was Christmas morning and I just knew I got the Barbie dream house and all of Barbie’s accessories. Cum still dripping down my leg my thick thighs massaging my already sensitive clitoris as I moved to open the door. Imagine her surprise when in walked a sexy Khaleena. Her eyes grew as big as saucers.

"I bet you thought I would never come out of that coma. In fact you hoped I would die," Khaleena said.

KHALEENA

I may have been in a coma, but I was very conscious. This envious bitch stole my virginity from me. That night was hell on wheels. My body could feel every bit of pain. I felt disgusted having my sister go down on me. The vile substances she would have me ingesting made my stomach curl. Whenever I thought I could take the pain she would find worse pain to inflict on me. It was as if she could read my mind. I prayed many days and many nights with her so that God would listen to either of us or both and just let me die. I could understand why she hated me so much that she would hurt me like she did? I watched and halt my shell undergo this horrid experience while I was tied down with invisible rope unable to save myself. All the while she enjoyed it all. Revenge is mine, I assure you. Oh, and I didn't forget that this bitch confessed to me that she was the one that cut the breaks in the first place. If these hoes ever though I would forgive or forget, they were sadly mistaken. To every hoe that ever crossed me, she already signed her death certificate in blood.

TASHA

I couldn't believe Macy. How did I not know she felt that way?

I started to call her, but Brendan told me not to. She had quit working at the hospital, so I have not seen her since the chaos erupted. Poor Brandon has been running around town thottin' down. He leaves no holes unplugged. A true womanizer. Clearly he's either hurt or deranged.

Brandon and Brendan stopped by. Brandon is so in love with Anika. And of course she runs him around the house until they are both tired. As I'm in the kitchen cooking dinner I hear Brendan ask Brandon when he planned to return to work.

"I took a sabbatical." Brandon replied.

"Brandon you are a doctor." Brendan said.

"Well whatever bro, fuck, stop pressing me out," he retorted.

"I'm not." Brendan said defeated.

I came out the kitchen. "I could not help but to overhear you guys and I do not want to appear nosey or intrusive -- I just want to say she quit. She has not been back either." I turned and walked away before either could respond.

I went back in the kitchen, then Brendan walked in and hugged me. He gave me warm, passionate kisses while I stirred the food. "What's that for?" I ask.

"That's for being the addition to my family."

"Oh, are you just now seeing all of this beautiful perfection?" I joked.

"No, I saw it back in high school when your school had a track meet at ours and you were this sexy little cheerleader. I followed you on Myspace but I never had the courage to approach you. And then, imagine my surprise when I saw you that night at the bus stop."

My mouth dropped. I had no idea that Brendan had known or seen me prior to that rainy night. "What school did you go to?" I asked.

"I went to Gonzaga."

"Oh yeah, I remember that. We weren't even supposed to cheer there. We went for the practice. I remember having a huge competition that we were all nervous about... actually it was not too long after that. Our coach thought it would be good practice to be in front of a large crowd. But they wouldn't let us cheer."

"I must have watched you all day." He said.

"Why didn't you ever say anything?"

"When I was about to say something to you at the ice cream truck, I overheard you say something about being excited your boyfriend was going to be able to come to your competition. So I walked off. You had a man, there was no room for me."

"But you said you followed me on MySpace."

"I did because I couldn't stop thinking about you. But all I saw was pictures of you and Dame," he said, almost whispering.

"Yeah, I can believe that."

"I got off of social media after I ran home from school to see if you had signed in. I felt obsessed to the point that I closed all accounts and didn't think about you again until I saw you that day."

"Wow, I'm at a loss for words. I'm living in a world where someone else's world intertwined with mine and I never noticed."

"It's like that often," he said. "I knew you were for me when I saw you again. You disrupted my life without effort. I said that this is God's work."

I was so touched that I had tears in my eyes. This man looked at me like I was a blessing. Not just a blessing, but also his blessing. I felt so special and so appreciated. I dropped down on my knees and took his manhood out of his pants. He fought me a little, asking what I was doing. He told me that Brandon was in the other room.

I stick him in my mouth and said, "And in the other room he better stay."

I gripped his manhood with both hands as I reached up on the counter to grab the grapefruit I had just cut open and slid it around his dick. I rotated it up and down the shaft of his dick ensuring my mouth mimicked the motion. I gagged to make my mouth wetter. With my other hand I massaged his balls. Oh, daddy was running, but he didn't get far at all. I was on his ass like a hoe on a NBA player. I slurped and jerked as I circled the rim of his throbbing dick head. I kissed it and slapped it on my face a little. This drove him insane and turned me on. He came all down my throat I swallowed it. He picked me up and tossed me on the bar. He ripped my panties off. I mean like literally ripped them bitches off -- there would be no more wear out of those. He pulled my dress top down until my breast were exposed on the counter just dangling with no direction. He squeezed them aggressively while pinching my nipples. I was cumming all over myself prior to him penetrating me.

"Baby wait," I say, trying to grip the bar for balance.

"Wait for what?" He replied.

"Brandon is in the other room," I say, clearly turned the fuck on.

"Oh, now you care about Brandon being in the other room. What did you say earlier? He better stay his ass in the other room?" He forced himself inside my awaiting, juicy hole.

"Ughhh!" I cried out in more pleasure than pain. "Baby stop," I plead. "Wait…"

He pulled my hair back and fondled my pussy with his free hand. Shit, I was up on my tippy toes, sprawled across the counter, laying flat, biting the hand towel trying to hold in my satisfaction so my soon to be brother-in-law wouldn't hear me beg his brother for mercy. "Daddy wait, hold on," I said.

"Nah baby girl, talk that shit you was just talking," he replied, pounding me forcefully.

"Daddy… daddy… wait," I say. He flipped me over, picked me up in the air, and devoured my pussy. I gripped his head so tight and buried it in my pussy. "Yes daddy!" I yell out loud. I heard the door slam. I figured Brandon had left. I giggled slightly before Brendan spun me back around on the counter, allowing my breast to molest the cold surface while he pinned my arms behind me as if he handcuffed me. Only the bare walls heard my pleas. He pulled me by my bound arms as far back as my body would allow. I've never felt dick go so deep that it was penetrating my throat through my vaginal canal. The more I fought, the harder he pounded. I got scared for a minute, but decided that my man was my duty and that it was my job to fulfill his sexual needs no matter how extreme they were. I had never seen him this aggressive, but I conceded and enjoyed every thrust, push, pull, bite, whatever, until he came all up in my pussy. He finally released me and put me down. I held my torn dress up as I walked towards the living room, hoping not to run into Brandon. I hoped he had left but I had no confirmation. When I saw the coast was clear, I shot up the stairs to our suite to shower. I turned the hot water on and allowed the water to caress my body. It felt so soothing. I turned the massager aka the showerhead on full throttle and started to please myself while remembering Brendan ravishing my body in the kitchen just moments before.

"I didn't do it for you?" I head Brendan say, scaring me out of my thoughts. I moved the showerhead instantly, feeling embarrassed. I had damn sure enjoyed the session but I didn't get off enough. I still craved more, but I knew Brandon would be back soon and I didn't want to get caught.

"Put it back," he demanded.

"What?" I said confused

"Put it the fuck back." So I did as he said, the feeling becoming more intense. He said, "Don't move it."

When he entered me, the feeling became so intense that I lost my balance. He grinded in me slowly, but it still felt too strong for me. I tried to move the shower head but he wouldn't allow me to.

"No baby, you started it let's finish it," he said. His pounding got aggressive, at that point the showerhead couldn't stay in one place. It was making its point nonetheless. "Baby... baby, wait," I said.

"Nah," was all he said. Two more thrusts later, I came all over his dick and he pulled out and bust all over my wet ass. He picked me up and put my back against the wall as he slid me up and down the shaft of his dick. My vagina was so tender that the touch alone sent wild sensations through my body. "Oh shit," I said as he lifted me up and down, my hips being firmly held in place with every thrust. "Damn daddy," I said leaning in and biting his ear. "Fuck me daddy."

"Oh I'm going to fuck you baby. Long and hard," he says countering my thrust. My body started to quiver and if I looked in the mirror, I'm sure my eyes would be rolling to the back on my head. I couldn't take it anymore. My warm juices coated his third leg and violated his space with no warning as his trespassed against his will as well.

Finally, we showered, ensuring to wash each other down completely. He touched every crevice and every cranny. I've never felt so loved or attended to. He carried me out of the shower and dried me off. Soon after, we fell asleep holding one another.

I heard a little knocking at our room door. "Who is it," I asked, already knowing the answer.

"Aneeka," Anika replied.

"Come in, angel." Anika ran as fast as her little legs allowed her to and jumped on the bed with Brendan and me.

"Mommy, I played at the park I think," she said.

"You did?" I noticed a white washcloth being waved at the door. "What Brandon?" I laughed.

"Is it safe?" He asked.

Brendan said, "What do you think?" He began laughing himself.

I looked over because I thought he was still asleep. But I joined in laughter.

"All I know is my ass better stay in the living room. But hell, I wanted to visit not listen to porn. I got the fuck out of here. This isn't our teen years -- I couldn't call a lil slide over to please me, too. So I eased out the door and Anika and I got ice cream and played at the park. Well, until she had to go potty. She's all yours. Needless to say, she didn't make it."

"Oh God, she's on the bed!" I reached to move her, but it was too late. The bed was soaked. Anika looked embarrassed. I said, "It's okay sweetie, mommy isn't upset."

She smiled and followed me to her bathroom to get cleaned up.

"Alright fam, my bad. I'm out though," Brandon said to Brendan.

“Alright, later bro.” Brendan responded. The door slammed and Brendan said, “I picked Brandon up. How the hell is he getting home? Dammit.” I heard him rushing after him.

BRANDON

I'm not going to lie. When Tasha said that Macy had quit, I was relieved. Never in my life had I been so embarrassed. This girl gave me a high and took it away. I replayed that day time and time again. I just could not explain it. I even played myself and called a time or two, hoping she had felt remorseful or had changed her mind and was too afraid to reach out. Shortly after, she had changed her number. I found out she had had an abortion with my baby two months prior to me proposing, but I told myself she was a good girl and probably ashamed and afraid to have a baby out of wedlock. Behavior has away of sending warning signs that the heart seems to always rationalize.

I felt my phone buzzing. It was text from an unknown number. The text said "we got your lil bish if you want her back alive you better be at 1111 Rose Drive at 7pm."

I was scared for Macy. I had to help her. I ran out of Tasha's house and took Brendan's car. Brendan was calling me non-stop, but I didn't answer. I forgot all about riding over with this guy. Fuck it. It was 6:50 and my GPS said the place was 15 minutes away. When I finally arrived, there was a car already there whose lights blinded me. I received another text that said. "Simon says follow the leader."

We must have driven in ten unnecessary circles. I figured this was to confuse me, but this is my city. We finally pulled into a house near Southern Maryland. I use to visit my cousin Harvey here, but I played along. I texted Brendan "23-1" then I deleted it. He knew better than to text back.

I walked into the house and Macy was sitting in a chair, clearly free to go. I was confused.

“Macy are you okay?” I asked hesitantly.

“Of course she is.” Kelsi replied.

“Kelsi what are you doing here?” I asked agitated, figuring she was up to her usual shenanigans.

“Oh, I’m not Kelsi. I am Khaleena, Kelsi's twin. That’s Kelsi,” she said nonchalantly, pointing over to the bed that I hadn’t noticed until just then.

“What the fuck y'all crazy bitches got going on?” I was really getting annoyed. All the while, I was staring a hole into Macy. She wore a sense of pride on her face that told any other story than her feeling remorseful or broken.

“Seems like you are still thirsty,” Macy finally spoke. “You thought it was me in the trenches instead of the girl who stalked me, ruined my career, and stole my man. Got him strung out on drugs and forced me to get pregnant with your higher baby just to get even with her.”

“What the fuck are you talking about? Who did any of that?” I asked. “And what does that have to do with me?”

“Kelsi tell him,” Macy said. “Tell him that you are the reason he feels the pain he feels. Tell him how you were the drunk driver that killed his mother.”

As soon as she said that, I heard Braylin and Brendan say “WHAT?!” in unison. I had not noticed them sneak in but I knew they were coming. 23 said in trouble bring toys out. The 1 said look at vehicle one’s location. My brothers always came ready.

Macy looked disturbed when she saw them. I’m sure she wasn’t anticipating their company but fuck her.

“Kelsi, what is she talking about?” I inquired. Kelsi turned her head. She replied “You couldn’t love me until you had no one else to love. Your heart was full. I just needed to make room for me.”

“Brandon let’s go before we do something we will regret.”

“Fuck that Braylin, I will never regret avenging mom’s death. And if this conniving, deceitful bitch is insinuating that this trick bitch killed our mother, I’m here for it. No questions asked or explanations need to be had,” I replied.

“Brandon they are trying to drag you down, let God have vengeance. It is not ours to have.” Braylin replied.

“NIGGA do you fucking see God in this room right now? I only see the devil and his minions,” I said pissed.

“I know you are emotional right now, but this won’t change anything. We need to leave these demons here and focus,” Brendan said.

“Fuck no.” I replied. “You think they deserve to fucking live?” I said. “What emotions, nigga? My emotions left with snow white. Thank this hoe!” I shouted.

“I didn’t say these demons would be left alive,” Brendan replied.

KELSI

These bitches are going to die.

"Bitch did you say make room for you? You killed my mother to make room for you? What in the sick shit--"

"Your mother was a BITCH. She took my father away from me. He was in love with my mother. She was going to leave her abusive husband to be with him but your mother blackmailed our father into staying. She said she would not leave a breath of air of his in this world. She was going to kidnap us when my mom had us and kill all five of us including your father," I explained.

Braylin looked puzzled.

"Don't sit there judging me with your eyes. Your father agreed to stay with her and broke my mother's heart. She died despising that man."

"That doesn't make sense, our mother loved and adored us. Where would such hatred derive from?" Brendan asked.

"No one said she didn't, but your father feared your mother. My alleged dad found out we were not his kids when I was six years old and needed a kidney donor. Imagine me being a helpless, sick child that is dying, and my mother's secrets pour out of the closet and outshine my need for help." I replied.

"You said earlier our father. How do you know OUR father is yours?" Brendan asked.

"I was sure to go with my mother to meet him. He never confessed to being our dad, but I knew. I reflected back on conversations that I had overheard, but at the time didn't understand. I remember one very well. The last time we saw him I was six. It was right after I got terminally ill. He came to the hospital and it went like this.

My mom: She needs a kidney and I am not a match.

Your dad: How do you know I am?

My mom: I don't, but please try. I have to save her.

Your dad: I'm not sure. I'd rather have one dead child than five.

My mom: What are you talking about? So she is expendable? Are you sure you are concerned about four other children, or is it three that mold fear in your heart?

Your dad: No, Whitney I'm not saying that. All I'm saying is you and I both know the consequences could be deadly.

My mom: The consequences are already deadly. I am not afraid of her. You are. Now I stood back and let you make the choice you made, but I will not allow this witch to hinder you from saving our child's life.

Your dad: All of the protection in the world cannot save you from her.

Then he left. I don't know why that hurt but truthfully I knew then I was going to die. I used to lie in bed counting down from 100 to 0 thinking that when I got to zero I would flat line. Once I got better my step dad started beating me real bad. He said, 'I knew you wasn't mine. You should have died. You deserved to die for your mother's sins. I heard he even spit in his sister's face for donating a kidney. And that bitch of a mother of mine was no better. She allowed God to save me so the devil could punish me. That's why they both died together, so the devil didn't have to double back.'"

Khaleena finally spoke. "I remember that," she whispered. "I never understood what was going on because mommy would just take me outside. But I remember you being inside screaming. Why did you want me dead though? Why hurt me?"

"Because you were safe and I wasn't. Why did you get to live without pain? For years I suffered and you never tried to protect me, not once. My heart burned." I answered.

Braylin spoke, "Let's go, we are done here."

Brendan agreed and started to leave, but Brandon stayed. He didn't move; he was frozen in place. Braylin pulled his arm, and with that they were gone.

"Kelsi wake up!" I heard. I had fainted. Remembering trauma was no joke.

Khaleena shook my foot and said, "The devil is in you, but let's see if he is concerned enough to save you." Her and Macy left out and abandoned me. I wasn't afraid, but I was alone again. The loudness of the silence was penetrating. Then a light of hope shone in and I thought death seemed better than this.

For a week straight, different men had come in and out of the house plugging any hole they found suitable. I smelled horrible. I was in so much pain that I prayed to a God that I didn't know and asked if I could just die already.

I was obsessed with these four men, I thought laying there alone. Although different men came in and out, I was still a man on an island. I named Brandon, Carter. I knew that his name was Brandon, but Carter and I had unfinished business. And while conversing with Macy, I needed an alias for him. There is how Carter was reborn. The lie draped in the truth. Sadly in my seeking vengeance, I had actually fallen in love with Brandon. I just wanted to be a part of their family and I didn't care how. My family hated me. Maybe his could love me if that bitch ass mother of theirs was gone. Now I'm laying here wondering if any of it was worth it.

CARTER SENIOR

The boys came over all frazzled.

"Dad be honest." Brendan said.

"Who is Whitney?" Brandon asked, fuck the formalities.

I almost lost my balance. "An old friend," I replied.

"Dad, we're listening," Braylin said.

"Okay. I knew Whitney many moons ago. She and I fell in love. Her vibes were unmatchable but she was virgin. I was already having sex so when the craving got too bad I handled it. After that, I decided to have a girl to fuck that knew the deal and allowed me to return home to my girlfriend. I never wanted to press Whitney. I knew quality early on in life. So as you can imagine, I knew I wanted her to be my wife. Her virginity was something I wanted her to be proud to give me on our special night. Anyway, she went off to collage in New York. NYU to be exact. I would drive up on the weekends or catch the bus and we would tour the city. In her junior year of college, she came home for a visit. While at Ledo's over in District Heights, this girl I had been fucking named Allure came in and went to work on Whitney. I did my best to pull her off of her, but her friends jumped in to help. She yelled at Whitney, 'Bitch you better stay away from my man or else.' I rushed Whitney to the hospital, but after that she had refused to see me. Four years later, I had met your mother. She was Whitney and I all over again. She almost instantly got pregnant, but I asked her to abort it. Well she did. Two years later, I was at a red light on MLK and there she was. There was Whitney just as beautiful as I remember. I chased her down. When she finally stopped, she looked at me with desert eyes. Empty. I'd never forget it. She said, "Please move along we are old strangers who never knew each other."

I had to get my emotions in check. "I asked her how could she say that when she knew I loved her. I confessed my feelings to her. Whitney said, 'You loved me an inch from my life.' I told her that I had nothing to do with that, but she had already known. She said that she had gotten phone calls about me cheating. She said she wanted to focus on herself." I still remember the rest of the conversation like it was yesterday.

"Whitney, allow me to try to fix it."

"You did all I was going to allow once you continued your relationship with Allure after she had beat me mercifully for being with who I thought was my man."

"I was lonely. I used her to fill the void of you."

"And did she?"

"Did she what?"

"Did she fill the void?"

"I was young and dumb. I did what my immature reality told me to do."

"You knew right from wrong. You chose her over me. Don't use your age as reasoning for your behavior. Being with her was convenient for you, and you didn't care how it hurt me. I questioned your loyalty so much, but of course, it was all about you."

"It was a mistake."

"It was a choice, Carter."

"I can fix it in time. I'm not expecting overnight, but I never meant for this to happen."

"I'm married now. Time is up."

I finished telling my boys what happened. "That broke my heart. But I still loved her so bad. Two months later my homeboy asked me to come to the hospital and get him. I saw

Whitney at the bus stop outside the hospital doors, beat up and bleeding. I jumped out of my car to help her so quickly I forgot to put the car in park. I had to jump back in and put it in park. When I looked over your mother's eyes were so cold. She saw the love I had for Whitney and it caused her to grow enraged. Your mother started yelling, but at the time we really didn't have any titles. When my homeboy came out I told him to drive your mother home while I sat there with Whitney. I had finally convinced her to go home with me and she ended up staying for four months before her husband had coaxed her into coming back. She felt obligated to go back because she had married him. The day before she left, I was sitting in the kitchen drawn to a miscellaneous spot on the wall. Whitney walked over to me and asked what was wrong. I looked up at her and dropped my head seconds later as I told her my sister got shot in California by her boyfriend three nights prior. Whitney ran to my side. I didn't cry until that moment. She felt safe."

I paused. "Whitney asked what happened, and I explained to her. They had gone to a mobile testing center for HIV/AIDS awareness day. The test came back positive. My sister confronted her boyfriend about it. They fought, and he shot and killed her to protect his secret. She was a virgin before him, so she knew that he gave it to her. I cried when I told her that. Whitney just held me tenderly. Amour was only 19 years old. Whitney picked my face up and kissed me for the first time. I let her kiss me, afraid that if I moved the moment would be over. When she started undressing me I asked if she was sure. She said yes. I picked her up and laid her on the counter. I devoured her. She tasted so sweet." I stopped for a moment to reflect for myself, then continued the story. "Needless to say we had the most passionate, explosive sex known to man. When it was all over she left the next day. I was beyond hurt. However, I did not see her until seven years later --"

Brandon interrupted me. "Dad, really? Get to it, are these girls our sisters?"

"Don't you ever interrupt me again," I said firmly. He backed down. "By then, your mom was pregnant with you. We had decided to get married. But even after Whitney, your mom and I did not rekindle things until two years later and even then we were off and on for three years. I had let Whitney go completely by then and was very happy with your mom. One day I am walking into Georgetown Hospital to retrieve the same homeboy, it had to be a coincidence, and Whitney is outside crying. I assumed her husband was beating her up again. Nonetheless, I walked up to check up on her same as before. She looked like she had seen a ghost. She looked around frantically and she said I need your help. But she said it in almost a whisper like she was afraid that someone would hear her request. I was reluctant for a minute but finally I asked her 'with what?' She pulled my arm leading me into the hospital. She took me in a room with a little girl. The girl looked familiar but I couldn't place it. So I waited for Whitney's explanation. She said, 'This is Kelsi. She has a twin sister named Khaleena. She has kidney failure and needs a donor.'

'Oh is she yours?' I asked.

'No, she is ours,' she hesitantly said.

My head jerked in her direction. 'OURS?!'

She said yes and I was like, how? Now she was looking at me like I was crazy. 'I got pregnant by you, that's how. I know you are familiar with the process,' she snapped back. 'I just found out she was yours. By the time I found out I was pregnant I was four months. I assumed it was my husband's.'

'How do you know they aren't his?' I asked.

'They did a DNA test to see if he could be a match like a donor you know,' she replied. 'Needless to say he was not. Can you be her donor?' I froze and walked out the room. I walked to the nurse's stand and asked them to test me to see if I was a donor. When I found out that I was a positive match I decided to donate my kidneys two days later. When I finally healed up I went to Kelsi's room to check on her but she was not there. I asked the nurse and she informed me that her family moved her to a different hospital. I asked why and she said that it was just their request. I hired PI after PI and countless lawyers to find them. By the time I had found them they had moved to another state -- North Carolina to be exact." I sipped my glass of Hennessy. "The state recognizes the husband as the father if the wife cheats. The biological parent has no rights to the child. It was no mistake that they relocated there. Your mom was by my side the entire time. I loved her so much more because of that."

Braylin said, "Dad this girl says she came on various visits that you and her mom had but you haven't said you've seen her."

"I saw both of the sister's court ordered and I saw them individually. Khaleena was sleep one visit and the other she was too afraid to come to me. Kelsi was the friendlier one. She would sit beside me and play with her dolls."

"But did you ever look for them as adults?" Brendan asked.

"I never lost them. I paid their tuition, visited Khaleena in the hospital, and paid her medical bills. I sent birthday gifts, fireworks, Christmas presents, I attended all major school events and recitals. I have a copy of every report card and award. I just never had the chance to tell them who I was."

"Why?" Braylin asked. "Kelsi, by the way, has another story."

"Bring her to me," I said.

"Did mom ever threaten them or us?" Brandon asked.

"No, there was no reason to."

"Why didn't you tell us?" Brendan asked.

"We told you. Your mother and I did together, but I got overwhelmed because you asked to see them all of the time and you couldn't. When you finally stopped asking, it was easier to just let you forget."

CALLIE

Don said, "Callie, Braylin is waiting for you in your office."

"Okay," I replied. I sent up a Jack Daniel's and coke to ease his mind. He only came here when he was stressed. I attached a note that said "finishing up a meeting, enjoy these until I get there." I also sent up Jacks and Tip, his favorite dancers besides me. Thirty minutes later, I walked in my office and he was alone.

"Did the girls come up?" I asked.

He replied, "Yes, but I sent them away."

"Is everything okay?"

"I am not sure." I'm not going to lie, my mind has been all over the place lately, as well. I just haven't had the heart to explain it. He scared me out of my thoughts when he started talking. "I just can't identify the truth anymore. The more things come together, the more they fall apart, he explained. My father has a set of twins that he failed to mention. My brother has been sleeping with one of them, mind you she knew she was our sister even though he didn't know. She had something to do with our mother's death and Macy is involved because the very same sister who is fucking our brother, raped her twin sister while she was in a coma caused by an accident her twin created. Man the list goes on," he said throwing back what looked to be the third glass of Jack and coke.

The loud speaker announced, "Duchess, you have a visitor in the clear room."

I was confused because I wasn't expecting anyone, but business comes first. "Baby give me a second. I think we should go home and sort through this mess." He agreed and I left to head to the clear room.

I walked in. "Hi, I'm Duchess. My assistant said you would like to speak to me. What would that be in reference to?" I asked politely.

The moment this bitch turned around I knew instantly that this little meet and greet was about to be lit.

ANGELIQUE

I spun around when Ms. Duchess entered the room. Her guards were up, I could tell.

"My name is Angelique and I'm --"

"Shelia's mother." She cut me off.

"Braylin's ex-fiancé and the mother of our daughter." I finished.

"Really? I heard you never made it that far. Actually, I heard you were more interested in someone else's saddle," she retorted.

"Is that what he told you?" I asked with a grin.

"How can I help you? I need to get back to business and if it's not talking money it's wasting time."

"You can leave my man alone so our daughter can have her father back. Shelia deserves her whole family," I replied.

"MY man made his position clear as to where he wants to be. If he changes his mind I'm sure we will all know," Callie replied, very matter-of-factly.

"If that ring solidified your spot, he wouldn't be in my bed at night." I replied dropping a bomb on her Ms. Know-It-All ass.

She smiled back and stepped towards me. I didn't budge. I was on a mission and I refused to show weakness. I didn't care if she was intimidating.

She replied, "And if that baby solidified your position, I would not be wearing this paperweight on my ring finger. But you enjoy your day beautiful," and she switched her ass right out of there. Her ass looked perfect. So perfect, I almost recommend we all be one big happy family.

I can't lie. I felt a little foolish. That bitch had me in my bag with her slick ass mouth. As much as I hated her, I knew what she was saying was right. But how can I right my wrong if this bitch felt entitled to my space. I knew for sure that Braylin would give us a second chance once we sat down to talk. Problem is, he never wanted to talk.

BRAYLIN

Callie's TV came down on the wall. At first I thought I hit something by accident, but when it turned on I saw and heard Callie and Angelique. I started to go down there, however, Callie was holding her own. And although Angelique game face was on point, I knew from her body language that she was defeated.

Angelique and I had sex once two days after my first date with Callie. I told her then it was mistake. Angelique didn't seem phased by it either way. In fact, I thought we had finally a started to have a congruent relationship. I got up and went to the bathroom. I was in the restroom for a while but when I came out Callie was sitting on the couch purse in hand and her laptop bag in front of her.

"Hey baby, are you ready already?" I asked.

"Yes," she replies. "I'll meet you at your house."

"Okay," I replied.

We both went our separate ways. I arrived 25 minutes before she did. How do I explain to her that what Angie said wasn't true? Fuck. I cursed myself.

When she finally got there, she said, "Hey baby I picked up food. I figured you didn't eat." I was caught off guard because I expected her to be angry but she was calm.

"Thank you," I replied as I sat down to eat. I broke down everything that happened that day and her mouth dropped.

ANGELIQUE

I'm all prepared for this bitch to run and tell Braylin what happened. You see I plan to act clueless. Like why would I ever? I'll simply explain I wanted to throw my man a surprise party there and I had no idea she worked there. How could I when we have never been formally introduced -- let alone introduced at all?

Braylin called, as expected, the next day.

"Hello?" I answered

"Angelique is it ok if I pick Shelia up for the week?" Braylin asked.

"Uhm yeah, no that is fine." I replied.

"Okay, perfect. I'll be there in thirty minutes."

"Okay, I will get her ready," I said before hanging up.

Thirty minutes or so later, Braylin pulled up. I was half dressed hoping to lessen his rage. I had booty shorts and a tank top on. "Oh hey Braylin, I was about to head out."

"Oh okay, where is Shelia?" he replied.

"In her room taking forever to pack. Do you want to come in?" I asked.

"Nah send her out when she is ready," he said before walking back to the car. Then I noticed that bitch in the car. No wonder he wasn't taking the bait. I simply turned around and called Shelia. Ten minutes later, she came to the door. I kissed her and sent her out. Shelia ran right past Braylin and hugged Duchess. I can't believe my daughter even likes this stripper bitch.

I know my facial expressions need deliverance at this point because my heart is filled with rage and I'm sure I'm as green as the Grinch. I hope my daughter doesn't end up liking this bitch more than me. What if she ends up living with them and calling that hoe mommy? What would her future look like? Ughh. I wanted to stab this bitch in the heart right now.

I had to create a plan to get rid of this bimbo bitch.

CALLIE

I know this girl is mad, but I honestly don't care. I'm not sure if Braylin saw the footage or not because when I got back to my office he was up in the restroom. I didn't bother bringing it up because it didn't matter either way. What's to discuss about a catfight? I figured the information about the engagement caught her off guard, so I'll let this situation slide. No harm, no foul.

After Shelia hugged me, I walked up to her mom and said, "Hey Angelique, I'm Callie. We are having a cookout Friday and I was wondering if you would like to come. Her face read confusion mixed with jealousy. I turned around and blew a kiss at Braylin, then turned back to her.

"Sure, why not? Nice to meet you," she replied pulling me in for a hug. She whispered, "Bitch you have no idea who you are playing with."

"I guess that makes two of us," I replied, releasing the hug and turning around to walk away. "Oh!" I said as if I forgot and turned around. "By the way, it's at Meltdown this Saturday at 3pm. You don't have to bring anything, but you are more than welcome to bring a plus one. Anyone is suitable, however, let's have class. If your plus one is Mr. Malcolm Johnson you should come alone." I smiled.

She smiled and returned to the house.

That's what I thought. You are not the only one capable of being a messy bitch. I wrote the manual hoe.

BRAYLIN

These women need a Grammy, I thought to myself. Normally, I would respect my ex's space and not bring anyone over, but she stepped out of her lane and because of that, I needed to do damage control. Since Callie didn't make a big deal about it, I decided not to either. If and when she did, then I will address it. Until then, I will have Callie around when I pick and drop Shelia off. No confusion.

After the girls hugged, I got in the car and waited for Callie to join us so we could move on with our day.

After she got in the car, I thought to myself, *I still haven't heard anything from our sisters*. Triplet boys and twin girls. Wow. I wonder what happened that night when we left. None of us talked about it or considered what my dad asked. I've just been so uneasy since that day. Something was not right and I knew it was not over. I was not nervous, but I was not certain.

KHALEENA

I had so much to think about over the past three weeks. I wondered if what Kelsi said was true. It was clear she had a deep-rooted hatred for me, but her reasoning seemed like a huge conundrum. Nothing made sense. One constant was that I was going to find out the truth.

I've been observing the abandoned house we left Kelsi in for a few hours a day for the past week. I keep seeing men go in and out they must be having a blast with her -- as she deserves. Part of me hoped the bitch rotted there, but the other part of me wanted to rescue her surviving ass. I even contemplated seeing if she was alive.

Finally, I decided to go in. Just as I was about to exit my car, I saw one of those three men she claimed was our brother go in. I decided to sit back and watch. Five minutes later he brought her frail body out wrapped in a tattered cloth. He placed her in the backseat of his car shut the door, got in front, started the car, and sped off. I would follow, but I don't care anymore. I cursed myself for showing up and thinking about going in.

That bitch's soul has abandoned her. She's dead on the inside and nowhere can she hide from her own demise.

MACY

So I moved. I think I did enough damage in DC. I got Browdy from rehab and we moved to North Carolina. I bought us another identity. This is the second time I've done this, however, I know this time will be different. My new name is Amy E. Waller and Browdy is Jace B. Waller. We are married now, at least that's what our paperwork says. I adore this man. He's the only man that I've ever loved.

Anyway, I work in the school system here as a nurse. Browdy, I mean Jace, as I should get acclimated to calling him, works in construction. Life seems simple here. Of course I miss the fast life that the city provides, but I would give it up a thousand times over to be with my heart in human form.

I told Jace that I accidentally killed Khaleena and Kelsi so we had to move. Can you believe he still wanted sadistic Kelsi? He said they understood each other. He said with her he could be him. He could even be an assorted version of who he wanted to be. Whatever the fuck that means. "I killed them bitches, so how are you going to want two dead ass hoes?" I yelled.

My only real regret is that I did not kill these bitches. Luckily for me, there are 365 days a year so I'm sure I have time. Fuck a fuck ass bitch.

BRANDON

I went back to the house. I was not sure if I was going to find Kelsi, a corpse, or an empty house. But I haven't been sleeping and it has been tormenting me. So many unanswered questions. When I walked in I heard grunting. I almost turned around and walked out but I knew I needed to see for myself. When I walked in I saw Kelsi tied to a bed restrained getting fucked by some unknown dude. I raced to her side and pushed the guy off of her. "What the fuck are you doing?" the guy asked. He jumped up and said, "It is my turn, you need to wait yours. I'm almost finished."

"Nigga, don't make me do that to you for a nut." I responded.

He caught my drift and left. I saw an old curtain and I decided to wrap her in it. I took her to my house and I bathed her. It felt real awkward, but she smelled terrible. After I bathed her I made her a bowl of turkey broth to help baby step her to eating again. When she ate all that I could get her to accept, I carried her up to my guest bedroom and tucked her into bed. She still hadn't said anything. I called Dora when she fell asleep and asked if she could render her services privately. She agreed to and stated that she would be there in the morning.

For three weeks, Dora came over and talked to Kelsi. Kelsi started to regain her strength and moved around on her own. When Dora told me the gruesome stories that Kelsi had shared, I understood her rage and her divided way of thinking. I decided to invite dad over to talk to her before she got anymore distorted thoughts.

CARTER SENIOR

I'm sitting here with Kelsi, listening to her recap of what she recalled happening as a child. I just shook my head. So he was way off. I was so angry with Whitney for allowing this girl to go through so much and filling her head with so many lies. I sat that night for the second time and told her the truths that I had told my boys. I brought her the court documents, footage, and payments made over the years. I showed her the videos of her and her sister at different events, I even showed her the scar from being her donor. She just looked so confused. I could tell she was overwhelmed.

"I'm glad I killed those lying bitches," she stated out loud.

I was so shocked I had no words. "Whitney is dead?" I asked.

"As dead as a six-foot grave would welcome you," she said.

"Uh huh. And you did that?" I asked. The pain I felt was immeasurable. The pain I felt reminded me of the pain I felt losing my wife but worse. My first love was gone.

She said, "You think I'm bad don't you? For killing them, almost killing my twin, and for killing your wife. Oh and for fucking your son's brains out and sucking is soul out of his pipe and falling in love with my brother?"

This was the first time I was hearing about any of this. Brandon slept with her. "Hell is going to welcome me," I thought out loud. She even disclosed something about Macy drugging her.

This girl is a hazard to herself and you just can't undo that amount of damage. I hugged her. It seemed long overdue.

TASHA

This whole mess has all of us on stand by. I haven't heard any wedding plans of any sort. No family events minus that one cookout. It's been dry and uneventful. I did get a promotion at work and Anika is in daycare. Everything just feels routine.

Brendan called to tell me we were going out. He was always on the move these days. It seems like crime is at its peak, but a working man is a busy man, so I don't complain.

He arrived at 7:30pm sharp. Anika and I walked to the car. I buckled her up in her car seat and got in. Brendan was on a business call, which I figured because normally he gets out to open my door and buckle Anika in. He ended the call shortly after.

"Hey baby girl, I'm sorry." He turned to me.

"No worries," I replied. "Where are we headed?" I asked.

"To the altar, hopefully." He answered.

I giggled as I do anytime he mentions marrying me. Imagine my surprise when we pulled up to an exclusive boutique. When I went in, the designer told me to tell him my dreams and he'll make it a reality. Brendan smiled and said, "I'll be back in an hour."

An hour later, I came outside and Anika had at least ten bags of clothes and toys. He spoils her.

That night when I put Anika to sleep, I laid in Brendan's arms, relaxed, and told him how much I adored him.

He said, "I want you and Anika to move in with me. Anika starts school this year and I live in a better school district."

I was shocked. “Are you sure?” I asked him.

“Yes, I’m certain. Why would I ask if I wasn’t?”

The next morning, I woke up to packers and movers. Brendan had paid my rent up for the rest of my lease and I was on my way with my daughter to our new home. Life was sweet. I adored this feeling.

Brendan took Anika in the den with him to watch the news. He was very adamant about knowing everything going on around him. When my phone started vibrating, it scared me out of my thoughts. The caller ID read ‘unknown’. I ignored the call but they called back. I was curious, but I was not expecting the call, so I kept ignoring it.

“Who is that?” Brendan asked.

“I’m not sure. I don’t answer unknown calls,” I replied. Then the phone rang again.

“Baby, just answer it,” he said.

“Nope. I believe if you call me blocked or private, I should respect your privacy and not answer.” I replied.

Brendan took my phone and answered. “Hello?” he said.

“Where is that nappy-headed bitch?” A woman asked.

“Excuse me?” he replied.

“Latasha… I know dis is her phone,” The caller said smacking her gum. “Tell her ma died and the funeral is Friday. She know where.” With that, the caller hung up.

I heard it all; Brendan had answered on speakerphone. He looked at me with sympathy in his eyes. He reached out to me to hold me, and I walked into his arms. I cried softly, said a prayer, and I pulled myself together.

“I have a presentation Friday, but I’m going to see if I can reschedule,” he said.

"No need. I'm not going to her funeral. We said our goodbyes long ago," I said.

He looked confused, but all he said was, "Are you sure?"

I shook my head yes. "I'm sure."

BRENDAN

Tasha's background is something we don't discuss often. It just seems so painful for her whenever she talks about it. After her response earlier, I am convinced now more than ever it's time for me to figure it out. I didn't press the issue because I figured her response could have been a knee jerk reaction to tragic news.

On Friday morning, I let Tasha sleep in. I got up, fed Anika, and got both of us dressed. It was something I did often so I knew Tasha would not worry. I put her in the car seat and pulled off.

KHALEENA

I decided to apply for a few jobs a few weeks ago. Braylin helped me get an interview at Jo's law firm. They called me back rather quickly and my interview blew them away. I was hired on the spot. I had been working there for a few days and I enrolled at Howard at night. Grad level was very chill, but still demanding. I thought about my family often. I missed my parents, I hated my sister, I loved my new brothers and my biological father. Life was just different.

"Yeah bitch, I said on sight!" I heard someone yell in my direction. I turned to look. The girl was very cute, big but had a slim waist, and nice boobs. "Oh bitch you don't know who I'm talking to?"

I pointed at my chest and asked, "Me?"

She said, "No bitch, Casper."

Now I am confused, trying to remember if I knew her. I decided I didn't. So, I responded, "I think you have the wrong person."

"No bitch... I'll never forget you. You're the bitch that was fucking my man," she replied.

"Oh no, honey you definitely have the wrong one. I am not fucking anyone, let alone someone else's man. So, if your man fucked me it was rape," I said.

"Oh now you saying Khree raped you. Hoe you got more tricks up your sleeves than a five-dollar hoe," she bantered.

"Excuse me?" I asked, shocked.

"Oh you heard me, but I'm not here to talk about it." She lunged at me. I just started fighting back.

I was always a good fighter. It was Kelsi who could not fight for shit. Just as I had that thought, I figured she thought I was Kelsi. I grabbed the bitch by her hair and slung her to the ground while dragging her face across the cement. This heifer was a wild fighter. As she painted the ground red with her leaking pride, she rotated her body in a spinning motion to hit me with a haymaker. I have to admit… the blows that landed were definitely impact blows, but I got frustrated and started stomping the bitch out. I heard bystanders saying shit like "Damn sis working her," and "She too small to be slanging bitches like that." One guy even pleaded for me to release her and mentioned something about head trauma. She finally jumped up. I guess she was ready to start the fight now. She kicked me on my stomach so hard that I flew back and hit my head on a rock. I felt dizzy and I passed out. I woke up after I don't know how much time had passed to her blow after blow stinging my face. I used my feet to kick her off of me. She didn't go that far. She rolled my hair up in her fist and started giving me face shots… I could tell Kelsi really pissed her off because she was not that skilled of a fighter. I heard her yell, "I bet this will be the last time you think a dick that is signed for needs a cosigner." I was several other trick ass bitches before I heard sirens. She tried to run off but I tripped her up. I hear someone on the crowd say "Down goes Frazier." I punched her in the side of her head over and over. She kicked her leg up and fucked my thigh up. By the time the police had broke it up it was blood everywhere. I would call her a worthy opponent, but I could look into her eyes and see in her eyes it wasn't skill. It was rage I was fighting.

"I'm going to fuck you up every time I see you lil bitch," she yelled.

"Bitch how about you make sure you square up with the right person next time. Then maybe you won't be out here yelling through closed eyes, swollen lips and draglines. Scary ass hoe," I retorted.

"Oh I did," she replied knowingly.

"Oh you did?" I asked. "Well trick, what's my name? Who am I since you know me?" I taunted.

"A TRICK ASS, THOT ASS BITCH," she replied.

"Hoe you don't know me. You just fought the wrong girl because you can't keep your dog on a leash or a memory. Because clearly you just fought the wrong girl," I yelled out of breath.

"Bitch I can hold a man, but I refuse to be in competition with a hoe that thinks it's okay to sleep with another woman's man." She said.

"First of all bitch, your man must be a boy or a pedophile because you're clearly a child. You sound crazy. You're not in competition with a woman that thinks it's okay to sleep with another woman's man. Bitch, grown women don't fight over men. You should have beat his hoe ass. But no, you're out here looking crazy for some community dick. Bitch where they do that? I hope the nigga got you on his fucking payroll. You sweet for it."

"Bitch, age is for the mathematician not me. You can say what you want, but fact of the matter is bitch I owed you that on principle. My property is my property. If you come on it again bitch I will shoot you dead," she threatened.

"Principle collects interest or its worthless hoe. Money getting used and redistributed to be disseminated to potentially lose value and never grow. The bitch that is cumin on that niggas dick is probably where his interest lies. He's using you because you don't understand your own value, potential, or your ability to grow. You wasted my time over some nonsense." I replied.

"Khaleena Taylor," the officer called out.

"Yes sir?" I answered.

"Witnesses say you were the victim of Ms. Buffy Gains. Is that true?" He asked.

Now 12 got to be insane, of course that's true if that is what the people said. And even if it isn't, I'm still going with it. I finally replied. "Yes sir, I do not know her at all. She clearly has me mistaken for someone else."

"Would you like to press charges?" He asked.

"No sir, I would like to go." I answered.

Buffy's eyes grew wide. I guess she was shocked.

He said, "You are free to leave. I will hold Ms. Gains here for a while."

"Don't hold her on account of me. There's not a threat of fear in this body for a weak morsel such as herself." As I walked past her, I said in a volume only she could hear, "Bitch did you catch my name? I'm sure it's not the name of the woman you have an issue with. I know this because I've been in a coma for three years and only been out for a few months. But listen I'll give you a head start because the next time I see you it's on sight, petty hoe." I walked off.

BUFFY

When I saw the bitch that stole my solace I tried to murder her. Everything went black and no excuse would suffice. I just wanted her to feel the disrespect, hurt, humiliation, and brokenness that I felt. That pain that came from that episode broke me. I loved him harder than I ever loved any other man and when I found out he betrayed me, it took my heart away. The more I thought about it the more enraged I became. It scared me. I tried to calm down and to let it go -- to chalk it up but this pain was angry and growing. I was no longer rational or in control. No one should have that type of hate and rage in them. But I had it and it couldn't be calmed. There was Kelsi. I knew her face, her smile, her everything. I could smell random panties and know if they belong to her. My man wore her scent so often I was sure it was for purchase. The smell was forever etched in my memory. I wanted her dead, but I couldn't justify it. In a world were people brag about being cold hearted and savage or moving on to other fish in the sea, I knew they could never understand.

I felt pain that everyone has felt that not many had the courage to fix and for that they would call me insane and pretend to not understand why. Why did she have to die? Why couldn't she live? I was snatched out of my thoughts when the officer called her Khaleena something. I was so speechless that I had no sound. I had fucked up. But how could I be wrong? When the cops released me I felt like shit. I decided right then and there to get help. My heart needed help mending.

APPLE

Callie done found out how many trades were moving in secret and allowed me to start dancing in the Back Room. All pun intended. She told a few dudes how to get in the room and aww honey child that was it. I was paid. The clientele became too much for me, which lead me to hiring two transgender women. The three of us combined put us right on top. The trades would come through the back door and would deposit an entry fee of $600.00. They would then get a dark purple key card that they could put as much money on it as they wanted. It moved like a credit card and a hotel key all in one. They would purchase their booth. The booths were glass, but you couldn't see in them -- only out. Most trades preferred their privacy because they lived this side of their lives in secrecy. They had private entry and private exits. Once the booth was vacant, a new client would enter all the while never seeing the previous occupant. We would dance for them and provide them with any and all fantasies. We never had any form of sex with them, but they paid top dollar anyway. Everything was lit and we lived for the attention and the atmosphere. The clients would pick their drinks on tablets and swipe their card. The bartender would insert it in a hole cut in the door never seeing the guest. The guest loved how exclusive it was and they paid extra so no one ever saw their real name on the visitors list. They could even tip the dancers from the tablet. We were doing well. No, better than good; we were monopolizing the game.

Anyway, I'm on my way I'm on my way up to meet Callie.

"Hey girl," I greeted her when I entered the room.

"Hey Apple!" She replied.

"Someone is glowing. What's going on with you?" I asked.

"Nothing, but you need you to sign this paperwork."

"Okay what is it in reference to?"

"Nothing of much consequence, really. Just needed your signature." Callie was being very vague, so I breezed through the paperwork to get some clarity as to what I was putting my John Hancock on. Not that I didn't trust her, but life has taught me to be precious in all situations.

My mouth dropped when I read through the first paragraph. I did not need to read anymore. Callie had signed in the entire Back Room to me. We were now both owners of clubs. I was so elated that I burst into tears. "I cannot believe you did this for me," I said through tears.

"You did it for yourself."

She gave me the independence I never knew I wanted -- independence I never fathomed I could have.

CALLIE

Apple has been through so much that I only wanted to see him happy. I feel like I have neglected him since Braylin and I got together, so I felt compelled to do something nice. To me, money was a great gesture of appreciation. Please don't get it confused bitches, I am not trying to buy him, I'm showing him there are levels to support. Your friends let you watch them do great and might even throw some words of motivation or inspiration in there. My friends build each other up. When we get a step up, we pull our friends up to the next level. No shade, but we move differently.

Later on that day, while we were flying over the city, Apple yelled, "Oh my God Callie, I feel on top of the world!" I arranged a helicopter ride that toured the city and we landed near Ruth's Chris Steak House for dinner.

When we entered Ruth's Chris, everyone who was anyone was already there. At Apple's table was Phaedra, Teyanna, Candace, and myself. Oh and even Opal came out to celebrate. Those are his girls. They all looked like stunning women, however, I was the only one that was actually all woman in the group. Shout out to God's special talents. There were more like YouTube and ten years of being in the closet with fashion magazines and therapy/hormone assistance. No shade, but yeah.

Anyway, Teyanna had a cake out that said happy 24th birthday, Phaedra had 24 balloons -- and you know her extra ass got four massive balloons with confetti in them -- and Candice and Opal had the gifts. Apple was shocked, it blew her away. But it damn sure didn't stop her from a Grammy worthy speech and the infamous cry/flash fan of the eyes with both hands to prohibit tears.

We partied all night long, leaving no bar unturned and club untamed. From VA to DC, we partied hard. Calling it epic wouldn't give the stories we could tell any justice.

At the last club we got the fuck bored and Phaedra suggested that we play 'I Never' and combine it with dare... so basically someone would say something like 'I never kissed a random stranger' and everyone who has will take a shot of whatever their drink of choice was and whoever didn't had to do it. About six shots in, I realized I was lightweight and boring so I decided to quit, but not before Opal gave me one final 'I never.' She said, "I never walked the hoe stroll." So there I was on an actual hoe stroll, walking it back and forth. Bitch, my walk screamed 'take advantage of me, I'm wasted'. I must have walked for like two minutes before Opal was picking me up off the ground and putting me in the backseat of her car.

My phone started ringing obnoxiously and every time I push the button to reject the call, the caller would just call back. Finally, I rolled over out of my slumber and answered the phone. I'm sure my tongue was still drunk because my words were slurring in my head and not just out loud. I said something that was supposed to be hello.

"Hello baby," Braylin said in a taunting tone. Lord knows his voice awakened parts of me that until that very moment, I didn't know existed. My pussy must be drunk and confused because it's going to remain in the jar until wedding vows are exchanged. Better calm down.

"Hey baby," I think I said back.

"Baby, I'm outside. Come on down," he replied.

"Okay," I said rolling over. I must have moved too fast because wouldn't you know, it caused me to test my up chuck reflexes. I ran towards the bathroom holding vomit it my mouth. That's when I realized I wasn't even home. I'm at Apple's fucking house. I still made it to the bathroom despite my memory loss.

I rinsed my mouth out with mouthwash, washed my face, used the restroom, and headed out the door.

"Hey baby," I said when I got in the car. "How did you know I was at Apple's? I had to tip out the house to not wake her. Last night was wild."

Apple called me on his way to New York, asking if I could pick you up from his place and he told me where the spare key was just in case you were too inebriated to find your phone or too intoxicated to answer it," Braylin joked.

"Hahaha" I replied, unamused. "You could have at least let me sleep a few more hours. What is it like 5:30 in the morning?"

"Baby it's 9:40pm. That's why Apple left you. He said you were lightweight," he chuckled.

"I did not sleep the day away like that. And I had a meeting today with Samantha," I said upset at myself.

"Oh yeah, Apple said he rescheduled that until the end of next month. She's going to London for three weeks and that is her next availability. But to answer your question, you definitely slept the day away, but your body needed the rest. You have been working excessively and diligently on something. Time outs are necessary."

We pulled up in front of his house. He said, "I forgot my wallet. I'm going to run in and grab it so we can get something to eat and then I will take you home."

"What if I want to come inside?" I replied hesitantly.

"What do you mean? You can come in. I'm not going to be in there long though."

"Braylin listen to me. I'm saying I don't want to go home." I spoke slightly more confidently than I was a second ago.

"Are you sure?"

"I am."

We both got out and went inside. I looked around as if it was my first time there. Just taking in the before scene. Braylin walked up to me and said, "Would you like me to order some carry out?"

"No, I'm not really hungry."

"Would you like me to run you a bath or something?"

"No. Tonight I would like you to touch me in places no other man has touched me."

Braylin was shocked, but he led me to his bedroom. It was definitely my first time there. In fact it was my first time in any man's bedroom. I had never even stayed the night with a man. What was the procedure for the morning after? We've been together a good year and a half. Sex is okay at that point right? Question after question eased into my mind. I just didn't know if I was doing it for the right reasons. I was so petrified that I wondered if this is what they call liquid courage. Was I still drunk? I had to be still drunk. *Yeah, definitely still drunk*, I told myself. No wait, not drunk that would make this incapable of being consensual. That would be rape. *Oh my God would Braylin rape me?!* I screamed in my mind.

He laid me on the bed and undressed me. He kissed my body slowly and massaged every inch of me. I started to relax. Well, as much as a kid relaxes after their mother promises them an ass whipping when they get home and they have been home for four hours and still no whooping so they hope and pray she's forgotten. Okay, I guess I'm not relaxed. I was ready to just do it and get it over with. It couldn't be that bad. But then Braylin laid beside me and we both drifted off back to sleep. At once my nerves eased. The next morning I woke up to a note that said:

> I'll explore you when I have earned you. And until that ring on your finger is sealed and solidified with the states stamp of authenticity and approval I have not earned you. I want to work for you so I'll

> understand why I never want to lose you. I love you Callie there is no rush.

I blushed inside. I loved this man. I knew right then and there marrying him is the right decision.

Three Weeks Later

I had a blast booking venues for the wedding, bachelorette party, and the rehearsal dinner. I think I finally decided on the wedding style. A traditional wedding at the Ritz Carlton in Georgetown. That place was immaculate. The bachelorette party was a booked mansion in the DR with all of my pleasures included. Lastly, my rehearsal dinner would be held at this exclusive restaurant called Cappella. I knew the owner, he was one of my dancers at night... or should I say one of Apple's dancers in the Back Room. He had a wife and kids, so very few people knew of his secret life. Because he respected the fact that we respected him, he gave me the hookup. I booked my favorite makeup artist and paid in advance for each event. The optics needed to blow everyone away, and I knew she could handle that. I slid through my designer's house to get my second fitting for my custom wedding dress and rehearsal dinner dress. I paid the balance remainder once I was satisfied with his work. I did not want any worries, I just needed consistency and smooth sailing from here on out. With the wedding in six months, there was no room for error.

BUFFY

"Why are we here today?" Dr. Allison asked.

"Honestly, I feel broken. I can't eat, I cant sleep, my heart hurts. I feel things that scare me."

"Things that scare you?" He repeated.

"Yes," I answered. "My boyfriend cheated on me with his so-called best friend. This girl was hanging out with us, always on the phone with him, he was always going out with her, etc. I should have known, but I trusted him and I felt blindsided when he confessed it all to me. I just feel so enraged every time I think about the situation. I can't control my temper."

"Why are you so angry with her?"

"Because she was always around. She slept with him and smiled in my face. Then when he told me about it, I tried to deal with it in a mature way. I pretty much asked them if they wanted to continue to sleep with one another. They both said no and that it was over. Well yeah, you guessed it. It was bullshit. I told them if they wanted to sleep with one another they could and I would step back. And if they didn't, that I expected him to be faithful and her to respect our relationship. They both agreed. I didn't believe either, but I convinced myself to let the situation unfold as I knew it would. When they fucked again the first time, we had a fight. It felt like the ultimate disrespect. You can't compete with a woman that was that close to him. And when we broke up, yes, you guessed it, he was right between her legs again. He was bringing her around his family who, by the way, hated me because I could potentially do all the things to him that he did to me. Oh and they welcomed her. Of course they only did that to ensure I was out of the picture. She wasn't what they wanted for him either. She was a pawn in their master plan, but it didn't stop it from hurting any less. To add icing to the cake, he brought her around my family. He had more respect for the hoe that was okay with being the hoe and helping him destroy me, than me, the woman who loved him unconditionally."

"Are you angry with him?" Dr. Allison asked.

"I feel betrayed. I feel like he could have had any other woman in the world and he chose me. He treated me like I had hurt him. I flirt between the lines of love and hate with every thought of him. I blame myself, wondering if I deserve this. Like did I do something to someone to deserve this? Maybe this was karma or something. I feel disappointed and sick to my stomach whenever I think of him."

"So do you still love him?"

"With every breath in my body, I love him so much I want to stop breathing just to stop the pain in my heart. It hurts to exist. It hurts to wake up. When I close my eyes all I see is him. So I can't sleep!" I shouted.

He wrote things in his notebook.

"Have you tried dating again?"

"I did eventually, but I just compared them to him. I felt suffocated around them. Like I was trapped in someone else's body feeling this excruciating pain, forcing a planted smile. I would get agitated whenever they text me because they weren't him. Every day I waited for him to call or text but he never did and every time it broke my heart all over again. I wasn't even enough to him that he would call me when or if he missed me. Dating reminded me that I was not good enough to have him."

"Trapped... you said the word trapped. Let's explore that. Why trapped?"

"Trapped in a box. One that was see through but small," I replied.

"Why a box?"

"Four sharp corners no matter which way you turn it. For so long I felt like I was punishing myself for starting at his pictures. Listening to songs he played me. Just constantly remembering things we did. Wishing I changed things or held him longer when he laid in my arms. It just hurts." I sighed. "And I'm not doing well. Just recently, I beat up a girl I knew for a fact was Kelsi but it wasn't her. She kept screaming I had the wrong person but I saw my enemies face. After that I decided I needed help."

"If it was her, would you have felt better now?"

"I don't know, it wasn't her."

"Do you feel better now?" he asked.

"No, I feel like a monster. I tried to hurt and kill the wrong person. I'm just hurt, doc. I can't heal and I've tried. I've tried so hard," I cried.

"Okay this is what we will do. Take 30 days and write however you feel in a letter for each day. If you feel love, write it. If you feel hate, write it. At the end of the 30 days bring me the letters, we can either mail them or burn them." He ordered.

"What is that going to help? My pride is wounded enough from begging him not to go. He still left. Everything I do is for him. I post pictures so he will see them. I call him. I don't get into relationships hoping he will come back. I search for them on the highway. I skip family trips because he was once family. Why should I do anything else for him? I have nothing else left to give him." I said that, but really, I would give him my last breath.

"I understand, but it is a venting exercise for you. Not him."

"I've done so much of that... I have lost friends over it." I said, embarrassed.

"Lost friends?"

"Yes, people are your friends as long as you are happy or there for them. If you are sad and depressed or hurt, they have an expiration date on how long they will listen before it overwhelms them. You being hurt is too much for them to bear. And not in ways of your pain is their pain -- more like your pain is annoying and they have better things to do then to listen to you. But don't worry. If they are broken, they expect you to care and be there for them. If they need anything, you are expected to be there for them."

"Well if you feel that way, maybe they are not your friends." Dr. Allison replied.

"If only it were that simple."

"Just try the exercise."

I shook my head and agreed.

LETTER 1

Dear Mr. Wrong,

I wish God would step out and save me. I wish you would push me off the ledge that has been holding on to me lately. My emotions are so conflicting. I've been over and over again tormenting myself and it's so stupid... asking myself what I could have done differently. I blame myself even though I know this inconsistency has nothing to do with me. I'm broken right now and you seem to have the remedy to fix me but you won't have anything to do with me.

Signed,

Nobody

LETTER 2

Dear Mr. Wrong,

Remembering the times we used to laugh. All the times we had my back then have me smiling and gazing. Tracing the lines of us is the most amazing moment. I love you so much. I just want to hold you and never ever let you go. I try to block out bad or sad times;; there's only room for good times. The love I have for you is immeasurable everything you ever did for me changed my life and every time you ever hurt me changed my life. My life is forever changed because of you and you never know how good and bad that feels.

Signed,

Your Only Vixen

MACY

He still doesn't want me. Why did I not kill these bitches? But if he doesn't want me, I'm going to give him what he wants.

My regional name is Mary Ann Monroe. I met Bradley, originally Christoph Jensen, in my 12th grade year. He was the teacher's aide. When Mr. Denver saw my grades slipping in science, he asked Mr. Jensen to tutor me. Mr. Jensen and I would meet at the library everyday and review whatever chapter I was on. My grades started to pick up -- eventually they were the highest in the class. Mr. Denver then asked Mr. Jensen to tutor Dell. Dell wasn't as bad as me, so he only needed tutoring for a short period of time. Once he finally passed his class, school was concluded and graduation was the following week. I was more than ready to be done with it. One day I was walking to the food court when I accidentally bumped into someone.

"Oh I'm sorry," I say as I looked up. I realized it was Mr. Jensen.

"Where are you headed?"

"To the food court."

"Do you mind if I go with you?"

"No, I don't mind," I replied. "Let's go." We walked together and we both ordered burgers and fries. As I was eating my fries, he asked me if I was ready to go to college.

"Yeah, sure." I replied.

"That's good. So what are you going to spend your summer doing?"

“Just chill and relax, I guess. To be honest I haven't really thought about it.”

“I’m hoping to travel a bit.”

“Travel where?”

“Anywhere!

We continued to talk for hours. It was fun. I found out he was 20 years old and he graduated from high school at the tender age of 16. He had a bachelor’s degree from Carnegie Mellon University. The loud speaker disrupted our conversation, announcing that the mall was closing in fifteen minutes. I got up and headed for the door as he did the same. “How far away do you live?” He asked me.

“One bus ride away.”

“I can give you a ride if you want one.”

“Okay,” I said, a little nervous and excited. On the way home the ride seemed silent. Not like our conversation at the mall that flowed non-stop -- not even like our tutoring sessions. He finally pulled up in front of my house. Once he opened my door to let me out he said, “Well, have a good night.”

“Would you like to come in?” I asked

“I-I-I shouldn’t,” he stuttered.

“Okay, good night then.” As I was walking to the door, he caught my arm and pulled it back to him and kissed me. I mean he really kissed me. I gave in immediately. The kiss seemed to last forever. When the kiss broke he looked terrified and I’m sure I looked as shocked as I was. I tried to walk away again. He pulled me back again and said, “Wait, I’m sorry.”

“It’s fine,” I said. He looked at me unsure as to whether I was telling the truth or not.

“It’s fine.” I repeated.

He looked up at my house saying, “All of the lights are off. Why would your parents go to bed before you arrived home?”

“I live alone,” I replied.

“How?”

“My mom was in prison for killing her lover and my father travels in and out of the country so often that he decided to stay out. So I’m on my own and he pays the bills from wherever he is.”

“Oh wow I’m sorry to hear that,” he replies.

“No worries I’m use to it. I have been on my own for at least four years now.”

“Well enjoy your night,” he replied. “Let me walk you to your door first.” He walked me. When I opened it, he hugged me and started to walk off. This time it was me who pulled him back. “There is no school tomorrow, do you want to stay a while?”

“I told you I don’t think it’s a good idea,” he replied. Before he could say anything else, I turned around and walked off with the door left wide open. He walked in to follow me, but by then, I was long gone. When I came downstairs he was sitting at the counter in a daze. I had taken a shower and I was wearing a modest pj set. Nothing sexual -- just some ninja turtle pants and a matching shirt.

“I’ll pop some popcorn,” I said. “How do you feel about the three ninjas?

“I feel like you are too young to know that movie,” he joked.

“Nooo... really that’s my favorite movie. I use to watch it as a kid over and over.” I confessed.

I popped the popcorn and we watched several movies. By the end of the last movie I had fallen asleep on him. He tried to sneak from under me to leave, but I grabbed him.

“Mary Ann, what are you doing?” He asked. “I need to leave.”

“Can you just watch one last movie?”

“I've stayed long enough,” he replied in a not-so-confident-tone.

I got up to let him leave. When I walked him to the door, he turned around and hugged me. I welcomed it. He then kissed me and walked me back to the couch, lips never leaving mine on the way. He laid me down and continued to kiss me gently. He took my clothes off and started to kiss my other lips. I tensed up, but he pried my legs open and continued to go to work on me. He tried to stick two fingers in me but they wouldn't fit so he put one in instead. It was still tight, causing him to stop and ask me, “Mary Ann are you a virgin?”

“Yes,” I answered truthfully.

“Do you want me to stop?”

“No.”

He looked afraid and I was too. But he slid the finger in and out of me that was already there while continuing to eat me out. I then felt his thumb go in my ass. I was so embarrassed that I wanted him to stop.

“It's okay,” he replied. “You will like it.”

I was so afraid, but I took it. I eventually started grinding his face. “Your first time should be in a bed.” He said, “Show me the way.”

So I did. He laid me down on the bed, this time slowly entering me with his very large penis. The pain was extreme, but I enjoyed it at the same time. I grinded my hips like I saw in movies. He smiled at me while maintaining a gentle rhythm. I had so many mixed emotions, but my thoughts were interrupted when he said “I love you.” I was about to respond, but he quickened his speed and the pain was so strong that I couldn't process a thought -- let alone a feeling. I tried to pull away but he had a death grip on me. It was almost like he was someone else. He got up and walked off towards the bathroom. He came back shortly after.

"Are you okay?" he asked.

"Yes, I'm okay. Why?"

"Go pee," he said. It was more of a demand.

I did. I almost panicked when I saw blood on the sheets when I returned. I hoped he didn't see it. When I went downstairs he was gone. I'd hope to see him at graduation, but he had left already. Mr. Denver had told us that he had gotten a better job offer to go out the country for the summer and he took it. I was hurt for a while, but the summer was almost over and I was almost over it.

Two Years Later

I was a sophomore in college and I was walking through the campus and there he was. There was the man I loved. I walked right up to him and said hi. He looked nervous, but spoke back.

"Hey, uuuuummm... uuummm..." he tried to recollect.

"Mary Ann!"

"Mary Ann," he replied. "How are you?"

"I'm fine --"

"Hey baby," a slender White girl said as she walked up.

“Hey Beth. This is one of my students from back home -- Mary Ann.”

“Oh, hi. I’m Bethany Brooks!” She was too excited for my liking.

“Hi,” I responded dryly. I just turned and walked away before she could say anything else.

I was so hurt. How could he be with this girl? He just used me and ran off with her. ‘Til this day, no man has ever touched me. I found out a week later that he attended school here as well. So, I decided to revenge fuck him as well.

Carl “Man Man" White was 6’6", as dark as they come with teeth as white as snow. Boy was he fine. He had been after me since I got here, but he had had a reputation and I was not interested in being another girl on his resume. Last week I saw him getting head from another one of his teammates behind a bar in town. At first it confused me, but then I saw it working in my favor. That’s when I approached him about the plan. He agreed, afraid that if he didn’t I would out him, but truth be told, I couldn’t care less about his secret. I had revenge on my mind and anything else would a distraction.

It was Thursday night. I heard Mr. Jensen in the hall. Man Man was already in the bed and I climbed on top of him pretending to ride him. As Mr. Jensen entered room, Man Man called out my name. He said, “Damn Mary Ann, let me hit that from the back. Bro this room is occupied, come back later!” He pretended to be irritated. Mr. Jensen left. Because I wasn’t sure whether he was standing by the door or not, we continued the show. He jerked off in front of me so he could sound like he was coming.

“Damn, it got on my bra!” I fussed.

“My bad shawty, I got wrapped up,” he said.

“I’ll see you later babe,” I smiled.

"Alright cool. You need me to walk you to your dorm?"

"No," I said as I was walking out the door.

As I made my way out, I saw Mr. Jensen sitting at the door looking like a sad puppy. I walked past him as if I didn't even notice.

"Mary Ann!" he called out.

"Oh now you know my name, or did you hear him call it out and it jogged your memory?" I rolled my eyes.

He said nothing. The silence was deafening

"That's what I thought," I said. Then I walked off. By the time I got outside, he was hot on my heels.

"It's not what you think Mary Ann. That night I was attracted to you. I wanted you badly. Everything in my mind said 'hey away from her, go now' but I didn't. And after... after... you know... I mean I just got scared. When I was offered the job I took it and ran off."

"Don't blind me with your excuses. Now you were scared? Ha how convenient."

"Mary Ann you were underage. A fucking minor for heaven's sake. I was afraid of going to jail. I was your teacher. I shouldn't have put myself in that situation, but I was so into you. I saw it all happen and I couldn't stop it."

"So into me that you took my virginity and kept it pushing on to Bethany?" My voice revealed the pain I tried to hide.

"Bethany was two years later!" he yelled. "I just met her."

"I don't care if you met her two seconds later!" I yelled back.

"I can't get you off of my mind." I was so hurt that I couldn't take that confession. I replied, "That's what all the boys say."

He looked confused and angry. "So you out here giving it to whoever? You're a THOT now," he stated more than he was asking.

"Call me what you want. I am whatever you think I am." I walked off, but he snatched my arm back like he did the first night. This time much more aggressively and kissing me on the spot. I tried pulling away but he had a hell of a grip on me. Finally he let me go and I threw gasoline on his wounded pride.

"What kind of man wants to suck the cum of another man's dick off of a one night stand's tongue?" I walked off.

After that day he chased me for another year. Satisfied that I had made my point clear, I took him as my own. I'm not going to lie that last comment had me thinking I had lost him for good but he caught up instead.

Everything was great until Bethany came up saying she was pregnant. I almost lost my lunch and balance. She walked right up to me at work and threw soda in my face, saying "What kind of tacky hoe fucks with a man with a baby on the way?" This time it was me at a total loss. When I confronted him, he dumped me. One day, during her last month of pregnancy, I saw her walking from work and I sped up and hit her with a car I stole. I wasn't trying to kill her, but I was definitely trying to kill that bastard of a baby. Just in case the baby survived, I backed up and rolled over her again and again and a-fucking-gain. Naturally, Mr. Jensen ran to me in tears. How dare this weak ass bitch made nigga cry his polluted tears on my Guess shirt. But I consoled him for the time and told him he needed to find other ways of mourning. I told him it was his selfish decision and careless behavior that created this brokenness in me and now he wants me to sympathize for the loss of whatever he was mourning. He looked at me upset.

But the more he talked the more I reminded him that the dead bitch and her baby was the reason behind all of my hurt and pain and that I am not here for it. When I snuck into her funeral, I saw him sitting there looking pathetic. And do you know they had an infant casket there beside hers? They were so fucking extra. But whatever. I followed them to her grave and when every one left, I looked at her grave and said, "Ashes to ashes, you dusty ass hoe."

By the time Mr. Jensen found out I did it, he was long dragged into it. The car I stole was his. I had texted an argument using her phone. I had snuck into her job stole it out of her locker and returned it when I was satisfied with the text. I played all types of trucks on him and her that could easily get misconstrued to make him look spiteful and vindictive. So we both moved away. And there birthed Browdy and Macy. The next chapter to our love story. The modern day Bonnie and Clyde.

BUFFY

LETTER 8

Dear Mr. Wrong,

Everything we shared was a lie. Looking back brought out the pain that I had buried deep inside. I'm trying to move on because these feeling and these thoughts are unhealthy. The further I get into these letters, I realize you were a complete stranger to me. I couldn't find you if I lost you. I'm green with anger and color me red with rage. All the times you disparaged my name, all the times you played mind games. I'm smarter than you. I saw them being played but if only you knew they would one day come back and haunt you. The cheating, the lying and manipulation tactics. I only wanted to hold you longer and love you more. Who knew game over really meant over. Fuck did you lie to me for? Why sell me dreams and hope. For every lie you told me, you broke me. I'm so used and abused that I don't even know me anymore. I can't even look in the mirror because the reflection is that of the old me. The person I was before you destroyed the essence of me.

Signed,

Crying Away These Tears

LETTER 9

Dear Mr. Wrong,

The first night you left, I sat on the floor and cried the entire night. I remember laying on the couch for hours before eventually ending up on the floor. I called anyone I could think of because I wanted to die and I was at the point to make that happen. But no one answered. I had my mind set. I mean who would miss me? No one. I was so afraid, but even more hurt. The thing that saved me, killed me inside. I thought to myself, if you kill yourself, he will forever live with your blood on his hands. I saved my own life so you could have one. I didn't save myself because I deserved to live, I didn't save myself because my family needed me and cherished me or any of the other great reasons that people speak of. I saved myself so you wouldn't be consumed with guilt. For a year I sat and waited for the phone to ring, a text to arise with your name on it, but as I stated before it never happened. To think you were miserable when you couldn't call and text her after you cheated on me with her. You snuck and talked to her on the phone when you weren't in my presence, but you never did any of that for me. Not ever did you execute a phone call. I wasn't important enough. Your heart wasn't yearning for my love or touch enough to force you to call me -- or at least text. Loyalty, love, and humility were not attributes that kept you. I survived that night needless to say. In fact I survived this year but I'm a shell of my old self. I'm not as whole as I once felt. I grieve you as if I lost you. Technically, I did lose you and it hurts worse than death. You are walking the same plane as me, and I can't have you. At least I could explain death to myself and even come to terms eventually with it. But you are alive and consciously okay with moving on.

I would surrender my wings if God would release his wrath on my heart. Untangle these vines that cause me pain. This isn't love, but God knows I'll suffer through it all over again to hold you, to love you, to potentially hear you say and mean that I am enough for you. To be in a situation where I don't feel in competition with someone you say is insignificant. I yell because you made me feel like I was consistently competing for my spot. A man doesn't make his woman feel insecure, he makes other women insecure of her. But in your mind, you defied the definition of a man, you said you weren't an adult despite the fact that you had a career, owned a home, and have traveled the world. And for that reason, I was with a boy and not a man. I'll provide you with no excuses. You damaged me, you put me in the way of harm, allowed me to be disrespected and showed me what hell on earth felt like. I didn't have the courage to say this is not okay, this hurts, or to even walk away. To me, courage was fighting for you. To you, that was weak and undeserving of you. You felt trapped and was looking for ways out and I didn't see it until I was forced to see it -- until the darkroom that I was in shed light on it all.

You didn't tell me about her because it weighed heavy on your chest, you told me because you were hoping that I did the hard work for you and left you. You kept cheating and saying you didn't understand why you couldn't talk to her or why it was okay for your future mother-in-law and wife to disrespect and threaten me because deep down they said what you wanted them to say. You never cared how your actions interrupted my life, hurt me, or broke me. You said you did but you didn't. It's clear now but my heart is immobilized. It's too late. People don't accidentally hurt you; they intentionally hurt you and to ease their guilt they say sorry or say it wasn't on purpose. But if you can tell me how you accidentally ate her pussy over and over again, or how she sucked your dick over and over again or when it was her voice that moaned out for you and not mine while you hit her from the back, it could potentially make sense. I mean right before or right after when you FaceTimed me and she sat in the video or the room knowing that your cum was still dripping off of her tongue while you told me you loved me. Me sitting at home fighting to stay awake until you got home, afraid of you drinking and driving. And then pretending to be asleep when your keys entered the door. If you can explain how one time, let alone several, maybe I can understand. But I'll tell you how I see it. I see it as you did what you wanted to do and you didn't care how that would hurt me. The disrespect that your family and hers exhibited were communal because if you were lucky, I would leave you. All you had to do was leave. You asked me to be in this situation. I never asked you and yet, I'm the only damaged one. But seeing as though I hear you two are together now I guess it's safe to say she was worth it. No question there.

Signed,

A Shattered Heart

LETTER 10

Dear Mr. Wrong,

I'm so saddened to ever write this letter. Never in my wildest dreams did I ever imagine losing you in this way, but the day your family saw fit to discharge on our relationship was the day it all fell down. I found myself constantly battling with whether to fight back or be disrespected. No woman should ever feel belittled and attacked when her man is in her presence. I'm sure you knew what to do. Yet, you chose not to do it. In the beginning you pursued me. Yeah we both got the others initial responses misconstrued, but once the dust settled you certainly pursued me. You did this despite me saying that I felt like it was a horrible idea. I thought you were too young for me being as though there was a five-year gap. I didn't want anything bad to happen between us that would draw a wedge between you and your family or mine and me.

You told me your parents are over ten years apart in age and they will respect your decision in who you chose to date. Well, I couldn't hide the fact that my attraction to you became more than what I ever anticipated. I told you we would both have to go to our families and ask for permission. You said you did not need permission. I told you that I would not go any further without it, so we both set off to do it. While my family thought it was a great idea and encouraged it, your family felt like it was a horrible idea and did everything in their power to destroy it. They told you negative things about me that others proved to you was untrue. They tried to bring you closer to the woman that you were cheating on me with, knowing that they never would never accept her either. How could I compete with a group of people that you have trusted your whole life? How could I point out their schemes when you were so adamant that they did not exist? I was so hurt by your family's course of action that I felt like there was no undoing this wrong. The family I have had my entire life painted me as a horrible, desperate, hope with baggage. They labeled my children as baggage. However, two of your siblings have children are theirs baggage as well or did mine rank the bottom of the totem pole? Should they forfeit the opportunity to be with a good man or woman because they have children?

They said I'm a hoe. Well where is the proof? You have personally met my exes and know that they all want me back. That's not a trait of a hoe. Most times, you and I didn't have sex -- again, not the trait of a hoe. They said I had a low vocabulary, but their own flesh and blood had to Google half the diction I chose to use. I used to sit and discuss history with you nonstop and shared my ambitions. They said I was bisexual, but I haven't interacted with females in over 6 or 7 years and my ex-told you that when she was too drunk to lie. I'm proud to have been at one point open in my options; it made me choose who I was when I didn't have a clue. They said I was desperate, but you yourself have seen the nonstop date requests, heard the offers, and saw the turn downs. I respectfully declined and ensured that everyone knew it was you that I chose. Your family said I would hurt you, and in the end, it was you that hurt me. Even when they knew about the two pregnancy scares, the multiple women, the secretly fucking the best friend and the ex-fiancé behind my back, never did they feel that an apology needed to be made. Instead, it was better for them to pin her with open arms and push me away. I was scum, but the home wrecker was the light at the end of the tunnel. I would cook for you, wash your clothes, tell you all the reasons why I loved and respected you. I bought you and your friends concert tickets to see a rapper you liked, and I paid for them to go paintballing. I brought you tickets to go to amusement parks often, out of town trips. It was me who bought you courtside tickets to see your favorite team battle your favorite player. I surprised you at work in front of your boys. I gave you massages after a long day at work. It was me who begged you to bring your manuals home so I could learn them and teach you so you could get promoted at work. It was me that got you drawn as your favorite character.

I was at all of your games, I made you breakfast in bed, I taped love notes in the shape of a big heart on the glass so when you woke up you would smile. I wrote notes like 'you're the shit' and stuck it to the toilet. That silly string fight we had? I cleaned it up. Rock, paper, scissors was how we solved problems. I cheered for you even when the crowd was quiet. I paddle boated with you. The list could go on and on, but I treated you like a king -- even when I was hurting inside -- only for them to put me down. You always said that you knew they were wrong and told me to just ignore them instead of you defending me. These people I loved never loved me. Who told them they could sit so high and look so low on me? The worst pain of them all is that I didn't just lose you. I lost my family. I lost the family I thought I wanted my family to resemble -- the family that my family saw as family. No one ever apologized. No one ever felt wrong, but they all accepted an apology. Nevermind, that them hurting me hurt my children. The endless nights of the baby girl crying for you, or my son staring in the crowd for you. Him inviting you to his award ceremony and you not coming. Don't worry, I told him you wouldn't but he had faith that you would. Well, needless to say how that played out. They hurt my children more than you know, but hey, it was all worth it. I'm sure you are no longer with their worst nightmare.

Signed,

Buffy Got Played

LETTER 11

Dear Mr. Wrong,

Broken is broken no matter how you flip it. This letter is for the crying children that searched for you, that fiend for you. They survived, no thanks to you.

Signed,

Broken Promises Don't Mend

APPLE

I was making more money than I could count. Life was good... but there was a void. Where was my happy ending, where was my boy? Surely he was around. No he wasn't, because just like normal, that that bitch Callie fucking stole him from me. I hate that hoe. It was July 4th and I was supposed to meet Callie at a cookout. Well, when I got there I saw her hugged up with my man Travis. I just turned around and walked off.

Callie texted me an hour later like "Where are you?"

I texted back like "Girl I got caught up with some homies from back in the day."

"Who???" she replied.

I lied and typed "a trade I traded in because he was broke. But girl he gets some money now!" I put a laughing emoji at the end.

She wrote "LMAO bring me a Gucci bag."

I replied "Girl I got to break him in first."

She never responded after that.

For weeks I told her I was with a trade when I was with Travis. I told him I saw him and begged him to cut her off. But he wouldn't. He said he needed her for appearances. I said told him he had me. Travis and I would role-play and straight murder niggas. I would play in distress like he kidnapped me, I would trick niggas back to rooms with me, etc., killing two birds with one stone. We were close. I met Travis when he was 8 and I was 6, but we lost touch and by the time I ran into him again I was all woman. He should have loved me. But he didn't. His secret meant more to him than I did. So when Callie asked me to execute a hit on him, I did as Adam. He looked me in the eyes and I took his soul away as I pulled the trigger. I didn't kill him for Callie, I killed him for trying me.

TASHA

"Brendan where have you been all day?" I yelled as soon as he walked through the door.

"Whoa, slow down," he replied. "Grab Anika's bag." I did, looking at him wildly.

"I went to your mother's funeral," he replied.

"What? Why?" I asked.

"Because you wouldn't go."

"All the reason for you not to go," I replied backing down slightly.

"I'm going to put Anika down in her bed, and I will be back down momentarily so we can talk." He walked off.

I just waited. I felt completely ambivalent about Brendan going to her funeral and even more about him taking Anika. I feel like he should have asked me first and respected my decision. Ten minutes later he came back down.

"Come sit down," he said. I followed him to the couch. He said, "Sit down, baby." So I did.

"Now I know you are upset, but what is done is done."

"No Brendan, that's not how this works. You don't get to do something so massive and then decide that what's done is done!"

"That's not what I was saying."

"No? Then what are you saying?"

"I'm saying I've already done it, so let's talk future. Not past. I can't undo taking Anika, but how will fighting about it help?"

"Why would you take her when I already said no?"

"Because I thought you would regret it later," he said truthfully.

"And who died and made you the expert of regrets?"

"When my mother died, I almost didn't go to the funeral. I was angry with her for dying. It didn't feel like it was her time. In my mind I still needed her. I still had to grow. The night before her funeral, I had a dream that I was sitting in front of her at a Starbucks or something and she told me, 'if I have not given you the tools to survive on earth without me then I have failed as a parent. Are you telling me I failed as a parent Brendan?' She asked me. No never. I told her she could never fail. She said, 'then your brothers and most of all your father needs you be the strength in your own weakness.' I went to the funeral. I made it and I was relieved that I didn't miss it. I was afraid that if I had missed it I would have never forgiven myself. I guess I pushed my fear over to you."

"You don't get to make decisions like that for me. That's something I would have to live with -- not you," I replied.

"There is no more you. There's no more me. There is an us until you walk away from my proposal. Until then we are all that it is." I shook my head to acknowledge what he said. But I knew he would never understand the demons that hid in my closets. Way in the back where the light doesn't shine.

CALLIE

If someone tells you they don't fuck with me, trust me, it's the other way around. I'm so sick of people pretending to be my friend for their own personal gains. So I got something for these bitches.

Let me catch you hoes up. Braylin and I got married in January. We decided to have a beautiful outdoor winter wedding. It was very small and intimate. It couldn't have been any more than 20 people. I had previously arranged a grand wedding, but after a while, I decided it wasn't what I really wanted. So I scaled it down a bit. We actually gave Tasha and Brandon our space at the Ritz. She picked somewhere else for the rehearsal dinner. That's cool. Now here's where it gets lit. I'm just going to fast-forward for y'all.

On December 31st, Karina asked, “My God... who would have ever known we would be here celebrating such a blessed occasion?” Karina was my home girl, but she moved out of the country the year I met Apple. Her parents were both in the Air Force. We kept in touch over the years though, ensuring to still talk very often.

“What's so glorious about it?” Apple slurred.

“Girl you a trip,” Karina responded.

“Whatever,” Apple said and walked off.

Karina walked back over to me. “Where is Apple going?” I asked.

“Girl I don't know. Them queens are too much for my taste,” she replied. I brushed off her comment because I knew Apple could be extra sometimes. Plus, I didn't want either of my friends at odds on my special day.

“So what's on the agenda?” I asked.

“Well, I guess you'll have to wait and see,” Karina replied.

About 6 shots in I remember nothing.

I woke up the next morning at 10 am. I missed the New Years countdown, but hell, who cares?

I moved through my wedding day with grace, but I was nervous as hell. I wonder if my dad would approve? He was everything for so long and now Braylin is. I just hope he doesn't wipe out my memory of the greatest man to me. As I was getting dressed for the wedding, I heard a light knock at my door. “Come in,” I say. In walks Apple and Karina. The last time I saw Apple, he walked off from Karina at my bachelorette party. Maybe he came back. Maybe he didn't. I was wasted.

“Hey you guys,” I stood, feeling some tension.

“Hey my soon to be bride!” Apple yelled.

Karina side-eyed Apple. “Hey baby girl, I’m so in awe of your beauty,” Karina replied.

“Thank you guys.” I had become teary-eyed. Just as I was about to get extra emotional, there was another knock at the door.

Karina opened it and looked back at me saying, “It’s time, lady.”

As I filed out behind Karina and Apple, I could have sworn I heard Apple say, “I hope you trip up, bitch." I stopped and asked him what he said.

“I said I hope you don’t trip up or slip,” Apple said quickly.

Call it a gut feeling, but something was off. Today was my day, so I hoped nothing would be fucked up.

“Thank you, Apple.” Karina was still cutting her eyes at Apple. I made a mental note to ask her about it.

At any rate, to my surprise, when it was my turn to walk down the aisle, Mr. Dayton, Karina's dad, walked up and guided me down the aisle. I was so grateful. My dad and Karina's dad used to be best friends. He gripped my hand and said, "Are you ready, Cal?" My dad used to call me Cal. I felt his presence at that moment. I said "Let's do this."

On the way down the aisle I tripped and almost fell. I looked down and Phaedra had her foot out. She looked apologetic and mouthed 'I'm sorry.' I just kept pushing through and decided it wasn't worth my focus. I had a king at the altar waiting for me.

The vows were exchanged. And just like that, it was bye bye Ms. Callie Reed and hello Mrs. Callie Daniels.

During our first dance, I heard a loud commotion. "What is going on?" I asked. Nothing better not be going down on my wedding day.

I stormed through the crowd only to find Phaedra, Apple, and Karina fighting.

"What the hell is going on here?" Carter Senior yelled as he broke it up.

"This is neither the time nor the place," Mr. Dayton replied.

"Daddy this bitch is a snake, and I am going to expose his ass!"

"Bitch, fuck you. You can't expose shit but that cheap ass 99 cent store lace front," Apple yelled.

"You better grab you some bold hold, hoe!" Phaedra yelled.

"Sirs, don't try me. I'll read all you wanna be bitches," Karina responded. "In fact try me hoe!" she yelled. "Callie I am going to leave. I'm so sorry about this. I would never disrespect you like this intentionally."

"What is going on?" I asked confused.

"She's a hating, lying ass hoe!" Apple yelled.

Phaedra threw her two cents in as well yelling, "Fake ass bitch!"

"Bitch you emulate women all day and I'm the fake ass bitch... the irony to that statement is off the charts. And sir, a liar I will never be. Your conniving, weak ass is treading on ice right now," Karina yelled.

"Yeah, whatever hoe." Phaedra replied, dismissively.

"Bitch, your name is Phillip Dre Ryan. Carry on!" Karina yelled.

"No, fuck this let's go to the room! All of ya'll, NOW!" I yelled. Apple, Phaedra, Karina, Braylin, Tasha, Brendan, Brandon, Carter Senior, and Mr. Dayton followed.

Once we got to the room I turned around and said, "So wassup? What the hell is going on?"

Karina handed me her phone and pressed play.

It was Phaedra and Apple in their suite talking. Very loudly might I add.

"So are you going to walk down the aisle with this bitch?" Phaedra asked.

"You damn right. I'm going to live in all of this hoe memories. I'm going to even be there after the wedding shindig, putting my finger and fist in her ass. Sucking her niggas balls. I'll be there when her first baby is born all like 'aww she's a cute little cunt.' By the time I'm done with this, everything she does will scream me!" Apple replied.

They both laughed in unison.

"I just want to be a fly on the wall when you tell the hoe the real story about Ashton, Dame, and Kevin."

"Yes bitch, he tricked for treats and they were all my hoes in high school."

"How are you a pimp in high school?

"They needed money, didn't they? They were already getting raped, shit at least I paid their asses."

Phaedra died laughing.

"What's so funny?" Apple asked.

"You said paid their asses!"

"Girl you corny as hell." Apple chuckled. "But you know what it is, sell that ass or get evicted. Bitch, it's up to you!" Apple replied.

"Why you tell her that lie anyway about them raping you?" Phaedra asked. "Because bitch, I was there and that shit was consensual."

"Kevin was the only one I couldn't turn. He didn't care what his brothers did, he wasn't. So I helped them rape his bitch ass and you know he liked it. Then when he left he went straight to the station. Thanks again for pushing his ass on the tracks for me. You can never leave behind a witness or a victim," Apple replied cockily.

"Oh, you are so welcome," Phaedra said charmingly.

I was so shocked but I kept listening.

"I bet that hoe will learn the next time she fucks with my man. At first I needed her for safety, then I needed her to get my revenge." Apple sounded disgusted.

"How you going to make money?" Phaedra asked.

"Bitch, her little naïve ass signed over the club to me like the dumb ass I knew she was."

"All this for Travis though? I'm going to be honest, I never liked him. He was too busy putting all his shit in the closet... how was he going to ever get out?" Phaedra asked.

"Girl shut up," Apple giggled. "All I know is that hoe is going to regret the day she crossed me. Bet she focus on the horizontal and leave the zigzags to me for now on," Apple said.

I had heard enough. The room was silent. Apple and Phaedra looked at me and walked out of the room.

Braylin walked over and hugged me. I saw Tasha run behind Apple and then heard a loud thump. When we got into the hall, Tasha was working on Apple while Karina helped. I forgot all about Dame and the funeral incident until that very second. She fucking lost it.

KARINA

I hate that I had to expose Apple, better yet Adam, at Callie's wedding, but I had had enough of this two faced bullshit. I knew how much Callie cared for Apple, so it was hard but this nigga is a snake. Him and Phaedra aka Pedro to me are two snakes biting one another while they both strangle the other. They have no loyalty to anyone -- not even each other.

Callie looked so lost listening to the recording. I have been warning her about Adam since I saw him steal her money off of her dresser in junior high. But we moved to Germany not too long after, so I guess they rekindled their friendship. When she called me and told me the stuff about Apple being raped I did not believe it. My home girl Mia told me that Apple was a real pimp and that Ashton, Dame, Greg, and Tony all tricked for him. That shit sounded wild but that's why I believed it. Nobody is going to make up no wild shit like that. But when I was going to ask Callie, she told me Apple was hurt and raped. I just thought it was best to shut up.

Sometimes your friends don't want to know the truth about their friends. So if you tell them they look at you like you are a hate or you are jealous. I just don't have time to be fighting wars from across seas. I knew this snake would eventually show its other side and I was right.

APPLE

I can't believe that hoe attacked me. "Dame is dead now, why you still mad?" I yelled.

"Bitch I'm not mad, but how dare you lie on my daughter's father's name, trick!" Tasha yelled back.

"No boo, he was the trick. I was the pimp get your titles right. And that was so long ago. Your new man is right here. Why are you still fighting over the last one?" I asked taunting her.

"Bitch I'll fight for him until the day I die. Don't ask any questions!" She yelled, trying to break free from Brendan's grip.

"Awww boo, you big mad or little mad?" I said laughing as I walked away.

"Brendan, let me go! This trick needs a wake up call."

"Baby, it isn't worth it," He replied. "Karma is going to break him down in ways your fist never could," I heard Brendan say.

"Listen to your man bitch, he's trying to save your life!" I yelled, still walking away. Truth is, I was trying to get the fuck out of there. I didn't want any smoke, but I didn't want to lose face either. Walking and talking seemed like the best option.

When I was a safe enough distance, I took a sigh of relief. *I'm safe for now*, I thought to myself. Well, fuck it. The hoe knows. I would have told her in a more painful way, but shit, what's more dramatic than her wedding day?

"So yeah, what are we going to do now?" Phaedra asked.

"Bitch, get money, what we been doing." I responded.

"Did you see that trick's face," Phaedra laughed

"Oh you know I did. But she got what she deserved. Nothing is all about you boo boo." Truth is, I felt kind of bad. I was looking for confrontation but that hoe didn't even speak. If that nosey bitch Karina let me execute the plan, it would have been a fight. Then I could have sued the hoe and got me some coins for my distress. I always hated that bitch. Even in Germany she stayed in my business. She was there so much I could have added her to the payroll, but fuck her she's on my hit list.

Now I got this nigga Phaedra all in my business, but fuck his dick-sucking ass too. His trick ass think I don't know he was sucking Travis dick on the regular. Bitches got me mixed up, but I'm going to get with him real soon. Real, real soon. As for Callie, this fake friendship is for the birds. I'm tired of my life purpose being to be her sidekick.

Three Months Later

When Callie signed over the company to me, it said finalized in 120 days. Well it's day 121. A bitch gives no fucks on this day. Let all the hoes say amen.

CALLIE

"Meet me at the spot. I think it's time for a sit down," I said.

"Bitch we will sit down when I say so. I'm not your minion anymore," Apple replied.

"Be there by 8."

It was 8:10 when Apple walked into my office. No surprise at all. He was trying to make a statement, but his statement was weak.

"Fuck are they doing here?" Apple asked as he sat down.

"I'm here because I am. Any more questions?" Tasha asked.

"Who is he?" Apple asked, pointing.

"Oh him? This is our attorney. Jonathan Goode."

"Attorney for what? Did little Callie get Bamboozled?" Apple taunted as he shifted in his seat.

"No, he is our division of assets attorney," I colorfully replied.

"Oh okay, well let's get to it," Apple replied.

Jonathan handed Apple a stack of papers. He looked over them and said, "And this means...?"

"To sum it up... you own nothing -- not even your stage name," Jonathan stated.

"What?!" Apple yelled. "I know that's a lie because I have the contracts!"

"Well then you know the fine print says 120 days. Baby, I pulled the plug on day 62. You see, a spot on 4th Street opened up and I decided to give you your own spot. Given the nature of your business, I assumed you would prefer the more secluded location. I figured we could monopolize the market by separating. But look at God. Won't He do it?" I smiled and laughed. "Here is the documentation of the lease offer. A copy of the down payment. The remodeling bill and the voided contract that I was going to have you sign once I returned from the Cayman Islands for my honeymoon. Oh, it was beautiful too. You should have been there. Anyway, before I get side tracked... long story short, bitch you fucked yourself."

Apple looked stunned. I thought to myself, *checkmate hoe*. That nigga looked at me with pure disgust.

"This can't be true, I was never notified," Apple said.

"Mrs. Mr. Apple, no notification needs to be given. It says here the business will be yours upon the 120th day with both parties' signatures. You didn't even show up before or by the 120th day. It's the 121st day," Jonathan interjected.

"You are lying!" Apple yelled.

"Sir. No one can just put something in your name. You have to legally agree to it. What if it was a huge debt, do you want them to be able to just transfer it in your name? It's essential that both parties agree to all of the terms and conditions. So regardless of she had other plans for you or not you missed the day to sign it. Mrs. Daniel's can be lenient and decide to reinstate the process, but that's up to her."

Apple looked over at me and I said, "It would be a cold day in hell before I ever. Thank you, Jonathan."

Apple stood up to leave seeing as though his bitch ass was seated in a losing position, but before he did I said, "Adam why would you do this to me?"

He looked at me and said, "Do you really want to know?"

I replied, “No bitch. I just asked for the humor. I couldn’t give a fuck less. Explanations are for weak bitches and fake niggas. Get the fuck out.”

Apple left and he took Adam with him. “Baby are you okay?” Braylin asked,

I said, “As good as can be expected.”

“What are you going to do with the other club?” Braylin asked.

“It’s already done. I lied to Apple, there wasn’t going to be a spot for him. I been felt like he was on some shiesty shit. I just served him the bait. You learn who your real friends are when they don’t need you. I bought that space and turned it into Let Me Nail You. It’s a male spa. Women nail techs, male barbers, bars TV, all that shit.

“Why did you change it?” Braylin asked.

“I had this planned for a while. I just wanted a change from the sexual experience. I want our children to be able to visit where I work and be proud of me.”

Braylin smiled and kissed me. “They will be,” he said.

Jonathan packed his stuff and headed towards the door. Braylin and I took all the final copies of all the documents locked them up and headed out with him. We had already changed all the codes, locks, and passwords to everything, so I knew it was secure. But If I knew Adam the way I knew Apple, he wouldn’t take this one on the chin. We were at war.

APPLE

The nerve of this bitch... ughhhh. I just want to punch this hoe into oblivion. That damn Karina ruined it all. She had to run her mouth. That bitch was going to pay.

ADAM

A week later, I was dressed in blue jeans, a white tee, a pair of J's and a Michael Kors watch.

I stood on the porch and lightly knocked on the door.

"Coming," the person on the other end yelled. As she opened the door, she said, "Yes sir, can I help you?"

"Yes, I'm looking for Johanna and Todd Lane."

"Who do I have the pleasure of telling them you are sir?" The woman asked.

"Their son." The woman's eyebrow raised. I could tell she was alarmed.

"Wait here," the woman said, closing the door in my face and not waiting for a response.

Ten minutes later, she came back to the door and said, "The Lane's only child past away years ago. They said you should leave or they would call the police."

"I'm not dead, I'm standing right here." I was very confused. I had been gone for about six years now, but to say I was dead was extreme. The lady saw the look on my face, and I could tell she sympathized, but she didn't budge.

I walked off and looked back. I saw my mom looking out of the window. Her face filled with pure shock. She ran out the window and rushed out the door behind me. She ran up and hugged me and did some weird pat down like she couldn't believe it was me. Like my flesh was transparent or might disappear from right in front of her. She didn't trust her eyes.

She cried harder than I've ever seen her cry. She yelled, "Todd! Todd, it's really him." My father who I didn't notice until that second just stared in horror. The last time he saw me, he tried to suffocate me in the hospital for being gay. I told the doctors and they made up some documents that said I was dead. My parents, per my dad's request as I predicted, wanted me cremated. He wouldn't fare leaving behind any evidence. You never know pain until you have to play dead so your father wouldn't kill you. It was hard but I did it. My dad never even looked at the machine to see if I was alive or not. But whatever. I was here.

My mom ushered me in the house. She was completely elated. "Adam where have you been? If you were alive why haven't you been home? I don't understand." My mom said.

I explained to my mom that the person who hurt me also tried to kill me and they moved me into witness protection. I told her he died a few months back and here I was. I mean I couldn't tell her the truth. All hell would break loose.

The story was reasonable, and at the least my dad would think that I thought it was someone else who hurt me and they were after me because of my original attack. But I'm calculated, not stupid. He would be a fool to sleep with both eyes closed while I was moving through his home. This wasn't my home anymore. There were no pictures of me. My room had become a storage area for mom's shopping problem. The people around them knew nothing of me. I could come like a thief in the night and steal the lives. I was already presumed dead.

JOHANNA

My husband could not do anything right -- not even kill our embarrassment of a son. This sissy is sitting in our living room while his ashes are spread through the city dump. I hated this boy and now I have to fake for the cameras. Something told me to kill him myself. All it took was one air bubble injected in the wrong place.

Adam stayed over that night. I couldn't let him leave. I needed to know what he knew and who he told. I didn't trust anybody that I had to put a hit on. Fuck do I look like trusting a nigga I tried to kill. Or that Todd's dumbass failed to kill. Can't let a boy do a boss' job and that's it.

TODD

I could have given Johanna a Grammy for that performance. She originally turned his ass away saying that she didn't want anyone seeing him and risk her having or us having to repay the insurance policy. We cashed out big time. At the time she was in so much debt with some loan sharks for her gambling problem so she decided a dead son was worth more than a sissy. So here I was reminding her that she was the one that ordered the hit on him to begin with. She just couldn't stand the idea of someone knowing her son was a booty snatcher. I didn't want to do it. I always liked him, but I had bigger plans for Johanna. Plans that I can't even speak on. She doesn't know me like she thinks she knows me. For now I just had to be attentive. I know for a fact that Adam knows it was me that tried to kill him. Although I could have killed him, it was the message that I just knew he would get and disappear. But my mistake, because here he was.

Here I am watching my back while his mother acts like a saint. My phone ringing interrupted my thoughts. I moved outside to a more secluded area.

"Hello?" I answered.

"Why is the bitch still breathing? Not only is she alive, but also now her bastard of a child is alive?" Gemini asked.

"I cannot speak on Adam, but as far as Johanna, I'm certain she won't make it too much longer." I replied.

"It's been 28 years, what are you waiting for?" Gemini asked.

"That not fair Gem... mom ordered me to get close to her. Then once I did, she tried to pin the baby on me. Alex slid through and shot the girl's stomach up. Mom knew damn well that baby wasn't mine, but how that bitch survived is beyond me. How the baby lived was clearly at the hands of God. Mom said I went rogue. The cops would suspect me."

"Todd, again I repeat, 28 years. What's the hold up?" Gemini inquired.

"Mom is waiting on certain information to be provided."

"Nigga your real wife and daughter are over here moving along without you. Alex is sick and Nikki is expecting," Gemini replied.

"What?" I asked, stuck. "What's wrong with Alex? When did Nikki get pregnant?"

"Get the shit over with. Kill the dumb bitch, fuck what mom said, you got bigger problems," Gemini yelled and hung up. I dialed Alex immediately.

"Hello?" she answered two rings in.

"Baby, what's wrong?" I asked.

"Don't care now, Jihad. You've long been gone. You raised another man's child, all the while your child doesn't even know you are her father -- let alone that you exist. I'm dying from cancer, but I could beat that. I can't beat the pain I feel in my heart, though. I can't gain my youth back, undo sacrifices, and have a better choice in a husband and a child father. You ruined my life and truly wasted my time."

"I've been in a tough situation. I thought I was protecting you guys. I never wanted you in the crossfire... the enemy will use your weakness to destroy you." I said truthfully.

"Fuck you. I've been sick, through chemo, survived, and recovered. Where were you? Not here. I'm tired and I'm giving up," Alex responded with finality.

"Baby I will come to you right now, please fight it." I said.

“I don’t believe you, and I’m tired of waiting for you. I hate you for making me this way,” Alex cried. “If you come back, be here for Nikki, but I won't be here.” I heard the dial tone.

“So that’s your weakness?” I heard someone say behind me. I just pulled my gun out with the silencer, turned around, and shot her in the middle of her head. I walked around the house until I found Adam in the kitchen cooking breakfast. He was playing a role and I was not here for it. “Hey dad, you want breakfast?”

I looked at him and sighed. “Your mother ordered the hit. I am not your father, your uncle is. Clearly, he isn’t your uncle. I would let you live, but you have run out of lives with me.” I shot him in the head and in his heart. Just for insurance. Didn’t need this nigga coming back to life yet again.

I hit 4 on speed dial. I said, “17” and promptly ended the call.

After the clean up crew was hired, I went upstairs, grabbed a few things, put that in the briefcase and walked out the door.

“Hey Mr. Lane!” my neighbor called out as she waved.

“Oh hey, Doris!” I waved back before getting in my car and driving off.

GEMINI

My brother has me completely fucked up. My mom knew Chrissy Moore when they were teenagers. They were best friends, started hustling for Herald together, and even lost their virginity in a threesome together. Needless to say they were as thick as thieves. One day my mom, Armani, met a guy named Genesis. Long story short, they fell in love and got married. First came my brother Oasis, and then came me, Gemini. Everything was great until my mom lost her third baby in her 7th month of pregnancy. She became depressed and unresponsive. Nothing Genesis did worked. She was in a living dead state. One night my mom called my dad and he didn't answer. That was very unusual so she tried again. Still nothing. For three days she called and text, hit hospitals, morgues, and called the jails. Nothing. She feared he was dead. She walked around the house all day trying not to worry us. She had had enough. She went out in search for him. No one in the streets knew his whereabouts, his family had no idea she was starting to give up. She drove to Chrissy house just to tell someone what was happening. When she pulled up the first thing that she noticed was Genesis car parked three houses down. Immediately she knew what was up. She used the spare key under the flowerpot and went in. Once the coast was clear she walked around the house quietly. She stood when she heard voices.

"Baby when are you going to leave Armani? You are here everyday and you have been held up with me for three days. The bitch hasn't even called me to see if I knew anything. Why isn't she worried ?" Chrissy asked.

"Man, the only reason I'm here is because you wouldn't get the abortion unless I stayed. I'm not your baby and this shit isn't anything. I should have killed you for that stunt you pulled slipping a Mickey in my drink, bitch. But I couldn't see my woman depressed anymore. And I couldn't hurt her and tell her the truth about your conniving slut ass," Genesis said.

"Really? Like wow. I don't want your fucking baby. I'd flush that bitch if I could," Chrissy responded.

"I'm going to be generous and offer you some advice for the next nigga you try to trap. Bitch swallow," Genesis said.

"You can go home to your weak ass bitch. That hoe can't even hold your baby she spat."

Genesis choked her and said, "That's the last disrespectful thing you will say about my wife. She carried and delivered two of my babies, you are beside yourself."

"Okay, okay, I'm sorry. I just don't understand... why her?"

She had heard enough. She had decided to leave making sure to leave the door wide open when she did.

Dad walked into a war zone -- one he knew existed. Once he saw the door open, he and Chrissy both knew she had been there. "Hello baby," he said to my mother. "I know you are mad, but I had an unexpected run in with the connect and he requested me ASAP. They took my phone and drove me to him. Everything is good now but I sense a war is coming soon. I think I need to move you guys for safety purposes."

My mother knew good and well what her man was saying was bullshit and that he was playing with her intelligence, but she went along with it. She always played her position really well and acted concerned. They both knew she knew, but that was dad's way of saying he didn't want to talk about it and mom's way of handling it. What she didn't ask, she couldn't prove.

ARMANI

I recall telling my son to wait. He had made a move and he was very close to being rewarded. But, no he killed the target and her son. The shit was hella messy. When did he start being so careless? The clean up crew took their money out my account after the job was done. You know, the one that I didn't authorize. Tisk, tisk, tisk.

Some of you might not understand but let me tell you.

The night we moved, I had the house raided. Yeah I had it raided. I knew they wouldn't find anything, but it helped with the Alibi. Then a month later, Chrissy mysteriously got pulled over due to an anonymous call saying she was a drug mule trying to smuggle drugs into another state.. after being in jail for two years she finally went to trial. At the end of the trial she was found guilty and charged with kingpin charges. Three life sentences. Aww my poor friend, I stood by her side through it all. Even after she was convicted. She would write me complaining about her cellmate, and I would write back pretending to sympathize, but really I was enjoying her torment.

In her final letter to me she cried about prison being so hard. So I had had enough enjoyment. I wrote back, "You should like it. It sounds about as hard and long as my husband's dick. I hear you like to ride it, so this should be no contest to you." She never wrote back, however, of course she was lingering in the shadows. About three years after the letter I guess poor little Ms. Chrissy couldn't take it anymore because she made a deal with the District Attorney to get out of jail by turning in Genesis and his connect El Diablo. Little did she know, I was now in charge and I had a whole new connect. The government took it, nonetheless, and Genesis and El Diablo was indicted and sentenced to life in prison. By the time we all found out it was her because her name was blacked out in the discovery packet, she was long gone.

The only reason the FBI even allowed her to get out is because she accused him of killing an undercover CIA agent. El Diablo ordered a hit. Who knows how Chrissy knew about that or where to find the weapon. Genesis isn't known to have loose lips, so I know he didn't do it. That nigga is that last one to pillow talk -- he was too damn paranoid. But what's done is a death sentence now. If you play pussy, I guess you will get fucked. I made it my business to find this hoe. It took me two years. I had followed her for a while and then right before I could execute her, I lost her. Then her daughter came up on my radar when she was 22. That's when I sent Oasis, aka Todd. He was trained assassin. He dated her, finessed her, and played to her need to be in charge. I almost had her mother's location. Now all I know is the area. The bitch would always get me close and then she would go cold again. I started to hire a professional, but I just didn't trust anyone. Besides this shit was personal. She was a loose end. The last place this bitch went was San Diego, California. She lived somewhere in the heart and that's where I was going.

MARIE

"Doctor, this man seems to be recovering very well. It was touch and go for a while," I said.

"His spirit and will to live has him recovering at an almost impossible speed," Doctor Vellin responded.

"I've never seen anyone with these injuries survive. I know it's possible, but it's not something that is common. I've been keeping a close eye on him and I noticed that he moves his finger and that his eye twitches.

"Honestly, I've never seen it either. I hope he will eventually move in front of me. I have yet to see these movements you speak of," Dr. Vellin confessed.

After the doctor left, I just sat there. I had been reading to John -- the hospital names all unknown guests John or Jane -- talking to him and even singing at times. Anything to see signs of life. He seems to be recovering on the surface very well. Although I'm shocked, I'm very happy. He is very handsome and strong, even after being hospitalized. I lied to the doctor about seeing John move his finger and twitch his eye. Truthfully, outside of the machines, there has been no sign of life; I wanted to buy him some time. I knew sooner than later he would, but he just needed time. You see, when you are Black, in a hospital on life support, and unclaimed with no insurance, they see you as an unnecessary liability. They won't hesitate to pull the plug on you.

"Hey Marie," Tia said interrupting my thoughts.

"Oh, hey girl," I said back.

"How was the shift?"

"Girl... long but progressive."

"What are you about to get into?"

"Nothing. You want some company for a while?" I didn't want to leave John.

"Yes, always. These shifts are long when you don't have company."

"Don't I know it. But going home to an empty bed just seems counterproductive if you ask me."

"I know that feeling."

I sensed something was wrong. Tia and I weren't best friends, but we are pretty close. We always talk at work and hang out afterward. Recently she started working the second shift. I'm not sure why, but before we worked the first shift together. We would split the floor and meet up for lunch. We were the perfect team.

"Tia is everything okay?" I asked, truly concerned.

She looked up at me with sad eyes and said, "I'm pregnant." I think she thought I would be upset and that's why she acted sad, but I was happy for her. "Whoa! Congratulations, Tia. How far are you?"

"Five months."

"Why do you sound sad?" I asked after she didn't perk up once she saw me excited. "I honestly had no idea you were pregnant, you are so small." Her eyes dropped. I got mad instantly. "What aren't you telling me, Tia?! What's going on?"

She was barely audible. "Ray has been beating on me for the past five months.

"What?!" I yelled loud enough that it could have awakened John.

"He took all of the food out of the house and won't let me eat or go anywhere when I am home. That's why I moved to second shift. So that I could eat. Swing shift is from two to eleven. I'm usually okay after that."

I was so shocked and angry. I couldn't attach myself to one feeling. "Tia, you have to get away from him," I said.

"And go where? I have no family or outside connects. I know he's just trying to make me lose the baby. He doesn't mean any harm."

"Girl, are you crazy? At this stage, hurting the baby will hurt you physically and mentally. You can come stay with me until we figure something out."

"No, I can't place that burden on you. I'll just wait. I know once he sees the baby he will want it."

"Tia he's not going to ever want that many. What is to say once you have it he won't try to hurt it? Be smart about this. Tell him nothing. Just pack up and move in with me. I have a large house with more than enough room for both of you. I always wanted a niece," I said smiling and rubbing her belly to reassure her.

"What if it's a boy?" Tia joked.

"It's a girl," I said, not really knowing. "But wait you are telling me you don't even know what you are over here toting?"

"No," Tia responded. "Ray won't let me go to the doctor's and he looks at my pay stubs so he will know if I went in an hour late or something."

"Hold on." I called Allie. "Hey Allie can I swing by with Tia for second? Okay thanks, we will be there shortly." I hung up and told Tia to come on. She followed me all the way to Allie's office. "Hey Allie, can you do an ultrasound on Tia? She's pregnant and has been keeping it a secret for unsaid reasons. We need you to keep it on a low profile if you know what I mean."

"Girl come on, I knew you had a bun in that oven! The weight is all in your hips and butt," she joked.

Tia blushed.

"Your man must be loving on you all the time. Alright you know the procedure -- come lay down on the table when you are ready," Allie said.

Tia left to get undressed. Allie was a nursing student, but a licensed ultrasound technician. She was very educated and only 21. I enjoyed her company because she always had interesting topics to discuss.

"So Allie what is today's topic?" I asked.

"What would you like to talk about?" Allie countered.

"ABORTIONS!" Tia yelled.

"Honey, the black community doesn't need abortions or birth control. That's just a way to willingly contribute to mass genocide." Allie responded.

"Girl, every nationality gets abortions and uses birth control, Tia said, rolling her eyes.

No, but did you know Margaret Higgins Sanger -- a known racist, founded planned parenthood to help the Black community stop reproducing? They were not in White communities originally. Everyone knew, but no one cared. Once they no longer needed us it was better to kill us. The United Nations only cared after the Jews went through their ordeal."

"That sounds crazy," Tia said.

"Google it, I'll even give you a starting point. Look up 'United Nations passed what law on December 9. 1948.' You never have to believe what I say. I could be wrong. Google it for yourself and for your own clarity and understanding. It's important to educate ourselves. Black people will contest the facts but never research them. Don't doubt it because you have been told otherwise. Just find out," Allie nonchalantly replied.

"Anyway, moving along.. look at that. There's your beautiful baby girl," Allie said.

"A girl?" Tia asked as she started to cry.

"Yup, a baby girl." Allie confirmed.

Tia looked over at me and I said I told you. Allie helped clean Tia up, printed the ultrasounds, and gave her some sample prenatal packs. Tia thanked her, took a pill, and put the rest in her locker.

CALLIE

I have not heard from or seen Apple in months. I expected a war, not him just going M.I.A., but you cannot knock me off of my square. I'm just patiently waiting. Braylin and I decided to let someone else micromanage the club and the salon since I was expecting a baby girl in another four months. We have been married for two years now, and everything is good. If and when that traitor comes back, I will be more than ready for his ass.

Today I decided to clean house and start moving the rooms around so that the baby can have the room beside ours. Braylin said he's going to help, but he's so busy he hasn't moved a thing. I guess I'm nesting because my patience has been long gone. I'm ready to decorate and prep for our angel.

I heard the doorbell going off, so the movers must be here. I waddled down stairs to the door, and yes, I said waddled. I wasn't fat, but the baby is somewhere in my vagina. This has been going on for like three days now. I'm going to schedule a doctor's appointment for sometime this week.

I open the door and noticed two males standing there talking to one another. One of them starts speaking to me but all I feel are these Braxton Hicks, so I grab my belly and bend over.

"Are you okay?" The shorter one asks me.

"Yeah, I'm fine." I replied.

We are from Alexander Moving Company and we have an order to pack two rooms and move them?" The shorter one says.

I'm still bent over, never really looking up. I said, "Yes. I'm Callie and I just need you to pack and move one room to another room."

"Ma'am, are you saying move it to another from in the house?" He asked.

"Yes. I am pregnant and I can't do it myself. I'm not allowed to lift anything so I need someone to do it for me." I grabbed my belly harder. "These fake contractions are hell," I thought out loud.

"Oh sorry, ma'am. We pack and move to different locations -- not the same location."

"Sir what is the difference?" I asked.

"The boxes and the mileage pay us. We wouldn't make a profit if it were in the same place."

"Okay, I can understand that. I'll give you both $200 a piece to do the task for me," I replied.

"Well, lead the way," he said. The other never spoke. I was so focused on the Braxton Hicks that I didn't even notice right away.

I showed the men where to start and where to finish. It took them four hours and they even put the crib and the changing table together for me. I paid them and they helped me cover the crib and the changing tables. The painters would be here in the morning. I had already washed the babies clothes and folded them. I decided to watch Netflix and chill.

BUFFY

"Okay, Doc. I initially wrote all of your letters and I felt the same," I said.

"Do you feel the same or do you want to feel the pain," the doctor replied.

"What kind of question is that?" I asked, irritable.

"A rational one," the doctor said. "A lot of people hold on to pain because it allows them to hold on to the person longer. Without the anger, hate, and emptiness, there is nothing left."

"Even if that were true, no one wants to feel that pain. Who would hold on to that feeling?" I asked.

"I'm asking if you are." He said simply.

"No. Why would I? Come on, I'm just really hurt. I'm tired of people acting like I brought this on myself, saw it coming, or overstayed my time. No, I was in a one-sided relationship that felt so real that to this day I question its authenticity. This is a feeling that I can't resist and every time I think I am over it, something happens that shows me I'm not. It could be something as fragile as a song he sung to me or a feeling I felt with him. I would think that this is God telling me not to give up. This is a sign that it's not over," I confessed.

"This is temporary pain. I know it feels like forever but it never is," Dr. Allison said.

It doesn't feel like forever, it feels indefinite. It feels like if I die my soul will live and search through every plane for his. It feels like the world is happy and I'm stuck in pain. It's fucking suffocating me. Why aren't you listening? I can't function. I WANT TO DIE SO I CAN LIVE. But I'll still tormented. He cut me so deep breathing feels like the end," I yelled. "Everyone would rather me sit and pretend so they can be comfortable."

"Buffy, deep down I know you can conquer this. You have to fight back mentally." Dr. Allison said. "You are limiting yourself by focusing in on a person who hurt you like this. Take your power back. Focus on you."

"You must have gotten your degree from Oprah. It's been said, it can't be done or it would be. I pay you to fix me, but you can't. The only person who can fix me dismissed his need for me." I said sadly.

"Buffy fight back. Don't give in," he said.

"Dr. Allison, all this entire situation did was show me I don't have any real friends. I've been suffering alone for too long. None of my friends care enough to call me, check on anything or me. But for each one of these bitches I was there. I call they don't answer, I text they don't reply. Fuck 'em." I said for the last time.

"There comes a time in everyone's life that they have to reevaluate their friendship and relationships," Dr. Allison said. "This is yours."

"I know," I replied.

"Did you bring your letters in?"

"Yes, but I decided not to mail them. Today I want to mail a letter. Do you mind if I use a sheet of paper and pen to write my final letter and send it to him, please?"

"Sure, here you are," he said while handing me pen and paper. "Speak from your heart."

I had no idea what I was going to write but once my pen hit the paper, whatever went on it was what was being sent.

FINAL LETTER

Dear Mr. Wrong,

I realized recently that I was holding in a lot of emotions. Some good and some bad. The more I think about the situation, the more I realize I've just been searching for answers. I know now that you will probably never be able to give me the answers I need to move on and that's something I will have to be okay with. You may never apologize or feel remorse, and I understand that. I've started therapy because the feelings that I was having were very unhealthy and I needed someone to help me transition through this rough time and move into a healthier situation.

I just wanted to say I forgive you. I don't wish you any harm, bad luck, karma, nothing. I sincerely wish you well. I forgive the both of you. May we both live in peace and enjoy life to the fullest.

I left no signature because if he has no idea where it came from, that was on him. I sealed it in the envelope, put a stamp on it, filled it out properly, gave it to Dr. Allison, and left for good -- hopefully to never turn back. Dr. Allison understood. And what's understood doesn't need to be explained.

CALLIE

The damn painters woke me up early as fuck. I wish Braylin ass hurries up and gets the fuck back in town before I hurt somebody. He's been gone on a business trip for two weeks and it's starting to piss me off. I know he needed to pitch this big idea early to this large corporation out in Cali so he could go on maternity leave with me, but hell, I need him here to answer the door for the painters I secretly hired.

I flung the door open and walked away. "Upstairs, the first room on your right," I yelled, pointing towards the steps and yawning.

About fifteen minutes went by before one of them yelled, "Ma'am can you come show us where you want the stripes?"

"I'm coming just give me a second to get up there." I was very grouchy.

When I walked up the stairs finally, I felt uneasy. The closer I got to the door, the more uncomfortable I got. I brushed the feeling off though and walked to the door. Just when I was about to push the door open, somebody grabbed me from behind. I started screaming and kicking as the other guy grabbed my feet. They forced me into our guest bedroom and threw me on the bed. "Let me go!" I yelled. One of them punched me in the face. I felt so dazed. I think I temporarily went unconscious. Well, clearly I did, because when I came to, my clothes were off and one guy was laying under me with his dick in my virgin ass. I started screaming from the pain it was unbearable. The other climbed on top of me lifting my legs in the air as far as they would go and entered my vagina.

They were both humping away. The tears rolled down my face non-stop. One guy even had the nerve to say the pussy is tight I'm about to nut and then go back in there. I felt like somebody was trying to rip my body to pieces. I just hoped they used a condom for the baby sake and me. I even found myself praying to make it out of the situation alive. A part of me thought Apple might have something to do with this, but then again this wasn't really his style. He was a more of an I-want-you-to-know- it-was-me kind of person. I heard one of them grunting, interrupting my thoughts. He pulled out in just enough time to nut on my face. I was so ashamed that I didn't have any power. The baby must have felt my pain because my stomach started hurting and got hard as a rock. "Suck my dick bitch," I heard the one who came all over my face say. I refused and he grabbed a knife. I contemplated death for a second but then he said, "Suck my dick or I'll stab this baby in the head bitch. Try me." I hurriedly put his salty dick in my mouth. It smelled like he hadn't bathed in days. I closed my eyes and tried not to vomit. He pumped in and out of my mouth until he came. He held my nose so I would be forced to swallow his acid filled cum. I swore right then and there if I ever saw either of these niggas again they would die. The assault lasted three fucking hours. By the time they finished I was out. I blacked out. The next thing I noticed is when I woke up in the hospital. I couldn't remember if I called for help or if someone found me. A stranger talking to me interrupted my thoughts again.

"Oh, good morning. I am Tia your nurse," she said sympathetically. "You are at Howard University Hospital."

"How did I get here? What happened to me?" I asked, confused.

"Well you were raped in your home. I'm not sure on the details, but there are two detectives in the hall waiting to speak to you, and then the doctor will come in and speak to you as well," Tia replied.

I was so confused. I remember being raped but nothing after that. Two women detectives came in and asked me a series of questions such as do you know what happened? Do you know who did this to you? Is it okay if we take the rape kit? Have you ever seen your attackers? It was just question after question. I did find out that the neighbor had called the police when he saw my door open for too long. He asked for a wellness check and when the police came, they immediately got me to the hospital. I thank God for that neighbor. When the detectives left, in walked Doctor Kay.

"Hi, Callie how are you," she asked.

"I'm lost and hurt. How is my baby? Did those people give me something? Where is my fucking husband?" The questions flew out of my mouth.

"Well, fortunately, we did not find any STDs. We did not know any of your relatives' contact information so as of right now no one has been notified about your whereabouts. I am sorry to have to inform you of this, but your baby did not make it. You were in labor when you arrived and you birthed her at 2:21 am. She simply was too early to survive on her own," Dr. Kay said.

I burst out into tears. I couldn't believe this was happening to me. "How... what did I do to deserve this?" I cried.

"Would you like me to call someone for you?" Dr. Kay asked, as if she had spent enough time with me and she was ready to move along and deliver more bad news to another good person.

"No," I replied, refusing to let her see any more emotions. "When can I go home?" I asked.

"You can go home tomorrow."

I just looked over at the window. That was my polite way of dismissing her.

Tia walked back in and that's when I noticed she was pregnant. "How far are you?" I asked.

"Five months..." she responded, dropping her head.

"What is it?"

"A girl."

"I know you are excited," I said.

"Not really. I know I shouldn't say this, but I don't really want her. I don't even have a safe place to take her." Tia admitted.

"What do you mean?"

"My boyfriend doesn't want a baby. I can tell. He tries to starve me. He pushed me down the stairs once, he beats on me. He use to love me, but now things are different," Tia replied.

I took it all in. This bitch was carrying my baby, and some nigga was trying to kill her. Instead of telling her I would take that bundle of joy for her, I decided to sit back and wait. If she gave her up for adoption I would be right there.

BRAYLIN

I walked in the house and Callie was in the kitchen making cookies.

"Hey baby," I greeted her. She flinched a bit. I said, "I'm sorry, I didn't mean to frighten you."

"Oh no, baby, I was in my mood and I wasn't paying attention," she replied. "Baby, I would like to move. I'm thinking the Georgetown area."

"What? That's random," I replied. "We have not been in this house that long."

"I know, but the other day my phone died and I had to navigate through Georgetown on my own. Long story short, I bought a house."

"You bought a house?" I was shook. "Like, you purchased a new house?"

"Yes."

"How? I mean you didn't even consult me. And then what about this house Callie? I'm still paying the mortgage on this house," I replied, obviously frustrated.

"Well I thought about that and I was thinking we could use this house as a place to hold battered women and children. We would essentially be providing people in need with a safe haven and it could be a huge tax write off." Callie nonchalantly added, "I already named it. We are going to call it Love's Freedom House."

"Baby what are you saying?"

"I'm saying we are a team. Let's move in unison from here on out. I apologize for making such a huge decision so whimsically, but baby I couldn't let this offer get by me."

"Tell me about the house Callie." That woman had me intrigued.

"I'll show you," she replied. "Go get back dressed."

"Baby, I am dressed." I reached for her stomach but she moved away. I said, "You must have baby brain." I walked away to drop off my bags upstairs. That's when I noticed this tiffany blue room. It had a big bow painted on the wall and it said Tiffany & CO. I thought it was adorable. Finally, I headed back down the stairs to meet Callie.

"Are we naming the baby Tiffany?" I asked.

"No, I'm just painting the rooms with different themes," she said. "I thought it would be cute."

"Oh, I thought it was our baby's room."

We both headed out the door and to the car. It was cold, but it felt good still. We arrived at this beautiful colonial style house with a two-car garage. Now this, I like. My baby had great taste. She said, "Come on, get out."

I looked at her like she was crazy. "We can't just walk around this house, they going to call the cops on us."

"Baby, we own this house. This house will raise our children."

I looked at her suspiciously. "We own it?"

"Here is your key, daddy. No pun intended," she said slyly.

"Oh I bet," I said, taking the key. I walked up to the front door and unlocked it. Literally, it was beautiful.

"Baby… do you like it?"

"Baby, we are staying here tonight." This place exceeded all expectations. It was so impressive I couldn't even complain.

"Baby, let's break this house in." I advanced towards her. She backed away.

"I am in pain, baby. I'm not in the mood. Rain check," she said.

I was slightly disappointed, but I just walked around instead. I found the man cave. "Oh fuck..." I said. This girl had a mega ton down here, a big TV in the middle of the wall surrounded by smaller TV's. There was a bar that was fully stocked, a pool table, game systems, surround sound, theater style chairs, and LED lights. I mean this girl had the works. Oh she did that. She even had a built in studio and it was the real deal too. I walked around and noticed she had a guest bedroom attached to a full guest bathroom and an office space at the end of the hall. The room had a nice desk with law books everywhere. And I'm not surprised, but there was a stage with a stripper pole in the damn office. Fuck kind of work was we about to do? Maybe auditions for the club.

I heard her say, "That is for when you feel stressed and overworked. There is a sauna and a massage area in the next room."

"Thank you baby," I said. "I'm very pleased and if this is how you moving when I'm not here by all means do your thing."

ADAM

I'm awake and I can't wake up. I don't know what's going on, but its like I hear everything and see nothing. I've been trying to force my eyes open but they won't open. There is a girl that talks to me, sings to me, and reads to me. She tells someone that I am moving but I don't feel any movement. I felt her suck my dick a few times. She has strong jaws like a man, so it's easy to fantasize that she is a he -- specifically Travis. For some reason, Travis means something to me. I don't know him, nor do I remember him, but I dream about him and in my dream I call him Travis. She calls me John so I know my name is John. Clearly I'm gay. But outside of that, I have no idea about the body I'm trapped in. I think maybe this girl loves me. That's what she says, so I think I love her back. I hope my eyes open soon.

TIA

I felt so bad talking to that lady after she lost her baby. I pray she heals and gets through this. It was stupid of me to say I didn't want mine after she lost hers, but I got pregnant for my baby and he's not happy. I was for sure he would be, but he isn't. I didn't want to hurt it, but I didn't want it either. I wanted to get an abortion, but after paying all of my bills and my baby phone bill, child support, and car note every month, I just didn't have the money to do so. When I asked him to pay for it, he looked at me like I lost my mind. Fearful that he would hit me again, I just scurried away and never asked again.

I had no idea what I was going to do... but I couldn't take this baby home. I'm tired of faking happy. I'm more excited about cheese curls than I am about this baby. I wish I could take this baby out of my stomach and put it in hers. That way I didn't hit it and it was gone forever.

My shift ends in two hours and I can't reach bae. Like where the fuck is he? I decided to call him again one last time. Okay six more times. No answer. I'm worried.

"Hey Tia," Marie said.

"Hey." I replied sadly.

"What's wrong? Nothing is wrong with the baby is it?" Marie cared more about the baby than I did.

"No, the damn baby is fine -- an extra burden even. I just hate this damn baby. It's the reason my man won't answer his phone," I yelled immediately regretting what I said. I looked around and saw everyone staring at me. So I yelled, "Mind your business, you nosey bitches!" Then I stormed off.

The next three months seemed to fly by. Still no resolution. This baby is still baking and I grow more and more depressed by the day.

I decided to drive home an hour early today. I'm driving down Florida Ave when I decided to pull over for a second. I ran into the store to grab some pop and graham crackers. I decided to drive to my mom's house. I can't spend another night alone. I'm going to go crazy if I do. I turned the radio up when I get back in the car. I hear Krazy Bone's song -- The World Has Too Many Freaks. That beat does something to me. I get on 295 and merge onto 210. I swerve a bit trying to dance with my fat ass, but its cool because 210 is a desert right now. Ain't shit on it but dust. The next thing I know some car comes out of nowhere and swerves into my lane causing me to swerve as well. I slid right off the road. It was so dark and my nerves were shot. I couldn't move and I wasn't sure if that accident was intentional or not. I'm not going to lie -- I was scared as fuck. My passenger side door opens and the person says drink this or I'm going to cut the baby out of you. I hurried up and drank whatever it was. I drank the whole bottle because they didn't specify where to stop. Immediately my stomach started hurting.

"What did you give me?!" I yelled out in pain.

"I'm helping you solve your problem. Look at me as your savior," the person said. I thought the voice sounded familiar, but I also knew how hard I hit my head. The person dragged me out of the car and pulled my scrubs off. I thought they were going to rape me. I started fighting because bae checks my vagina every time he sees me. He will know if I had sex and he won't believe me if I said I was raped. He will kill me if he thinks I was with someone else. The pain in my stomach felt sharp like menstrual cramps and then I felt myself crowning. I reached down between my legs and felt the baby's head. "Oh shit!" I yelled out. I screamed in pain as I delivered my baby right on the side of the road. *What am I supposed to do with it*, I asked myself. After the baby came out, the person took it and ran off. I heard the wheels speed off. *The baby never cried -- maybe it was dead,* I thought. I don't know and I don't care. God sent someone who wanted the baby to get it and that was fine with me. I just needed to find Ray. I picked myself up and got back in my cart and drove off, heading home. I knew I couldn't go to my mother's house now, she would have too many questions. I sat in a hot bath for hours. The water would get cold and I would refill it.

I returned to work two weeks later. As soon as I walked in, Marie ran up to me. She looked down at my stomach and said, "You had the baby!"

"Yeah, but it died."

"Oh my God." She could barely get the words out. "I'm so sorry."

I said, "It's fine, I've dealt with it."

She hugged me. "Where did you deliver it? Were you here?"

"No, I was at Southern Maryland Hospital" I replied. I had all the answers. At least, I hoped I did. I practiced and rehearsed. There was no point in calling the police. They might return the baby to me if I do. The way I see it is that somebody did me a favor, so why get them in trouble? You can't pray and ask for help and then get mad when you get it because of the way it was delivered. This is how I rationalized with myself.

Marie tried her best for a few months to comfort me, but she was trying to heal my loss of a child when I was really sad that I lost Ray. I missed him and he was still missing.

"How about we go out tonight?" Marie asked.

"No, I don't think I'm in the mood," I responded.

"You say that every day. I need to cheer you up. I can't watch you depressed."

"I'm depressed and you can't watch it." I repeated, irritated.

"I didn't mean it like that."

"I'm sorry. I know you didn't. It's not a good time," I said walking off.

"Tia wait," she called out. I stopped and turned around. "Please don't shut me out. I only want to help," Maria said. "Is Ray there for you? Is anybody there for you?"

"Bitch, mind your fucking business. Stop trying to use mine to entertain your dull ass life. I don't fuck with your messy ass. Go back to the patient in 204 and suck his dick like you have been doing. Your whore ass keep acting like you give a fuck. Truthfully, I'm your only friend you thirsty ass, trick ass bitch. Who are you to ask me anything? You over here lying on a corpse and bitch don't think I don't see your protruding belly. You stupid ass hoe! I know you are pregnant with that nigga in 204 baby. How are you molesting or, excuse me, raping a gay ass corpse? His anus is wide open and his eyebrows look like God came down and kissed them himself. You suppose to be handling his IV and pulse, not riding his dick. Damn, did the intern in neurology leave you already, hoe? I guess even he could see your ass is fucking lonely. Stoic my ass. How many STD's is Donna going to help you get rid of before you learn to wrap it up or just close your legs? And don't pretend like that wasn't you down on the hoe stroll down Union. Bitch I saw you. Matter of fact, bitch I know you. I will read you don't try me stay the fuck away from me before I make it bad for you. And bitch if you get your PH levels together your pussy will stop smelling like the Wharf every other fucking week."

With that I stormed off. I was done. Not done. But done done. That was my breaking point. I hope these hoes got a good enough show. Stupid bitches always spectating. I walked out of the hospital and never returned. I had better things to focus on -- like finding my man. A bitch could give a fuck less about anything or anyone else. I love him.

When I walked in my house, I picked the mail up off the floor. There was a jail letter. The writer was... OMG my baby was in jail! No wonder I couldn't find him.

I called the jail and found out his visiting days are Monday through Friday 5pm until 8pm. So I decided to get dressed and go up there. I waited a whole hour only to get to the check in point and they tell me he already has two visitors. That was impossible, he was waiting on me. I slipped the guard a $100 bill to find out who. She informed me that it was his wife and daughter Malaysia and Alaysia Green. My soul dropped.

"His wife?"

"Yeah, they have been together for years."

"How do you know?"

"You think this is his first time here?"

"He has never been in jail," I said. "We have been together for four years. I would know."

"Well I've been here for 10 years and he has been in and out of here. Sometimes for months and sometimes for years. That's his wife and daughter. I remember when she was pregnant. Not to mention they got married here while he was in jail for a two to three year bid," she replied. "I see a lot of you over the years. He gets them and leaves them once they get pregnant. All of you wear the same face whenever you find out the truth. I really hate to tell you. I see that you love him."

I was devastated. He must be trying to leave her crazy ass though. I'm going to help him. I slid the guard another $100. "Could you come out and talk to her when she leaves so I can see what she looks like?"

The guard looked like she was hesitant about it. I said, "I just want to see what I am up against." She agreed.

I sat in the car for two hours before I saw the guard come out talking to a woman and a young girl. This bitch wasn't that cute. In fact, she was a little average if you ask me. The little girl was cute in a baby monkey kind of way. The way this bitch smiled made my skin crawl.

TASHA

Brendan and I went over to Callie and Braylin's house to finally see the baby. They named her Caitlynn Brynn Daniels. She's very adorable but ummmm...

"Baby..." Brendan said as soon as he got in the car.

"Yes?" I answered.

"Is it just me or does that baby have completely different genetics than Callie and Braylin?"

"No honey... I was about to ask you the same thing," I laughed.

"Do you think Callie cheated?" Brendan asked.

"Either that or the baby was switched at birth."

"It couldn't have been. Braylin told me Callie had her at a private facility," he said. "They were the only ones there."

"Honey, this one is suspect," I said.

"But why lose her virginity to him and then cheat? That doesn't make sense," Brendan said.

"Something is afoot."

"I know you didn't say afoot. No more Lifetime for you," Brendan said while dying laughing.

"What?" I had to laugh at that myself.

"You know what. Where did you get that word from anyway?"

"I don't know what you are talking about. I'm just out here living my best life, expanding my vocabulary. Being profound and shit." I responded nonchalantly.

"You are too much," Brendan joked.

"Let's grab some food."

"Okay, where would you like to eat Anika?"

"Why does she get to choose?" I asked, faking an attitude.

"Because I'm a princess and princesses eat at Chuck E. Cheese," Anika replied.

"Well, I guess we are off to Chuck E. Cheese," Brendan said.

"Yay!" Anika yelled.

That girl is so spoiled and easy to please, I thought to myself. I can't help but to wonder about the Braylin and Callie situation. It was so odd. Maybe the baby favors somebody in her family. I just decided to dismiss the whole thing.

"So, we should go out tonight," Brendan suggested.

"And what are we going to do with Anika?" I asked curiously.

"Drop her off with Brandon and Pops," Brendan replied, as if it wasn't a question.

"Is Kelsi still there?"

"I mean she's there, but she's at Brandon's. Brandon is going to be at Pops house tonight."

"Doing what?"

"Normally they watch the game together. Brandon loves all sports just like Carter. Braylin likes football and I like baseball," Brendan said.

"So who will be watching Anika while they are watching sports?" I asked.

"Carlotta will be there as well. Just go out with me. Do you really think I would put Anika in an unsafe environment?"

"No," I answered honestly. I just felt some kind of way after finding out through Brendan that Kelsi's sick psychotic ass was staying at Brandon's place. I will never trust her with my child or children. I'm a true believer that some people are wired wrong, and she for sure is one of them. Not to mention she was fucking Brandon -- her own brother. I'm not sure if she should be staying with him, seems suspect if you ask me. I would not be surprised if somebody told me she was pregnant with his baby. That's some sick shit. But who am I to judge? This family has a lot of secrets in their closet, and I am almost certain that they are about to fall out. That why I keep Anika close to me because somebody isn't saying something.

We arrived at Chuck E. Cheese in no time. Anika pulled at my sundress. "Can I go play mommy? Please?" She begged.

"Anika let us check you in first," I said calmly.

"But mommy I am going to miss all of the good games. I don't want to have to wait forever to play," Anika cried.

"Aww let the girl have some fun." Brendan said. He handed me a hundred dollar bill and said, "Enjoy. I'll get the snacks." Anika damn near snatched my arm off while pulling me to the game area.

"Wait Anika, we have to get coins," I said.

"Okay, mommy," she said moving all around. I inserted the money and put all the coins in a bag. Those little cups didn't hold much of anything.

First she got on the train. That entertained her for all of two seconds before she hopped off mid-ride. Then she wanted to ride a clock. Thirty-five minutes into the festivities, Brendan finally called us over for pizza. Thank goodness because I was tired.

"Y'all look like you are having fun!" He teased.

"Do we, now?" I asked.

"Yes, baby," he said happily.

I said, "Anika... Mr. Brendan is going to take you to play again once you are done eating."

"Yay! Let's play basketball." Anika said. "I bet I can beat you."

"I bet you can, too. I am getting old!" Brendan joked.

"No, those are excuses. Anika, he is trying to trick you," I interjected. Anika eyed Brendan suspiciously. After inhaling their food, they both ran off about fifteen minutes later.

A woman sits next to me and says, "These bunnies will wear you out won't they?"

"Yes, child. It's like their energy levels never decrease," I replied.

"I'm Marie," she said.

"Hey Marie, I'm Tasha."

"Where is your baby?"

"Oh I'm here with my niece, Kia. She is eight, so I don't have to chase her too much, thankfully," she replied.

"I hear that," I said. "When are you due?" I asked after I noticed her continuously rubbing her belly.

"Oh, I am not sure," she said. "I just found out I was pregnant."

"Oh I thought for sure you were a few months in," I said, hoping I didn't offend her.

"I'm sure I am. It's just such a complicated story. I haven't had the chance to digest that this is happening to me."

"Your focus should be on the baby, not the situation. Take it from me -- that baby is coming either way and it's better to be prepared than unprepared."

She looked like something was weighing her down. I didn't want to pry but hell I felt bad for her. Clearly she was in a tight spot. I simply said, "I'm here for a few hours if you want to talk about it. Anika has millions of those coins."

She smiled at me. She said, "Recently I had a friend, well someone who I thought was my friend, snap on me in front of my entire job. I was literally trying to be a good friend to her and out the blue she attacked me. It really hurt me. But what bothers me the most is that I want to reach out to her," Marie confessed.

I looked at her, understanding the feeling. I felt that way when it all hit the fan with Macy. I continued to listen. "She told the whole job that I was liar, a whore, and a rapist."

"Why would she say those things about you?" I asked, knowing that usually there is some truth behind all statements.

"She was pregnant and then she came back to work and she wasn't pregnant. When I inquired about the baby she said it was still born. I didn't believe her at first because I over heard her tell a patient she didn't want the baby. So I assumed she had gotten rid of it by way of adoption. But she was so sad and depressed that I started to believe her. Long story short, I tried to get her to go out one night and she got disgruntled. That's when she spazzed on me. I was so shocked that I had no response. I've been placed on mandatory leave until the investigation is over."

"Oh damn, that's a lot," I said. "Were any of the accusations true?"

"A few were true, but most were not. I lied about seeing a patient move because I didn't want them to take him off of life support. They tend to do that when a person has no family, no health insurance, or is on a HMO. It becomes a burden and a bill to the hospital. My brother moved to Texas and two years into him living there he got into a bad accident. Well, he was in the hospital on life support for all of two weeks before they pulled the plug. No one notified us because they didn't know who his next of kin was. When we sued the hospital, their lawyer's rebuttal was that if he wanted us to save him he would have listed us as his next of kin, but since he didn't, he must not have wanted our assistance. They claimed that we were just trying to make a profit off of a tragic situation. No one saved my brother or attempted to save him. I just wanted to save someone else from going through this. Because I showed interest in him, she claimed that I was sleeping with him and pregnant with his baby," Marie said.

"Wow, that is a lot." I responded. "Is it his?"

"No I got artificial insemination," she replied. "I picked an entire person out of a catalog."

"Do you have proof?"

"How could I not?"

"Well, problem solved. You already discredited everything she said with that one document."

"I'm not sure I want them to know. They are so judgmental. I just wish I knew she had duplicitous intentions before I had gotten so close to her."

"Well how will you prove you are innocent?"

"I'm not sure yet, but I hope it doesn't end up with me having to tell a bunch of shady people my business."

"Yeah I can understand how you feel overwhelmed. None of that sounds easy," I replied sympathetically.

She took a deep breath and said, "I'm going to get through this. I just have to wait it out. As soon as my name is cleared I'll be good again."

"I agree," I said as Anika ran up to me.

"Mommy, mommy, mommy. Look at all the tickets I won. I'm going to get a cool toy with these!" Anika yelled.

"Oh wow, look at you. You must have beat Mr. Brendan real good."

"I did. He is old mommy," Anika replied.

"That he is, baby. That he is." I replied, laughing so hard.

"Hey some of these tickets I won, too." Brendan said defending himself.

"Mommy he won two rows, but he only got four tickets because I counted." Anika told. Everyone including Marie fell out laughing. Anika looked at everyone baffled. She couldn't understand why we were all laughing.

Marie said, "She is so adorable."

"Thank you." Anika said. "I am cute as well, and my mommy said I am intelligent."

"You are certainly all of the above," Marie said.

"Aww thank you. You are such a doll," Anika said.

"Brendan get this child!" I laughed.

Brendan said, "What... she's your mini me, don't get mad at genetics."

"Y'all two are a mess. You see how they gang up on me?" I asked Marie.

Before she could answer, a little girl ran up to her and said, "Auntie, I need more tokens."

"Kia... be polite and say excuse me before interrupting." Marie scolded the young girl.

"My apologies. Excuse me," Kia said.

"Yes, Kia, how may I help you?" Marie asked.

"May I have some tokens, please? I am all out." Kia asked.

"Just a few more. We will be leaving shortly," Marie replied. She pulled out ten dollars and handed it to Kia.

"Thank you!" Kia replied before she jetted off.

"Mommy she is almost faster than flash. I can still see her though. You can't see Flash," Anika commented.

"She must be Flash's sidekick," I joked along.

Anika eyes grew wide. "Really mommy?" She asked.

"I don't know... she has to hide her identity, so we may never know," I replied.

"She put her fingers up to her lips and said, "Shhhhhh mommy. Someone might be listening." And with that, she was gone.

"I guess I'm still on duty," Brendan said.

"Looks that way," I replied

Marie's phone started ringing. She looked down at it and rolled her eyes. She excused herself and walked out to the front of the establishment. She returned fifteen minutes later.

"Everything okay?"

"Yes, everything is fine. That was my sister getting on my nerves again," Marie replied.

"Oh, she's wondering when you are going to bring her daughter back?" I asked mostly to make conversation.

"No, this is my other sister Helen. She heard about what happened at the hospital and wanted to know what was going on," Marie replied.

"Oh okay, that's a good thing. She is worried about you!" I said.

"No, she is nosey. What can a section 8 hoe do for me," Marie asked agitated.

“I… I don’t know.” I was caught off guard.

“All she does is show up when there is drama. The only reason I answered is because she would just keep calling,” Marie explained.

I don’t even know this girl and she seems messy. I hate to judge her, but I'm trying to be drama free and she doesn’t seem like the avoiding type, I thought to myself. I had to hurry and make an excuse to dash before she asked to exchange numbers. Just when I thought that, Marie said, “I need to use the restroom. I will be back.”

“Okay, sweetie.” I replied.

I texted Brendan and told him to prep Anika to leave. By the time Marie came back from the restroom, we were headed out.

I said, “Well okay, it was nice meeting you Marie.”

“Are you leaving?”

“Yes, I have to go. It was nice meeting you and I hope everything works out for you,” I replied, hoping she got the point.

“Yes, you as well.” She turned to look for Kia. I took that as my cue to push on, so we did.

Brendan said, “What’s up with her? She seems nice.”

“Of course she is, that’s Girl Flash’s aunt.” Anika said.

“Girl, hush.” I replied.

“That girl is a trip,” Brendan said.

“Oh, now you agree?” I joked. “Anyway, she seemed nice but she has a lot going on and I don't really need the extra right now.”

"Why do you think just because you befriend someone you will have to carry on his or her burdens?" Brendan asked.

"I don't know, that's usually what happens. When your friends need you you are there for them." I replied.

"Yes that is true, but you have to be there only as much as your sanity, finances, and free time will allow. Don't stress yourself by putting yourself in stressful situations. Their problems are still theirs, if you can help help. If not, you can't. Pray for them and keep it moving," Brendan said.

I knew he was right, but I was growing somewhere between positive vibes and positive energy. The wedding is a few weeks away and I'm not sure I am there yet. I need a level of equanimity to get through. She exuded stress. *I'll pass*, I thought to myself. Nothing is more irritating than not following your gut and realizing later that you should have followed your first instinct after shit has hit the fan.

MARIE

"Oh damn, Marie are you okay?" Donna asked.

"That cum-sucking hoe has some nerve to embarrass me like that. I never did anything but try to help her weak ass. I see why that nigga is at home going upside that hoe head. Fucking cunt," I yelled.

"Girl she said the most. Why didn't you say anything. Now you look guilty, and what STD did I clear for you?" Donna asked.

"I really do not know what she is talking about. She is a bitter bitch. That nigga probably dismissed or ditched her. A hoe stroll?" I yelled. "Why would I need to?! This bitch makes me so sick," I said rolling my eyes again.

"Girl calm down. She is just throwing words. Nobody believes her. She exaggerates air," Donna joked.

"I'm just so confused. I was a phenomenal friend to her -- why would she attack me like that?" I asked no one in particular. I was just thinking out loud.

"She just mad because whoever performed her C-section hacked her up. Look like the hoe did it herself," Dona replied.

"Hacked her up?" I asked.

"Girl you didn't see her stomach? It looked like the chainsaw massacre!" Donna laughed. "I walked in on her in the bathroom changing. She thought she locked the door. Then had the nerve to scream at me for not knocking on a multiple stall bathroom. I thought I saw her replacing the stitches but I wasn't sure," Donna said.

"Screamed at you?" I inquired.

"Yes honey, called me a nickel and dime hoe. Told me the next time I enter without knocking she was going to knock my head off. I told her if she feels foggy leap, bitch. I said lock the door if you need privacy. I said, who cut you Edward Scissorhands? She slammed the door in my face after that." Donna shook her head while she recapped.

"What?!" I said.

"Yeah," Donna replied. I left Donna shortly after. I stopped at a payphone and called in a possible crime. I said that I suspected a girl of killing her newborn baby. No doctor in 2018 -- rushed or not -- is hacking at you. I have always suspected her of doing something to her baby, but only a crazy person would do that right? Then again, lately her sporadic behavior and aggressive outburst definitely says she's a candidate. She's been acting quite deranged. I hoped I was wrong though.

The detectives came up to our job inquiring about her. My coworkers and I all stood back and watched/ listened as the lead nurse told the detectives about the accusation she threw at me a few days prior. She also told them that she has not reported back since then. She said she didn't believe that she would return.

They thanked her and left a few cards before exiting. A week later, I saw the same detectives there requesting documents. This time they had a subpoena. After the hospitals attorney reviewed it, they turned over whatever documents were requested. Then they started to interview nurses, doctors, and other personnel. They were asking questions like did we know she was pregnant? Did we see her stomach protruding? Did she exhibit signs of pregnancy, etc. I guess they didn't find any documented proof that she was pregnant.

Donna walked up to me. "Girl did the detectives question you?"

"No not yet. What is this about?" I asked, playing clueless.

"They think she hurt her baby," Donna said.

"What? No." I gasped, pretending to be shocked.

"Girl they asked if I knew she was pregnant. I was like yeah I saw the ultrasound right after Allie did it. She was definitely pregnant. I saw that the baby was a girl. They asked if I knew what happened to it. I said no but I saw a scar or something on her stomach. I said I think she was stitching it up in the restroom one day when I walked in. Then they asked me about her behavior and how she was acting. I told them other then yelling at me and her yelling at you she seemed quiet as usual. They just kept trying to get information from me. I told them I don't know anything else and they finally let me go. Why they tried to give me a card talking about some call if I remember anything else. Girl, I said okay and walked out. I never even grabbed the card. What I look like calling twelve?"

"Damn, I don't want to talk to them," I replied.

"Well you better want to because too many people told them about your fight so I know they are going to ask you, and I heard Isabella say you dumped her after finding out she was pregnant. These bitches and their rumors, ugh."

"Where the fuck did she get that from? I'm not even like that." I replied. "I never exhibited that behavior or anything. These motherfuckers are on their best bullshit I swear," I said annoyed.

"Excuse me... Marie is it?" The detective asked.

"Yes, that's me."

"Hi. I am Detective Ho and I am investigating Ms. Tia Wells. We would like to speak with you if you don't mind."

"I do mind." I replied. "I'm not the one for getting into anyone else's business. Not to mention it's time for me to check my floor."

"Well I understand your position, however, we can wait. There's no rush," the detective replied.

"Your choice," I said as I walked off. Six hours later my shift was complete. As I headed out the locker room, I bumped right into Detective Ho. "Oh, excuse me," I said before I looked up and realized it was her. I rolled my eyes agitated.

"No worries." She replied with a fake smile. "Are you ready now?"

"Actually I'm in a bit of a rush as you can see."

She firmly said, "Well slow down and sit down." Instantly I got agitated. I didn't want anyone to suspect me of calling the police on her out of malice.

"Fine, let's get this over with," I replied.

"Okay, well here's an empty room." We both walked in. Even though I was at work, I felt like I was in the house. A cold empty sterile room. I got nervous immediately.

"Did you know Tia?"

"Yes, we were coworkers."

"How close would you say the two of you are?"

"Coworkers. As close as coworkers are."

"Did you think she was pregnant?"

"I know she was pregnant," I replied.

"Okay, how do you know?"

"I could see her stomach and I was in the room when Allie did the ultrasound and told her it was a girl."

What happened to the baby she asked?

"She said it was born a stillborn," I replied sitting back in my chair.

"Where was it born?"

"She said Southern Maryland. But I don't know."

"Do you think she would do anything to intentionally hurt the baby?"

"I don't know. Who would know that? She told me she switched to swing shift because her boyfriend wouldn't allow her to eat at home. She never said anything directly to me about the baby."

"How would you describe her recent behavior?"

"Do I look like Doctor Phil?"

"Any reasonable person can describe a person's behavior."

"Well, I guess I'm not that observant."

"Even after she accused you of raping a patient?"

"I've been cleared of all of those accusations."

"Was that something she normally does, go on rants and tirades about her friends?" The detective was prying.

"As I have said, we were coworkers -- not friends. Try not to get the words misconstrued," I replied as I started to walk out.

"I will try not to. One last question," she said before I got all the way out of the door.

"What?" I asked looking back but not turning around fully.

"Would you help your co-worker hide a baby?"

"What? No. Why would you ask that?"

"Well didn't you help sneak her prenatals and didn't you coerce Allie into giving here a sonogram?"

"Yeah, because making sure she has a healthy baby and delivery does coincide with a baby murder or an accomplice. I am gone. Have a good night Detective Ho," I replied and left.

"I will," she replied just in time. "But stay close, try not to get traveling ambitions." It went in one ear and out of the other. I'm the one that called them, and now I'm somehow an accomplice. "Stupid bitch," I huffed to myself.

Those detectives aren't getting shit else out of me. The audacity of that BITCH to try to implicate me in a crime. What the fuck do I look like saying, oh yeah I did it? I'm the one that called. Man this place right here is a bad place to be in. You cannot help anyone these days. Not even 12.

KELSI

Yeah, I heard about Buffy beating Khaleena's ass. So the fuck what! She lucky it was her and not me. This dumbass therapist is trying to get me to feel like I did all of these people wrong. Why would I ever feel that way when I was the one that they did wrong? And now I should be sad because I decided to return the gesture? Hell nah!

Anyway, fuck that hoe. Moving along to more pertinent situations, I have been following this bitch Buffy around for weeks. She is dating this guy. He is cool, but I would not ever turn my head around to look if he walked by. I see she's not going to therapy anymore. They must have fixed her crazy ass. Leave it to me though and her therapist will be a millionaire. I got a plan for this hoe. She just walked into a convenient store in her neighborhood, so I decided to call it a day and go home to Brandon. He always got on my nerves when I was out too long. He ask questions like: Where have you been? How was your day? Anything out of the normal happen? My answers are always the same -- out living my life. My day was motivating. I survived it again. You would think he would just stop asking, but noooo. He is ambitious.

On Monday morning, I started to execute my plan to destroy these bitches.

"Hey Brandon, can you buy me a laptop?"

"There is a desktop downstairs in the office," he replied.

"Yes I know, but I have been keeping a journal and I thought it would be good to write a book. Some fiction mixed with nonfiction. Maybe it will help someone else out," I responded.

"Why can't you do it on the desktop?"

"Because I feel most creative outdoors, at the bookstore, in the train station, etcetera." I replied. "I just don't want to limit my creativity."

He looked at me suspiciously but agreed. "Okay we can go down to the HP store in an hour."

"Umm..." I said.

"Ummm what?"

"I was hoping for a Mac. It is more compatible with the phone you got me. You understand right?"

"Yeah sure. I guess." While we were in the Mac store Brandon, got distracted by a cute manager. I used that opportunity to ask the sales associate all the questions I needed to know.

"Hey handsome, can you help me?" I flirted.

"Sure ma'am, what do you need?"

"I am in the process of writing a book and I want to ensure the book's content, as well as the pictures, are hidden within the computer. Hidden from nosey people's view." I said. "Is that possible?"

"Yes ma'am, it is." He began downloading things to my new laptop and showing me how to use them. He also made it so you had to verify with my fingerprint and my iris to open it.

Satisfied with my login information and new software, I decided I was ready to go. Everything I needed was now complete and I understood how to use it.

"Thank you love! I greatly appreciate your help," I said.

"You are very welcome," he replied. "Also if you should need anything further here is my number. Don't hesitate to use it."

I flirtatiously took the number and said, "Will do," as I switched away from him. By the time I left the store Brandon's flirty ass brought me a brand new laptop, a cover for it, a case to put it in, a printer/ fax/ scanner, paper, the newest Windows software, as well as the Adobe Suite. I was ready to be on my best bullshit now.

“Thank you Brandon,” I said when we left.

“No problem. We all need a hobby”, he replied.

“You are right about that. I think I'm about to head on down to the waterfront and see what Pops is up to.” I replied excitedly.

As soon as we got home I started charging my laptop. Once it was fully charged, it was late at night. I decided to try again tomorrow. I took a long hot soothing bath. I sipped Moet and listened to my music. I felt calm and relaxed while my body experienced a sense of ease that it hadn't felt in the past few months -- which is a great thing since you need to clear your mind to be bad.

I got out the tub, soaking wet and walked down the stairs to grab my frozen grapes. “Oh shit... what the fuck are you doing Kelsi?!” Brandon yelled. “Why are you walking around the house fucking naked?”

I walked past him very sexily towards my room, not saying a word.

He snatched me by my forearm and said through clenched teeth, “Next time I have to say this, I won't. Don't walk through this house without respectable attire. Do you understand me?”

I slyly smiled and said, “What I understand is that its either here or Carter Senior's house. Do you think he's able to resist all of this? Well let's just hope he is for your sake.”

“What is wrong with you? That is your father,” Brandon said with a disgusted look.

“That is your father. We just share DNA.”

“Hey bruh what's taking you so... what he fuck?!” Brendan yelled.

"Get off of me!" I said while snatching my arm away. "I won't stay here if I got to fuck you." I sighed. "Just when I thought your ass was different."

"Bitch what?" Brandon said, advancing towards me.

Brendan pushed him back. "You have to be out of your mind if you think I'm going to buy that story. He knows we are all here in the basement. Why would he make a move on you now? And why are you walking around your brother's house naked?" Brendan asked.

"Is this your house?"

"Bitch don't question anybody in MY house. You just mad because your hoe card got pulled. It's something truly wrong with you," Brandon said.

"I am asking because clearly he doesn't know about you sneaking in my room at night. He doesn't know about you feasting on this goodness often. So who is he to question me?"

"You trick ass bitch. I don't give a fuck who questions you. You better put some clothes on before I drag your ass. Don't nobody want that trash ass pussy. To my understanding the whole crack house done had it. Fuck ass bitch!" Tasha said coming out of nowhere.

"Awwwwww what's wrong? You afraid he might want a sample. Them titties looking dried up... fuck you producing powder milk?" I said, chastising her.

"Bitch if I ever thought it, you wouldn't be breathing," Tasha replied.

I started laughing hysterically. "Good night lovely people." I ensured that my ass bounced with every step I took.

"Brendan let's go before I catch a case. Brandon you need to get your house back, this bitch is evil. What kind of woman knowingly entices her brothers?" Tasha asked.

"Hey y'all, don't leave," I heard Brandon say.

"You are more than welcome to come to our house," Tasha said.

He better not, I thought. I spiked his drink. He will die in transit.

"Yeah fam, I think I'm going to do that." Brandon replied.

Welp, it's his funeral, I thought. But I cannot lie, I was looking forward to getting me some of that dick tonight. Next thing I know, I heard the door slam. I decided to go to bed after that.

The next morning, I woke up well rested. I slept naked all night long. It felt so good. I ate bacon and eggs for breakfast with a glass of orange juice. After I got dressed I headed out.

I found myself in Union Station intrigued by the renovation. I spent a lot of my time here as a child. My grandmother worked for Amtrak. I decided to sit and build up the fake social media accounts necessary to help my goals. I posted a bunch of pictures of Buffy and a few random people. Then I went an added all of her friends to my new account saying the old one was hacked. I had so much fun playing with the site that I almost lost track of the plan. I had to get back to the shenanigans.

For three weeks, I impersonated her. She was completely unaware.

Our old boo popped up in my suggested friends. For a while he did not accept my friend request. But with some help of some provocative photos in his DM he came around. The message didn't hurt either:

> I brought some vibrating panties, and I'm sitting here at work controlling the speed wishing I were riding your dick again.

He added me instantly. “Is that right? You use to hate riding me,” he typed.

“That was then, let's talk about now.” I replied.

“What is different now?”

“That mouf work is different for starters. I have not had sex with anyone in a year or so. Need you to cum knock these walls down and remove these cobwebs.”

“My dick is getting hard talking to you.”

“Harder then it gets when Kelsi is talking to you?”

“Ughhh here we go. Why are you always in competition with her? You haven’t found a hobby yet? Damn.

“She has you and I want you. What am I supposed to do?

Then I tweeted and said: My friends tell me to leave him alone, but they aren’t the ones that loved him. Then I put a picture of us up and shared it on IG with the same caption.

He finally replied, “My wife of 10 years has me.”

“What?” I said. Not that I really cared -- I was only fucking with him to get back at Buffy’s boyfriend stealing ass.

“You were so focused on her and her on you that you never saw the real threat. Neither of you ghetto bitches can secure my wife position. I left you alone cuz all your mouth did was talk back. If that mouf sucking my dick humming on my balls and swallowing cum we could have still had something.”

“How do you say these things to me? I was nothing but good to you. I don’t deserve to be treated like this,” I said playing the part.

“You deserve whatever you allow.”

“I’m so hurt.” I replied. “I thought we had something.”

"I'm sure you had a lot of some things. Your ass probably lived in the clinic. Truthfully, you want an apology and you won't get one. You bitches don't want forever you want a Ken doll. Someone you can flaunt around and brag about what they do for you. You are just mad because I used you before you used me."

"I did want forever."

"A woman who wants forever will know when a man is otherwise engaged with another female. You didn't notice because it wasn't a concern of yours. You were good as long as it didn't interrupt you flow or your needs. You women are treacherous. You will step all over another woman's heart, disrespect her home, and yell 'I didn't say I do to her'. You didn't but what you don't understand is we did and we aren't losing our home, our family, or our money for temporary pussy. So when the wife find out about you... you are done. Respect your pussy and niggas like me won't come and run through that bitch."

I was hot. This nigga now was lowkey to be disrespectful. "You don't respect your wife any more than you claim I do. If you are so happy, then keep your dick at home. Her shit must be dry if you got to come out to play."

"I come out to play because real life is stressful. You have no expectations, so it's easier to relax with a bitch that don't want shit. My wife is at home talking about the future. I'm for it, but a nigga be needing a break. But if you think I come out for pussy you are lost. You are just easy, it takes no effort. Why not lol"

"This is too much. Keep your apology. You didn't deserve me."

"I'm sure that was supposed to be a negative thing, however I'm glad about that. You are weak and this discussion solidifies that."

"No, you mad because while you were fucking us, your wife was fucking your best friend. Yeah, the wife that I have always known about. Oh and she knew about us too, she asked me to keep you busy and I did. The gag is she has no gag reflex. She swallows. You done tasted your best friends kids with your gay ass."

"BITCH when I see you on site you are dead."

"Nigga talk to me with lowercase letters until you can backup all that aggression. All I had to do was call you daddy and you came in seconds. Hell I should DM your wife and see if she will give me Joe's number. I heard he could go a few rounds. I heard he got that TAPOUT!!!" I typed vehemently.

"I use to choke you with this nine."

"You must be referring to that 9-5 because I know you are not talking about that dick size. That would be like nine minus five, and how you going to choke me with that?" I laughed with emojis.

I blocked his dumb ass. Buffy should be thanking me. I actually did her a solid. And guess what his homo ass did? He made a fake page to stalk my fake page. This nigga is crazy. But I'm crazier. Y'all know I screenshotted all those messages, added his wife and all of their friends to my profile. I posted the screen shots and a caption that said, "here's a real look back at it type of situation" and tagged her profile with it.

She tried to inbox me but I screenshotted that and posted it with a caption that said, "he knows sis, no more private, behind the doors conversation. Oh and Kelsi said that pussy is sweet, keep sucking pineapples."

She blew up, then he blew up. I'm like when y'all going to yell at each other. Typical FUCKUATIONSHIP -- they'd rather fight the innocent fuck buddy then the cheating spouse. Well time is up. I saw my target, no more time for social media. Real life action is underway.

TIA

Donna called me saying something about a detective who was interviewing Marie. I knew that bitch was a snake. I went ahead and fed into the bullshit just to see what they knew.

“So what happened?” I asked while watching Malaysia go in the house.

“Girl, I don’t know. I just heard her asking about if she knew you were pregnant and what happened to the baby.” Donna said over the phone.

“I'm tired of saying this -- the baby was a stillborn.” I replied.

“Girl, I know, but I think after you read Marie ass she lied and told them some bullshit.” Now I know for sure that this girl is messy. Why would she throw her friend under the bus like that? Then I started thinking that she probably with the feds right now. Let me hang up before she has my ass in jail.

“Alright girl, I gotta go.” I said, just to test the waters.

“Wait you know Misty is pregnant, right?” Donna asked.

Yup she was a rat, not Marie. I hung up and threw the phone in the Potomac while driving back to my hideout. I made mental note to pay that bitch a visit.

At 2am, after I collected all of my tools and changed into my get away attire, I headed back out to Malaysia’s house. I broke in the back door. No one saw or heard me come in. I headed upstairs and looked around. First I woke up Alaysia. I put the gun to her head and told her to keep quiet or the thump will be what wakes her mother up. I took her downstairs, tied her up, and went back upstairs. Shortly after, I returned with Malaysia. I tied her ass up, too.

"Hello family," I said.

They both looked at me very confused. "Well, you stole my man, bitch, and hoe your ass is the reason he didn't want our child," I informed them both.

"Who is your man?" Malaysia asked nervously.

"Apparently, your man. I went to the jail to visit my baby and they rejected my visit because you bitches were there."

"Look, you can have him. I was at the jail asking for a divorce and letting his daughter say bye. I use to be a loving and faithful wife to him but he kept cheating on me -- he was never there for our daughter and I'm..." she hesitated to say.

"You are what, you lying bitch?" I said calmly.

"I'm pregnant."

"Oh! So they can cut my baby out of my stomach and kidnap her, and you can birth his second child?" I yelled. I was completely confused.

"It's not his baby, though." Her head lowered in shame.

"Bitch, you will say anything."

"Look, over on the table the divorce papers are right there. See for yourself; I'm not lying."

I did as she told me. Lo and behold, the divorce papers were right there signed. Clearly, he loved me and not her. He signed the papers. I thought about letting them go but they had seen my face. There was no turning back. I shot both of them in the dome. I'm sure they died instantly. Good for them, because I was about to have some real fun with these bitches.

What do you do with a broken heart? Simple -- you break shit. The next day I went through the whole process only to be put at a computer screen to talk to him. *What the fuck is this?* I thought. Later after that, he just picked up the receiver.

"Hey baby," I said

"Hey," he replied dryly.

"I got your letter. I have been looking for you. I was so worried."

"I sent that to you by mistake, it was for someone else. But yea. I'm good."

"Are you sure? Do you need anything?"

"I need my sanity."

"Me too," I replied, putting my head down.

"What's up with the baby? Your stomach jive flat." He was unusually observant.

"It's not a worry anymore," I said truthfully.

He perked up and said, "Good."

"Hey did you slide through here the other day? A guard said they denied one of my visitors."

"Nah. It wasn't me, I just found out where you were."

"Oh okay, I was on lockdown anyway for punching a nigga teeth out. He wanted my damn Ramen... had a real nigga confused."

"I can buy you more, you want anything else?"

"Bae just send me some entertainment in a word form. A nigga need company up in here."

"Say less, I'm here for you."

"I know you're the only one I can count on," he said. "I thought I had two other riders, but they done jumped ship on a nigga."

"That ship sank last night."

He looked at me confused but responded with, "Say less."

The visit was filled with small talk and dirty hypotheticals. I was just enjoying him being here with me. I was sick in love with the dick and the man. His hand cannot do what my warm pussy can. I was all prepared to pay the guard for a few minutes with him in the bathroom. Shit, I would suck the guard's dick if he guaranteed me some time with my love.

"Five minutes," the guard called out.

A lot of people started filling out. I waited until the last second of the last minute. Then, I sent him $100 via Western Union. I knew he would be glad. I just had to do what I had to do until my baby was back home again and safe with me.

"Whatever daddy wants, daddy gets," I said out loud.

I decided to become an escort by day and nurse by night. Of course that nosey ass detective found me. It was a quick conversation.

"Hello Tia. I am Detective Ho. I have been looking for you."

"Keep looking," I said.

"Well I do have just a few questions," she replied cheerfully.

"I do not care if you had a half of a question or a whole. I don't have shit for you," I said.

"Did you kill your baby or did you sell it on the black market?" Detective Ho asked.

"Did you charge me?"

"No. Should I?"

"You are smart enough to know that without meeting your burden of proof there is no discussion," I replied.

"I have the burden of proof," she said.

"Then charge me," I said. "Go ahead and arrest me right now." I was calling her bluff.

"Why? I'm just here to ask you questions."

"Call my lawyer when you find a body or something concrete and not a moment before," I said.

"Ms. Wells, you do realize you said 'when,' right?"

"I also said contact my lawyer. I do believe that that means we are done here. That is, unless you want to read me my Miranda rights."

She looked at me menacingly. "I'll be back."

"Hopefully with an arrest warrant and not another round of 21 questions," I replied sarcastically.

"You need to watch who you are talking to," she replied.

"You are right. Talking to twelve can prove to be very detrimental to my health. The way y'all are out here murdering innocent Black people. I'd hate to be the next victim. If you don't mind," I said excusing myself.

"I do mind," she replied.

"And I'm in fear of my life. You are harassing me and your hand hasn't left the butt of that gun since you've been standing here." I yelled down the hall, "If I go to jail, I did not commit suicide."

"Cute. You might want to be more polite next time." I walked off with my hands up in case her trigger finger got happy.

Without turning around or dropping my arms I stuck my middle fingers up in the air and said, "You might want to be more prepared next time Ho -- I mean, Detective Ho. Who is your pimp -- I mean partner? Never mind, keep his ass away from me too. I have not heard from her since our girl talk. Well, I must not be your speed."

The nerve of these bitches. Nothing gets my heart but the nigga whose dick I'm riding. I quit the escort service before I could even get started. My baby put in a request for me to handle his cellmate's co-defendant. Basically, his cellmate's baby mother. That pillow talk is the real killer. Six bodies later, we were both paid. I was ready and willing to do whatever for my man. While I was watching the news they nicknamed me Lullaby Barbie. I just rocked them bitches to sleep. The news said they suspected some type of gang wars occurring, I didn't care what they thought as long as they stayed out of my way.

At work I started bonding with a girl in the morgue. The things I learned from her would scare the devil. That bitch is crazy. I started taking her on hits with me. The first time she went in, she sawed a girls leg off from the kneecap. We've been working as friends. The bitch had a few loose screws. I liked it.

One night after we took care of this snitch bitch Ava, my new buddy went home with me. We started watching Netflix waiting for our pizza. The next thing I know this bitch picked my ass up, sat me on the counter, and started giving me head. She ate me out like I've never been eaten out before. She put her fingers in my anus and pressed down in my vaginal hole. She turned my body around and ate my ass.

Now I've never been into girls, but this girl got my mind blown. I was letting her play with my juicy pussy. My head fell back and she pulled out a massive strap. I swear I thought that was a gun in her pants. She jammed it in my mouth and I gladly deep throated it. She said, "Come ride me ma." I did as I was told. I jumped down right on her penis. I ride her to the beat of sex room. She started to moan, I started to yell. Oh my God. That shit felt so good. Fuck how we get here, but I'm here and I'm for it. I almost told this bitch I loved her sadistic ass, but the bitch won't keep me. She better bring that King Kong dick before that happened. I started my speed fuck. That bitch couldn't hang. She and I both came all over the place. She pulled my pussy right on her face. *I need you like twice a week*, I thought. I moaned out in pleasure, too.

TASHA

If that bitch Kelsi didn't have me fucked up, I don't know who did. Her sick ass wants to fuck her brothers. I told Brendan let's go. I was done talking at that point, and he knew it too.

"Man, thanks for getting me out of that house. Something is off in that girls head," Brandon said. "Get this. She said if I put her out she is going to move in with Pops. She even went as far as to say he would not be able to resist her good pussy."

"Man something is really wrong with this bitch. Who wants to fuck their brother or father?" Brendan's tone revealed his disgust.

"Oh hell no. Did you tell Carter Senior?" I asked.

"I'd rather not. He is so happy to finally be able to get to know them... finally able to tell them his side." Brandon said as he shook his head.

"Well getting to know them means just what you said -- getting to know them. He can't meet a fake person. You need to tell him what this monster is all about," I replied.

"I'm just not sure now is a good time to speak on it," Brandon said.

Brendan chimed in, "Yeah I have to agree with Tasha. Dad is a strong man but he is still a man."

"I'll get to it, but give me some time. This shit isn't easy," Brandon confessed.

"It never is." I said, understanding his dilemma.

"I'm thinking about renting her a place and paying her rent for a year or two," Brandon said.

“As much as I dislike her, I think that is a good idea. It gets her away from both of you. It's like killing two birds with one stone,” I said. “I'll help you decorate. She can have my old furniture, and Brendan, you can put groceries in the refrigerator.”

“It’s not a problem either way, but I’m going to go ahead and pay two years of rent to keep that bitch gone. Sorry to call her that, but she is sick as fuck and she needs to be far away from me and Pops.” Brandon said.

“My thoughts exactly,” I said.

The next morning, we all got up went to Denny’s to eat, and started apartment shopping. Place after place we turned down. I really couldn’t believe how picky these dudes were.

“Can y’all just decide already?” I asked. “The next one better be the one or I am taking an Uber home,” I said.

“Awww baby, be patient. We need a nice place or she won’t go.” Brendan laughed.

“She better take what you give her. It's free for the next four years,” I said annoyed.

“Let's ensure she does. Once it’s done, it’s done.” Brandon said.

“She’s not going to be happy with anything that she didn’t pick out,” I said.

“You know what, you’re right! Tasha you should go get her and let her pick out a place,” Brandon suggested.

“Uh no. I’m good. I cannot deal with her or her disrespectful behavior,” I said, growing agitated. I’m not doing it.”

“How about a realtor?” Brendan suggested.

“That’s your best bet.” I pointed off in their direction.

“You are so stubborn woman,” Brandon joked.

"I'm not, but seriously. That girl is off!" I laughed back.

"If you are scared, just say you are scared." Brandon said.

"Boy, go away." I jokingly replied. "You should be scared, not me."

"Oh, don't get it twisted. I'm definitely scared. That girl is playing mental wars and her unstable ass does not have a sense of logic." Brendan spoke in a serious tone.

"You are right about that," I said. "Drop me off at home please. Princess Anika's bus will be home shortly."

"Oh yeah, no problem baby." Brendan replied. "I didn't realize it was this late."

"No worries," I replied.

Two hours later, Anika was running up to me from her bus. "Mommy," she yelled. "I knew all of my sight words today! All of them!"

"You did? You don't say!" I encouraged her.

"Yes I did. My teacher said I'm very smart," she replied.

"Yes you are." I waved to the bus driver and we walked toward the house.

"I know mommy, but is it okay for my teacher to make an observation?" Anika asked.

"Yes, observations are good." I said laughing. "Where are you getting these words?"

"My teacher, mom." She said it as if it were obvious.

"I got up and went to play with Liza and my teacher called me. I said, 'Yes, Mrs. Lewis.' She said while reading over my observations from last week's group activity, she noticed that I chose Liza as my partner. I said, 'That's nice Mrs. Lewis.' She said why? And I said why, what? And she asked me why I only play and work with Liza! I told her, because I like Liza and she's my friend. Then I asked Mrs. Lewis before she could make me play with one of the other kids, why do you use words like observation when I don't know what it means? And then she said because I know you are smart enough to ask what it means. And then I said okay Mrs. Lewis, I will play your silly game. And then... um... and then I asked her what does observation mean. Then you know what she said to me?"

"No, baby. What did she say?"

"She said I am not telling you!"

"What? I can't believe it!" I said as I put on my best shocked imitation.

"Yes, mommy. So I said okay Mrs. Lewis. And when I got on the bus I asked Mr. Poor what the word observation means and he said I guess in these simplest form it's something you noticed or saw for a period time. So now I know what observation means. And when I get to school tomorrow, I'm going to tell Mrs. Lewis I made an observation as well. And I saw you wear the same dress twice last week, but the second time you put on a sweater."

"Girl, you better not say that," I replied, trying not to laugh.

"I should say that because it's true, mommy." Anika said.

"Baby, some things you just don't say and that is one of them Anika," I said sternly. "That's not nice."

"Ok mommy. I learned that we used to be slaves today at school. Why didn't you tell me? I had no idea," Anika said, holding her chest.

I almost choked on my soda. I quickly recovered though. "Ummmm what exactly did they tell you slaves are?" I asked.

"Unpaid workers, mommy. You didn't know that?" Anika asked.

“Baby, they are really watering down history. Why tell you if they are not going to tell you?” I said sadly.

“Well you will tell me right?” Anika asked.

“Yes, we will expound on the true meaning and history of slavery this weekend,” I replied.

“Okay mommy,” Anika said.

CALLIE

I had not seen anything on the news about a missing baby and/or a dead mother. I took my baby from that woman's womb, but it's too late for tears. I see everyone looking and inspecting her, but Braylin has not once questioned her. She is beautiful, I swear she is. She is so damn dark and chocolate. That glow is everything. I guess she really didn't want her or maybe she was going to try to blackmail me later. I'm not sure and I don't care as long as Braylin never finds out. I'll go to war for baby girl.

"Hey," Braylin said, scaring the shit out of me.

"I'm sorry. I didn't mean to scare you," he said apologetically.

"Oh no, I was just in my own world," I replied. Truthfully, I had been jumpy and on my toes since the rape. I still haven't told Braylin about my shame. I thought I could deal with it and handle it on my own. Hopefully I could.

"Did you make dinner?"

"No, I'm tired. I can make something quick, though."

"Don't worry, I'll cook. Get some rest." He kissed me on the forehead.

"Thank you baby," I replied very gratefully. I ended up drifting off to sleep in the rocking chair while watching my angel sleep.

I had nightmares of someone with a painted face holding me down and forcing himself inside of my virgin anus. He heard me screaming in silence but he didn't care. He told me how good it felt to him. The blood intrigued him and he pounded harder and harder while the other guy held me in place. I fought, but I was no match against their strength. I kept pleading, it was in my eyes but they were soulless and didn't care. My baby griped in anger as and fought through my stomach to protect me, but again, they didn't care. Pump after pump. The humiliation was embedded in my pride. The one that was pumping ferociously at my anus stood up and put his foot on my face while jerking off all over my body. The other laughed and said, "she's really enjoying this Don."

"Don?!" I yelled.

"What about Don?" Braylin asked.

"Nothing. I think I forgot to mention to Don about an event this weekend." I replied anxiously.

"Oh," he said, looking at me with side eyes. "Well dinner is ready. Why don't you freshen up and come downstairs when you are ready."

"I will as soon as I change Brynn." I replied, smiling.

"Let her sleep," he replied.

"No. She will get a diaper rash."

"Okay." He gave up with no fight at all.

For some strange reason, I was about to text Apple, but I caught myself. He was the enemy now and that was not to be debated.

"Baby on second thought, this cannot wait. I need to swing past the club. I will be back shortly," I said, moving like it was a big deal.

"But I made dinner," he said in a low tone.

"I'm sorry, but we can eat when I get back or you can go ahead and eat now."

"But it's ready now. Let's eat first and then you can go to the club."

"Baby it would be unprofessional for me to not handle business first. I thought you knew and understood how essential my organization is to me. Things happen that need immediate attention I said. I made a mistake and I need to go fix it before it develops into a bigger problem," I said.

"I do understand. I will wait up for you." He replied.

As I was driving I kept asking myself how I didn't know Don was there. I knew him. I know his face. I was so preoccupied that I didn't notice the face under the low worn hat. I walked in and sat in my office. Don didn't know I knew it was him because I kept going in and out of consciousness. Speak of the devil.

"Hey boss lady, what are you doing here?"

As uncomfortable as it was, I fought through it.

"Just reviewing the books."

"I thought you do that at the end of the month," he further inquired.

"Normally. But the baby would not give me any peace, so I used this as an escape," I lied.

"Been there plenty of times." He replied before walking away.

Oh he was confident. *He just knew he had covered his tracks,* I thought to myself. I knew this was they type of job I had to do alone. No witnesses necessary. This was going to be a slow satisfying fuck with no lubrication. It helped a lot that I knew my attacker not because I felt better, but because I knew who to not be relaxed around. Two people close to me hurt me and both harbored duplicitous intentions from the start. If I had my way, this one was going to suffer and he wasn't going to enjoy any of it.

"Hey baby, I'm home," I said walking in the door.

"Oh hey. That was fast," Braylin confessed.

"I told you. I just needed to delegate some tasks while disseminating some pertinent information. Then back home to bae." I said very flirty.

"Oh is that right?" He walked towards me.

"Yes baby, that is absolutely right."

He wrapped his arms around me and leaned in for a passionate kiss -- which I happily accommodated him with. After that, clothes flew every fucking where. I dropped down to my knees and sucked his dick. When I pulled his dick into my mouth with my jaw muscles, he quickly backed up. I said, "Uh uh daddy, bring that dick here. Baby you taste so good," I moaned. No doubt he was running. It was very amusing. I can't lie it boosted my ego way up.

"Slow down girl, it's been a while," Braylin said.

"If it goes down, I'll get it back up. No worries", I said as my tongue circled his balls.

"At least bend over and let me cum inside of you," Braylin suggested.

I bent over the couch propped one leg up and leaned forward so he could hit it from behind. He started pumping and images of my attack popped up. I pushed through though. I even threw a few 'yes daddys' in and a 'damn, oh my goodness I'm about to cum.' Right there he busted all in me.

He collapsed on the couch. I went to the washroom, put hot water on a cloth, and returned to lay it across his penis. I said, "Keep calm daddy, I will go make your plate." I sat there for like two more seconds and I was off to make his plate. I knew he felt more relaxed.

As soon as I got in the kitchen, Braylin ran up, picked me up, pinned me against the wall, and started eating dessert. I moaned out loudly. It felt so good, and there was no faking that. I felt awkward -- like he was sucking another mans cum out if me. It did not matter how many showers I took, I just never felt clean or pure. I felt dirty and touched. But I leaned against the wall and did everything in my power to enjoy this feeling. With a lot of work and focus, I finally came all over his face. He slid me down right on his dick and bounced me up and down and down. Now this I enjoyed and had not one flashback, I was fully in tune with my husband. I threw my head back and grinded into him. He sucked on my nipples and gently nibbled at them. I dropped my head back as he sucked his way up to my neck. I started bouncing on his dick and then it got a bit aggressive. He flipped me over and ripped my shirt all the way off. He entered me from behind and pulled my hair back towards him. "Daddy stop." He said, "No now, don't you run". He picked one of my legs up and placed it on the counter as he forced me to lay over it. The other heel was still on the floor begging to be free. He entered me and with each thrust he yanked my hair towards my ass. I was leaking juices all over the counter while I enjoyed my husband having his way with me. "Yes daddy, right there, don't stop!" He sped up his pace and fucked me with all long strokes. My body went insane. I was cuming all over his dick in seconds. But he wasn't ready, he was still going. He knocked on my g-spot done and then bust that bitch down. I was screaming so loud in ecstasy. He heard nothing but "go harder" because that's exactly what he did. Finally, he bust all inside of me.

"Baby it seems like you were waiting for me," Braylin said.

"More like feinin'." I replied.

"Let me know next time. No need to fein'," he said. "I figured you would let me know when you were ready."

"I was just afraid the kitty lost her elasticity. I was in no rush," I said covering up the truth, with a partial truth.

"That thang felt tighter than before." He confessed.

"Really?" I was kinda shocked.

"Really."

"Braylin, I love you so much. Thank you for being so patient with me."

"Baby, I will be whatever you need me to be, whenever you need me to be it," he said.

We cuddled and fell asleep. We never did eat dinner that night. Well, we ate, but not what was prepared.

That morning, I woke up and immediately started brainstorming a plan to get the one that got me. First, he was going to suffer. Lastly, he was going to die. In that order. Those two things were not up for debate.

"Hey. Good morning beautiful," Braylin greeted me.

"Mmmm, good morning handsome." I purred at him.

"How was your sleep?"

"Blissful," I replied. "I need to go check on Brynn because she did not wake up not once through the night."

"Alright. Well actually, let me go check on her because I just want you to sit back and relax," he said stopping me.

"Okay baby, whatever you say." I laughed. I was really grateful because that gave me more time to focus on the plan. Soon enough, Braylin came back downstairs with a happy, giggling Brynn.

"What was she doing?" I asked, immediately obsessed with her smile.

"Playing with her toes." He nonchalantly hunched his shoulders.

"Why was she so quiet?" I asked to no one in particular.

"Callie before I yell.... I mean you yell... I love you," he said.

"What?" I asked, growing alarmed.

"I forgot to replace the batteries in her baby monitor," he said.

I calmed down and said, "Oh okay, try to replace them today please. Can you make her a bottle?"

He looked at me confused. "Why aren't you breastfeeding her? Bottles are for when we go out, remember?"

"Ahhhh yes. I am sorry I just have a lot on my mind," I replied.

"I know baby," he said sympathetically.

I popped out my right breast and Brynn went to town. I thought it was cute how she squeezed each side of them like it would push more milk into her fat cheeks. She also wiggled her little toes. It was adorable. Some days, I would stare at her searching for Braylin's features and I never found any. It broke my heart every time. *She's carrying around another man and woman's face*, I thought. But back to planning. I thought long and hard. I bounced ideas around all day. I think I finally decided on what to do. I wasn't going to write anything down because no evidence is the best evidence. Part A of my plan is going to be implemented asap.

Two Weeks Later

I was sitting at my desk in the club when Tracy bust in. "Oh my God, Duchess did you hear?"

"Hear what?" I asked anxiously.

"Last week, Don's mother got killed in a hit and run accident. He and the cops suspected a drunk driver. They buried her yesterday."

"What?"

"Girl yes!"

"Why didn't anyone call me?"

"Don didn't even tell me until Sunday night. When I asked if he told you, he said he did not want to be treated different and was not ready for people to know."

"I AM NOT PEOPLE! I replied, offended.

"I know, but I respected his wishes. It was a private funeral. No one was invited."

"That's so sad."

"No, but wait. Girl, somebody gave his daughter soy milk and she is allergic to soy. No one knew what was happening. Needless to say she ended up dying right there on the spot. She never had a chance. That baby was only six years old." Tracy said sympathetically. I just gasped for air and held my chest.

"Don is a wretch. This is two back-to-back deaths."

"This is just tragic." I finally replied.

"Who are you telling? Damn." Tracy cosigned.

"I'm just wondering why he did not tell me."

"I don't know. I saw the report about Asia on the news. It broke my heart when it said she was holding her chest. The camp did not even know she had allergies."

"Yeah I did not know either. That explains why he never ate carry out though."

"You are right, he didn't. I never noticed that," Tracy confessed.

"I just assumed he saw them fry a rat."

"Are you going to call?" Tracy asked.

"No, it seems like he doesn't want me to know." I pretended to be sad.

"I am sure he is just trying to cope," she replied before walking out. I just let her go. He didn't tell me because he knew what he did. He may not have known I knew, but I am sure he thought it was karma for him hurting me so he decided not to tell me. *Guilty behavior*, I thought.

I got home in the wee hours of the morning. Braylin was still awake with Brynn fast asleep in her playpen.

"Hey baby, I did not expect you to be awake," I said.

"Me either," he replied. "Just trying to finish these briefs before the weekend."

"You work so hard for us baby. I love you so much for that," I said lovingly.

"Anything for you baby," he replied with a sleepy smile.

"I am going to go take a bath and come back down to grab Brynn and put her in her bed," I said.

"Okay baby," Braylin replied.

I ran my bath, dropped in a bath bomb and undressed. I stared at myself in the mirror for a while. I no longer had the admiration I once had when I looked in the mirror. My pride was gone, my strength was stripped, and my heart was hardened. I just did not see myself anymore. I turned off the water and got in the water that felt so soothing to my body. I just relaxed and shed a few tears for my baby girl that didn't make it. I soon fell asleep.

I was awaken to someone lifting me out of the water. I immediately started fighting. I was throwing punches and kicks like my life depended on it. The person dropped me and I started throwing whatever was in reach. A glass bowl hit him upside his head and heard him cry out in pain asking why I was attacking him. Then, I came to I realize that I had beat up and attacked my husband. There was blood everywhere. I ran to him. All I could say was, ‘I’m sorry baby. I don’t know what came over me.”

He called Brandon over to give him stitches. When Brandon arrived he looked at me and then back at Braylin and said, “What happened here?”

“Nothing man it was an accident,” Braylin said.

“What the fuck? Are you a battered woman? Nigga I am not stupid. Do not insult my intelligence,” Brandon fussed.

I just walked off and went upstairs. I was too tired to defend myself. Braylin came up behind me and said, “Baby, do not worry about him. He doesn't mean any harm.”

“Braylin you are gushing blood everywhere, go get stitched up. It is fine. I truly apologize.”

“I forgive you. I know you would never intentionally hurt me,” he said.

“Thank you baby,” I replied. He sat there until I drifted off to sleep. I woke up when I heard Brandon say, “It sounds like the actions that rape victims exhibit after being assaulted.”

“Nah, I would know if my wife were raped.”

“Braylin, that baby looks nothing like you, she won’t have sex with you, and she is fighting you when you try to carry her to bed. That’s not normal,” Brandon pushed. “I think she was raped.”

“Man that is my baby and my wife was not raped. What are you saying?” he yelled. “This was just an accident.”

“No, it was domestic violence. She needs help if she's not going to tell you about it,” Brandon replied.

“I should have just gone to the ER.” Braylin said angrily.

“And tell them what? That you ran into a wall Braylin?” Brandon shook his head.

"I can't with you. You are beyond facetious." Braylin countered.

Just then, Brynn started crying.

"Go get the baby, but swab her later. I guarantee you are not the father. You just cannot handle the truth. The lie is more beautiful, that is probably why she did not tell you." Brandon retorted.

I got up came downstairs, grabbed the baby, and walked off.

"Dammit man, she might have heard you." Braylin scolded Brandon.

"That's the least of your concerns," Brandon replied while finishing up the stitches in Braylin's head.

I head Brandon say just above a whisper, "Put your pride to the side and make sure your woman is okay."

Then I heard the front door open and close. Braylin never came upstairs that night, and he was not there in the morning when I came down to make breakfast. He must feel disgusted with me too. I broke down on the floor crying.

"Baby what is wrong?" Braylin said, scaring the shit out of me.

He jumped behind a wall. His reaction hurt me. He was afraid of me now. I felt like scum.

"You don't want me anymore," I said still crying.

"Why would you think that?"

"You weren't here when I woke up this morning."

"I was asleep in my office. I couldn't sleep, so I kept working on my briefs. I must have fallen asleep there." I cried harder. I cannot explain it, but when the tears started I could not stop them. It was like opening the floodgates.

"Baby tell me," Braylin said. "I know you heard Brandon last night. Is he right?"

I just broke down and told him everything. I never told him about the nurse, me stalking her or taking the baby. I told him the rape happened right around the time I got pregnant. I explained to him that I thought that I had a miscarriage with the baby the day I got raped but I was not sure because I had never had one. I told him that when I finally went to the doctors they told me I was pregnant. I just assumed I was wrong.

He looked at me so hurt. He said, “Why didn’t you tell me. I could have helped you. We have the guy’s DNA.” We could run a match for it in the system.

I said, “I don’t know who hurt me and I never want to find out. For all of our sake, just drop it. Please.”

He shook his head up and down and said, “Okay, I understand. I just want you to agree to get help and we will figure out the rest from there. Brynn is my daughter no matter what a DNA test says, don’t ever question that.”

“I won’t,” I said, happy I got the weights off of my shoulders and he bought the lie. This buys me some time to work out the kink. I know he loves me, but I also know he believes in the law. Hell, his whole career is built off of it.

DON

Shit has really hit the fan. I am a shell of my old self. I lost my mom and my daughter within days of each other. My wife has broken down completely. She cannot even say our daughter's name. I felt like shit. The calls keep coming in, followed by flowers and sympathy cards. I am just fucked up right now.

"This is Asia's favorite doll. She is going to be scared without her doll," Amour said.

I was shocked because she said Asia's name. "I'll get it to her baby," I said, reaching for the doll.

"No, I have to give it to her!" She yelled, snatching the doll away from my reach.

"Okay." I was caught off guard by her reaction.

"I just need to give it to her." She said, slowly calming down.

"I understand baby," I replied. "I am going to go for a walk. I feel like I am suffocating."

"It's better than feeling dead inside," she said before turning and walking away.

I had no response. I just walked out of the door. I had to fix it, but I did not know how. I was too broken myself. I walked for hours. My daughter's funeral is tomorrow and I needed to pull it together for Amour's sake, as well as my own. When I returned home, Amour was not there. I do not know where she could be at this hour. *It was 1 am, maybe she went to her mother's house*, I thought. I walked to the back of the house and I noticed the back door open. Of course she went outside. I walked out back and I did not see her. Just as I was about to turn around and go back inside, I heard moaning coming from the shed. I instantly got angry. I was going to kill this bitch if this was she in my motherfucking shed fucking another nigga and my daughter is not even in the grave yet.

"Bitch, I'm about to kill you and whoever is in here with you!" I said storming in the shed and turning the lights on. But instead of seeing her fucking a nigga, she was tied up like a bull. Her feet and hands were tied together behind her back. It was blood everywhere. "What the fuck happened?" I yelled racing to her aid.

It was blood everywhere. I called an ambulance immediately. By the time they got her to the hospital, I was damn near about to beat up the doctor. He took her back to the operating room. It seemed like an eternity went by. When he finally came out to talk to me he had two detectives with him. They were asking me all types of questions, none of which I heard.

"Doctor what is wrong with my wife?"

"That is what we would like to know," Detective Smith said.

"Nigga fuck you. Bitch investigate and stop looking for me to do your job!" I snapped.

The doctor intervened, "Amour was brutally attacked with some sort of foreign object. She has three broken ribs, two black eyes, and her anus has been ripped open."

"What?" I said collapsing to the floor. "Who would do that? Our daughter's funeral is tomorrow. Will she be able to attend?"

"Unfortunately, I will not know until tomorrow." The doctor replied.

"Can I see her?"

"She's out cold and will not come to until at least until tomorrow," he said. "Is it possible to postpone the funeral?" He was genuinely concerned.

"The funeral is only a few hours away. It is at 9am. It's 4:45am right now. I just don't see how," I said, finally defeated. The doctor and the detectives walked away after that, but not before the detective gave me his card to call him once things died down.

I contacted the funeral home and told them what had happened. They allowed our family to view the body but held off on burying her a few days to give my wife, her mother, a chance to say goodbye. I lost my lunch when I saw the doll in the casket. The very doll my wife would not let me touch. So I knew damn well she did not let anyone else touch it, either. Her attacker was here or had been here. I was on guard. No one looked out of the ordinary. I tried to focus on my bae, but my attention kept getting divided.

When everyone finally exited the church, I asked the directors about the doll. They said a little girl had dropped it off and they claimed the mother wanted it buried with her daughter.

I was even more confused. *Who was the little girl?* I asked myself. I went ahead and headed back to the hospital. I went to my wife's room but it was empty.

"Excuse me?" I said to the nurse.

"Yes sir, how can I help you?" She replied.

"Do you know what happened to the women who were in here this morning?"

"No sir, I do not. I just came on shift," she replied.

"Okay, well is there someone that I could talk to that would know? Or is there some paperwork you could check?"

"Sir that is not protocol."

"My wife was in this room and now she is not and I am just trying to find her. What is the protocol?"

"Sir, standby and I will find someone that can possibly assist you."

"Don't find someone that can possibly assist me, find someone that can assist me," I said sternly.

She looked at me sideways and walked off. *What the hell was that about*, I asked myself.

Forty-five minutes later, I was still sitting in the same spot and no one had come to talk to me. I got up and walked back to the nurse's station. "Excuse me, I have been waiting for forty-five minutes for someone to tell me my wife's whereabouts or her location." I said.

"She has been moved to protective custody," the nurse responded.

"Oh thank God." I said, relieved. "When can I see her?"

"Sir, she is in protective custody. No one is allowed to see her," the nurse nonchalantly said as she reviewed documents.

"What do you mean no one? I am not no one, I am her husband," I said.

"Sir, at this point you could be God's most trusted source and we still couldn't give you any information."

"This is not the time to try my humor," I replied. "I need to see my wife."

"Sorry sir, I can't help you," she replied.

"Well, when the fuck was y'all going to say something?" I asked frustrated.

"Sir we would have come to you when we had a moment. Please watch your mouth," the nurse requested.

"Bitch who are you talking to? I am a grown man whose mother died, daughter just died, and my wife is in the hospital. Be happy that's all I said." I walked off. Saying it out loud just hurt even more. I cannot figure out how all of this happened to me.

I almost went to the club, but I was too broken to go. I talked to Tracy once or twice about everything, but no one knew outside of her what was going on. She wanted to tell Duchess, but my wife always hated Duchess and I didn't want her to come offer help or support and shit end up hitting the fan. I decided it would just be best to tell her later. Duchess and I were close and I felt bad to not tell her, but if Amour found out she was helping in anyway -- especially for our daughter -- she would never forgive me. I never knew why Amour was jealous of Duchess, but I figured they knew something that I did not. I just dropped it. The money was good, so I continued to work there but never have I ever wanted or looked at Duchess in a provocative way. I kind of wish Amour was more driven like Duchess, but I kept that to myself.

As I was walking in the house, I hear someone say "so I guess calling your big bro back is too much to fucking ask for." I knew the voice instantly. I tried very hard to stay clear of this guy. We use to be close, inseparable even, but now we are more like oil and vinegar.

"I got bigger things on my mind than returning phone calls," I replied.

"I have been trying to reach ma. Funny thing is she is not answering either. I guess both of y'all are traitors."

"Traitors... wow. The only time you call me is when you need something and the only time you call our mother is when you need shelter. So it sounds like you need both right now, am I right?"

"Oh you think you have me pegged don't you?"

"Am I right?"

"Nigga, fuck you. We are not that much different. We use to do the same shit."

"There's an emphasis on the 'USE TO' part."

"It was not that long ago, bro."

"Look, I don't have time for this. So state your business or move along because I don't have anything for you," I replied.

"I came to see if you could help me find a job," he said.

"Nah bruh, I got bigger fish to fry. Can't add that to my pallet right now. Fill out some applications, drop them off, and see what bites. You know the process."

"Man, I knew you wouldn't help." he said. "Where is ma?"

"She cannot help you," I replied.

"Fuck you. If you do not want to help me, don't. I don't need your sadity ass. Fuck you and the horse you rode in on."

I chuckled and started walking away. "Your mother resides at 1801 E Street SE."

"When the fuck did she move?" he yelled.

"When she got tired of her miscreant son embarrassing her and tarnishing her legacy," I replied.

Our mother was one of the first Black women to join World War 1. She was never respected or honored for that. Back in 1918, things were a lot different, color still defined class. She never allowed that to get to her. She used to teach us all about the revolution and the Black Panther Party. She was so moved by Assata Shakur and her strength. She used to tell us about everything that instilled pride in our culture. She said the thugs on the corner were brainwashed into killing their own people instead of preparing and protecting our brand, our history, and our influence. She said the White man would steal our color, pride, and strength if he thought he could get credit and collateral for it. Authorities called my mother an extremist and for years we were so embarrassed by it. But now I know better. They were trying to wage war amongst us and encourage self-hatred. What she taught people went against that. It modeled unity and power.

My brother and I used to resent her because we wanted to be like everyone else. Conformists are what she would call us, but she refused to allow us to be so. We eventually turned to a life of crime to spite her. She would get out of bed in the wee hours of the morning and walk the streets to find us after we snuck out to hang on the corners. I started laughing to myself. We use to think she was nuts for yelling, 'No devil, the streets cannot have my sons.' Embarrassed, we would just go home. When I was fifteen, the cops arrested me because I looked "suspicious." They beat me so bad that I was in the hospital for weeks. Of course my mom filed police reports, went to news stations, and told the community, but no one cared. Nothing ever happened to them because it was just another day in the ghetto. Now there is a whole Black Lives Matter movement. That is beautiful. Finally, something signifying strength and unity. I wish I had some sort of media help back then. The power that we have is much greater than the power that we think we have, but long story short, that incident deterred me from a life of crime. Dom, on the other hand, was influenced differently. I looked at it like, if they could beat me and get away with it when I was innocent, imagine what they could do and get away with if I were actually guilty. Too many injustices are happening without crime even occurring. Dom reacted like he's going to do what he wants and live as crooked as he wants. He said what is the point of following the law if they are going to still find ways to break the law at my expense. He said the law doesn't see good and bad in Black people, they just see problems. Hence, him sitting here asking a broken man for help. I walked him in the house and left him standing there.

Not too long after I fell asleep, I had a beautiful dream that put me at ease. My mom was sitting in heaven with my daughter on a cloud. She said, "Baby girl, we will watch over and protect our loved ones from here."

"Why nana?" Asia asked.

"Because, Banana. They are still in a world that doesn't appreciate their color and value. They're in a society that judges you based on classist reasoning and that is accepted. Money motivates love, hate, and everything in between," my mother explained.

"How will we protect them if they cannot see us?" Asia asked.

"We will guide them to do better. They can feel us even when they cannot see us."

"Ohhhh," Asia said. "I can do that. Mommy needs me, she is mad at daddy. She thinks daddy hurt others and that why they hurt her."

"Your daddy is a strong man. He will be able to right he wrongs to his own life story."

"But he did not hurt anyone."

"I know, Asia, but a face in someone's memory is a guilty verdict instantly," my mother replied.

When I woke up, I was relieved. My mother and my daughter both entered through the pearly gates and I was grateful. As soon as I walked in the club, I got a drink. No one knew what was going on so that was good. It gave me peace to enter a routine.

"Hey Don, I didn't expect to see you so soon." Tracy greeted.

"I needed the air," I responded.

"I understand," she said.

"How is Amour holding up?" Tracy inquired.

"So this is how I got to approach you in order to hold your attention,?" Dom interrupted.

Tracy looked and then double looked. "What the fuck?!" Tracy said out loud.

"Hi, I am Dominique. I am Donatello's twin brother. My friends call me…"

"Hey," Duchess greeted me interrupting Dom. I did not want to see her while this bitch was here.

"Hey," I said. I noticed that she looked twice like Tracy just did.

"Ahhhmmm... Don," Duchess said trying to figure out which of us was which.

"Yeah," I said smoothly.

"Who is this?" she asked, looking like she was disgusted. That look caught me off guard, but I think I was the only one that noticed she smiled quickly after. She hugged me while asking.

"Hi, I am Dominique. I am Donatello's twin brother. As I was saying, my friends call me Dom." Duchess grabbed her stomach when Dom reached out to shake her hand. She said, "Excuse me and walked off."

I followed her lead and stepped off too.

"Bruh you going to just act like I am not standing here?" Dom said as I walked off.

I am going to do you one better and act like I cannot hear you too, I thought to myself.

I caught up with Duchess in her office. I knocked lightly on her door and she yelled, "One second." I could tell she was crying but I had no idea why. She finally opened the door.

Hey what is wrong, I asked?

"Nothing, hormones are still off," she replied. I knew she was lying, but I decided not to pry. "How are you?" She asked.

"I'm holding up."

"Just holding up?"

"As best as possible," I replied. She stared at me very empathetically.

"What is going on?" Duchess asked.

"Nothing," I said.

"Tracy told what happened," she confessed.

"I figured." Intentionally, I said, "I'm not expounding any further."

"I'm not trying to make this about me but why didn't you tell me, she asked.

"There are too many moving variables that have conflicting end results, and I felt it was best to keep you out of it."

"Moving variables like what?" She said, "Speak English. Don't dress up bullshit with fancy clothes."

"I'm going to keep it a stack with you. My wife is intimidated by you. She always questioned our relationship. I just did not want you to donate, show up, or do anything that would upset her even more than the situation required. Especially with our daughter's de.... with Asia not here. I felt it was best to respect her feelings."

"Is that why? I never knew she felt any kind of way. I have only met her once," she said.

"I know but when she saw you, she never trusted me around you again. I originally left her when it first started but she text me saying she was pregnant. After Asia was born we got married. I love my family. Never would I cheat. She said it was not me that she did not trust, it was you. That was her logic and I wanted to minimize conflict."

Duchess' face said she understood, but something about her body language said she was holding back. Maybe she was secretly attracted to me and I never knew it. That would have made Amour right all along. I shook the thought off and asked

Duchess to turn on the cameras. She did and put it directly on Dom.

"What is up with this?" she asked.

"Nothing but trouble," I confessed, never turning to look at her.

"I sensed that," she said.

"I wish others did as easily as you," I replied. "They see our faces and how we look alike and assume we are the same. But we are not the same, we are one of two."

"What caliber of a man are you?" She asked me.

I looked at her and back at the monitor. I said, "I will let you know when I get over this." She didn't say anything more after that, and neither did I.

DOM

This bitch ass nigga going to tell me our mother moved and gave me the fucking address to a cemetery. I memorized it so I thought I had went to the wrong address, but when I went to her old address Ms. Lula Mae, the old lady that had the house beside hers, said she died a few weeks back. Said a car hit her. Little did these people know not even death could silence her. I had to tell her old looney ass to shut the fuck up.

She said, "You are the bad one. Your mother tried to right you, but the devil had a hold on you. You are going to learn the hard way."

"And you talk too much. I never did like your old ass," I replied.

"The devil is going to teach you a lesson that God will save you from if you are lucky. But everyone around you who knows you will suffer first because you are too hard headed and stubborn to exist. And don't think I'm not hip to you. You're like a piece of candy. Hard on the outside soft on the inside. With your sweet ass. Jail might suit you. You'll be able to just be yourself."

"Bitch, I will show you how much of a man I am," I said

"Baby I am not your cup of tea. Besides my back door has been a closed since Bartholomew died in '89." I just shook my head and walked off. That lady had always gotten under our skin with her sly comments and passive aggressive behavior.

Anyway, since my brother played with me, I went back to his house. I never saw Amour or Asia. I figured they were visiting relatives or she done left his square ass. So I decided to just follow him to work. He could have shitted bricks when I walked up. On the outside he looked calm, but I knew him. On the inside he was boiling over. We were polar opposites but we both shared that attribute. The cute little piece of ass that was standing there was comforting him for something. I'm not sure what, though. Maybe our mother's death. Then here comes Callie. Yeah, I know who she is. I now know her better than her husband will ever know her. You see, this is not the first time I followed Don.

I knew Duchess was his boss. After a little research, I found out where she lived and that she was looking for movers and painters. My man Rho had his own paint company. Well, not really he did it under the table. Being as though he was a convicted felon he had problems finding a job, so he started painting. I convinced him to talk to her and get her to hire us. He knew I was up to something so he put out flyers in her neighborhood instead. Sure enough, she called. When we got there we did the work. Surely, people would notice two suspicious black men walking in this woman's house. Anyway, I knew off the break I was going to rape her. I had to taste that juicy looking pussy. Shit had my mind gone just looking at it through those sweats. Rho didn't really want to, but when I started, he went with it. She kept going in and out of consciousness. Lil weak bitch. She acted like this was her first rodeo. Man, it was one time where she passed out sucking Rho's dick, he just held her head up and fucked her throat. He shot cum all down her throat. I just knew for certain she would wake up but she didn't. I decided to wake her up my damn self. Rho laid down and put his dick in her ass and I went into her anus too. His dick rubbing against mine was fucking weird but fuck it, this bitch was fine and tight. If I didn't know any better I would think this was her first anal. I pulled out and I put Rho dick in her pussy while I went in too. Her pussy was tight as shit too, it felt like her ass all over again. I had to pull out just so I would not nut early. I noticed she was bleeding but fuck this bitch. I'm taking this good pussy. I increased my speed ramming my dick in and out of her.

I felt like her pussy was going into convulsions. Shit kept gripping the dick and releasing it. Shit turned me on. If her pussy wasn't so damn good, I would have been done. I bet she wish her pussy was some trash now. Bitches always bragging about having trap-a-nigga-pussy until a nigga trap-that-pussy in a corner. I was about to cum so I pulled out and forced that shit down her throat. I groaned and moaned until I released the whole load down her throat. Then the bitch started choking on the cum. Can you believe that? She came too, so I know she wanted it.

I punched her in the face and she was out cold again. For hours we had our way with her. Together, apart, whatever... it didn't matter. The shit was so lit it made my mouth water just thinking about it.

I had to get Don. He moved around like he was God's gift. I needed him to see and understand that just because you did good don't mean good will do right by you. I was on a mission to ensure he saw the truth one way or another. I had so much malice in my heart, but I didn't give any more fucks than he did.

It's me against every motherfucker that loved, helped, or respected him. The amount of chaos I was about to put on him, I assure you none of y'all are prepared for.

CPSIA information can be obtained
at www.ICGtesting.com
Printed in the USA
LVHW081829050519
616671LV00035B/338/P